# SMOKE IN THE KITCHEN

# SMOKE IN THE KITCHEN

## A NOVEL ABOUT SECOND CHANGES

## GLORIA S. N. ALLEN

*AuthorHouse™ LLC*
*1663 Liberty Drive*
*Bloomington, IN 47403*
*www.authorhouse.com*
*Phone: 1-800-839-8640*

© 2014 Gloria S. N. Allen. All rights reserved.

*No part of this book may be reproduced, stored in a retrieval system, or transmitted by any means without the written permission of the author.*

*Published by AuthorHouse   03/28/2014*

*ISBN: 978-1-4918-7413-4 (sc)*
*ISBN: 978-1-4918-7412-7 (hc)*
*ISBN: 978-1-4918-7411-0 (e)*

*Library of Congress Control Number: 2014905282*

*Any people depicted in stock imagery provided by Thinkstock are models, and such images are being used for illustrative purposes only.*
*Certain stock imagery © Thinkstock.*

*Because of the dynamic nature of the Internet, any web addresses or links contained in this book may have changed since publication and may no longer be valid. The views expressed in this work are solely those of the author and do not necessarily reflect the views of the publisher, and the publisher hereby disclaims any responsibility for them.*

# Acknowledgments

I would like to express my deepest gratitude to God for inspiring and guiding me through the process of writing and publishing my first fiction story. Also, my heartfelt thanks goes to my siblings, including Mrs. Nora Wellington who read the original draft and Dr. Winston Allen who read the final galley draft, and to my many friends who supported this endeavor from its inception. I shouldn't forget to thank my niece Ms. Lydia Williams in the UK, we forwarded e-mails back and forth throughout the process. Their words of wisdom and encouragement spurred me to keep pressing through the challenges.

Special thanks to my original copy editor, Nancy Johanson, who got the ball rolling and did a fantastic job bringing my words to life.

To my friend and writing buddy Barbara Banta, thank you for introducing me to the International Women's Writing Guild, an organization that nourished this budding writer and gave me the opportunity to hone my literary skills.

I want to express my sincere thanks and appreciation to Professor Abioseh Porter, PhD, for reading the final manuscript and providing valuable input on its potential impact.

Finally, I thank my children and grandchildren for their continued love, support, encouragement, and belief in me.

To God be the glory!

To my children, Ronald and Henrietta and Lavinia and Danny, as well as my grandchildren, Jesse, Julien, Brandon, and Melanie.

I love you all so much!

## Disclaimer

This is a work of fiction. Names, characters, places and incidents either are products of the author's imagination or are used fictitiously. Any resemblance to actual events or locales or persons, living or dead, is entirely coincidental.

# Chapter 1

**Sierra Leone, February 1983**

Sara Moses was not unlike most West African women. She had a long-accumulated storehouse of fortitude. It was a good thing, too, because she was struggling with the obstacles created by three very different but equally testing issues. She was determined to prevail over all three. She had a few years behind her; in her forty-three years, she had already encountered and overcome a long list of challenges. Each victory had given her increased strength and courage.

Troubled by one of her newer problems, she slammed the door of her beautifully equipped, modern kitchen and marched resolutely across the yard to her beloved outdoor kitchen, a relic from the days of the home's original architecture. No one was going to stop her from cooking with firewood on the *three-fireside-stone* she treasured. Not even her new husband, Ben, who enjoyed the food she prepared on it and had never once made a negative comment about the quality or taste of any dish. She had listened to his arguments against using wood for cooking. She had listened objectively and with respect and fully understood his strong viewpoint about conservation of Sierra Leone's natural resources, but she felt no guilt over it. She was a wise woman, and her mind was constantly working on how she could still keep her outdoor kitchen fueled with wood while participating in Ben's passion.

Secretly, she was working on a plan—how to keep Ben happy and keep her outdoor kitchen fueled with wood.

With hands on her hips, Sara examined her well-organized outdoor facility. She loved this kitchen—as much as she loved children. Everyone else's children, that is. She would not be able to give Ben a child of their own. That was her second challenge. She was determined to bring children into their extra-large home. They had three empty bedrooms crying out for occupants. And quite frankly, she wanted to cook for more than one person. She had presented Ben with a solution to this dilemma, but he wasn't ready to commit.

Rubbing her face with her hands, Sara sighed. While she felt quite confident about the outcomes of her first two problems, she wasn't at all sure about the third. Because of a feud, her father, rather than his older brother, had inherited the family's auctioneer business. After her father's death, she had inherited the business. Now she had been informed that her cousin Thomas was resolute about recapturing what he felt was his birthright. Sara had worked beside her father as a young girl and had grown to love the auctioneer business. She would not turn it over to Thomas without a fight. The days were long over when men were considered more suited to own property or run a business because of birthrights. Even in Sierra Leone.

Sara trudged across the yard again and sank into the comfort of a chair under the spreading branches of a mango tree that was older than her great-grandfather. Leaning her head back and closing her eyes, she allowed her thoughts to drift back in time. Soon, a twirling montage of memories held her captive for much of the remaining hours of the afternoon.

Two years ago, she had been Sara John, single, lonely, and still grieving. She had dragged herself home from church every Sunday and slumped onto a chair on the top step of her porch, unable to keep herself from wallowing in self-pity. As her mind's eye drifted across the expansive ocean stretching out to the surrounding seaside villages, she had been reminded of the permanence of some things, regardless of the battering waves of storms. Very little in her life held permanence, and she had longed for it with every fiber of her being—the permanence that comes with creating a family that would carry on name and heritage.

Yes, Sunday afternoons had been the worst for such a long, long time. Other church members left for home with their loved ones to enjoy a midday spread, lazy hours of idle chatter, and long, cool drinks of ginger beer or cold beer. But such delightful pastimes were not hers to share. Most Sunday afternoons, she was on her own.

And then, something unexpected happened to change her life, for the better.

\* \* \*

### Freetown, Sierra Leone, March 1981

Sara dabbed at her moist face with her best Sunday handkerchief, knowing it was a useless exercise. Tucking it into the bodice of her dress, she rested her elbows on the dining table and stared at the wall in front of her, wishing she could magically transport herself to some part of the world she'd only enjoyed in pictures. But wishes didn't solve problems. She was stuck in Freetown.

Of course, she'd never cool off if she remained dressed up. She should get herself together and change into something cooler. Still, Sara hesitated, dreading to pull open the bedroom door and hear the absence of voices and laughter. On weekdays, she looked forward to returning to her house and didn't mind the silence that greeted her, but it was different on Sundays. On weekdays, she could embrace her empty house and her solitude at the end of each day she spent at her business, but never on Sundays.

"Deal with it, Sara!" she said aloud, admonishing herself for succumbing to what had become a weekly ritual. Pushing herself to her feet, she pulled open the door into her bedroom. Her church shoes clicked on the floral terrazzo, sounding much like the annoying woodpecker that awakened her every morning when it hammered on the mango tree outside her bedroom window. She tossed her red hat and green handbag onto the bed. Desperate for some relief from the smothering humidity, she yanked the cord on the ceiling fan and lifted her face to feel its cool breeze. Then, pushing her hat and handbag to the side with a sweep of her hand, she perched on the edge of her bed while unbuttoning her dress. Suddenly she broke into a smile as she stared at the bright red hat and emerald green bag. *They look like someone cut up a ripe watermelon into two halves,* she thought. *I must have been the subject of many a conversation this morning.*

Quickly peeling off the floral cotton dress that hugged her hourglass frame, she rose from the bed to drape it over the back of her vanity chair. She expected no visitors, so she might as well be comfortable. Unexpectedly, a few tears trickled down her cheeks. Giving in to them, she sighed and threw herself onto the rumpled bed.

Snuggling a pillow in her arms, she let the tears flow at will. There was no sense in quashing the memories; they'd come unbidden before the day was over anyway. There was no running from them. Memories came and went of their own volition. For ten years, they had put down deep roots into her psyche, regardless of her efforts to stifle them. Her fiancé, Willy West, had died unexpectedly only three months before their nuptials. She was unable to attend the funeral because she had been in the hospital, where the medical staff battled in vain to save their unborn child. A precious, tiny daughter.

As the painful memories intensified, Sara drifted into a restless sleep. She was awakened half an hour later by the ringing of her telephone. She almost ignored it. Then, leaping from the bed, she dashed to the parlor to snatch the receiver off the hook because the bedroom phone extension was damaged. "Yes, hello," she said, hearing the breathlessness of her voice.

"Sara John?" The deep baritone voice was that of a stranger.

"Yes, this is Sara."

"This is Ben. Ben Moses."

Her mind raced to fit the name with a face. "Oh, Benjamin Moses. Your cousin introduced you to me this morning. Near the entrance of the Ebenezer Methodist Church? That Ben?"

"The one and only. Hope I didn't catch you at a bad time. You sound surprised. I told you I would call this afternoon."

"Yes, but—"

"You didn't believe me!"

"To tell you the truth, Mr. Moses, I didn't."

"Ben. Call me Ben, Sara. I would have called even earlier, but wanted to give you time to relax after church. Are you still on the line?"

"Yes, I am. What is it that you wished to speak with me about, Mr . . . . Ben?"

"If you are free this evening, I would very much enjoy your company. I thought we could have an early dinner at one of the new restaurants along the beach."

Every Sunday during the dry season, Sierra Leoneans enjoyed the cool breezes blowing inland from the Atlantic Ocean while picnicking under the tall coconut palm trees that line the shore. Many also took to swimming in the salty ocean. Sara had tried to join them from time to time after Willy's death, deciding she could simply sit and people-watch, but she could seldom stay for more than a few minutes. It was too painful to observe and hear the happiness of other couples when her heart was still breaking. "It is so very kind of you to extend such an invitation, Ben . . . but I will not be able to accept."

"You've made other plans. Why would I expect otherwise?"

"I, uh, it's my sister. She was planning to stop by later."

"I'd like to meet your sister. If she is as lovely as you are, I would be doubly blessed. She's welcome to come with us, Sara."

Sara felt her bottom lip tremble and bit it hard to keep from bursting into loud sobs. She turned down so many requests to go on a date that she could hardly remember the last time she had one. She had forgotten what it felt like. If she remembered correctly, Ben was a nice-looking man. Very mannerly. But what were his intentions? Why was she second-guessing his invitation? Maybe he simply wanted to share dinner with someone. Maybe he was as lonely as she was. Maybe . . .

"Well, could I think about it and get back to you?" she found herself asking.

"Why don't I call you back after you've had a chance to talk with your sister?" he said.

"Thank you. You may call back in an hour." Sara replaced the handset and sank onto a chair. What had just happened? She had met this Ben Moses only a few hours ago. He had said, "I've heard many wonderful things about you from my cousin, and it's a great pleasure to finally meet you in person." He had given her his business card, and she had hastily shoved it into her handbag. She remembered the twinkle in his eyes and his warm smile that revealed perfectly aligned white teeth. He looked like an honest man. But she knew from experience that looks can be deceiving.

The loud ring interrupted her thoughts some minutes later. This time, it was Kelitia on the other end of the phone. "I'm coming over to see you, Sara. I'll be there in half an hour. We'll drive to the beach."

Sara headed for her bedroom again. On the way, she stopped to brush her teeth in the bathroom and freshen up. While she performed this ritual, she gazed out the small window at the bees on the burgundy bougainvillea that created a fence between her yard and the back neighbor's. She found herself counting them, and then watched as they flitted from flower to flower, not settling for the nectar from only the bougainvilleas, but sipping from the roses, jasmine, and lilies as well, although snubbing the hibiscus.

Back in her bedroom, she selected a purple and white embroidered Africana outfit and laid it out on her bed. *This will be appropriate for my date with Mr. Ben, if I decide to have dinner with him,* she thought. *But I won't. Not today anyway. I'm not ready.*

Deep in thought, she didn't hear the knock on her front door.

"Are you deaf today?" Kelitia stood in the doorway watching her. "What's up with the fancy outfit? Isn't that a little dressy for the beach? Or did you wear that to church? I skipped church today."

Sara laughed. "Can't you ever stop for a breath? You chatter like a magpie! You've got my head spinning. By the way, I like that pink jumpsuit on you. Makes you look great. I'm jealous."

"Like you have anything to be jealous about! Your curves are the envy of every woman and the object of every man's desire, I dare say, who passes you on the street. Too bad they're wasted."

"Wasted?"

"You know exactly what I mean. You've been languishing around this place for ten years, burying yourself in books and cooking for strangers, instead of finding yourself a man."

Sara expected no less from Kelitia; she was not one to hold back. In fact, she delivers the truth with brutal honesty. Sara pretended to ignore her rants as she proceeded to her wardrobe. She changed into a green tie-dyed caftan. *This is perfect for the beach*, she reassured her reflection in the mirror. "I haven't been interested in replacing Willy."

"Willy was only your *first* love, Sara. You don't know who the love of your life is yet, and you'll never find him if you keep to yourself. You've got too much to offer—"

"Guess what happened after church?" Sara folded her arms and glared at her sister.

"You know I hate guessing games. Just come out with it." Kelitia flopped onto the bed, running her hand over the patchwork quilt. "I never see this without thinking of Gramma Corinthia and the months she spent making it for you."

"Six months, to be exact. I treasure it. She let me choose the fabric from her leftovers and wasn't particularly pleased with my selection. I told her the tiny dots in each square patch reminded me of the grains of sand on the beach, while the larger one reminded me of the shells that wash ashore with the tides. That satisfied her. She completed it just in time for my graduation."

"That was such an important day for our family. Papa Solomon was so proud of you, Sara. He told everyone who stopped by the store that his daughter was the first girl in town to obtain a bachelor of arts degree in business administration from Fourah Bay College."

"It had been renamed the University of Sierra Leone by then. You know that. If Papa were still living, he'd be bursting buttons over your success, too, Kelitia. It's no small achievement to be the assistant manager of the Funkia Hotel."

"Okay, enough of this small talk. You're purposely getting me off topic. We're hardworking women and can hold our own in this complicated society. We know that. Other folks know that too. Now, what happened after church today?"

Sara ran a comb through her hair. "A fellow named Benjamin Moses asked me to have dinner tonight."

Kelitia leaped to her feet. "Really? You're not saying that just to shush me up? Are you going? What time? If I hang around, will I be able to meet him?"

Sara shrugged, smiling. "His cousin introduced us after the service. He called an hour or so ago to extend the invitation. Right before you called me. But I said I had to think about it."

"*Yu crase*? What's there to think about? Sara, look at me. You have to stop living in the past. You have so much talent, so much heart, and yet . . . How many times do I have to remind you that the value of any life doesn't rest on the number of days that person is on earth; it's based on how well we make use of them. Haven't you heard the saying that a man may live long, yet live very little? Don't let Willy's death define you! It's time to move forward."

Sara buried her face in her hands and turned away from the words she needed to hear, but found so difficult to accept. "I'm not crazy, I'm just hurting. Willy's death was devastating, and to later find out he was cheating on me with another woman, knowing I was pregnant with his child, ripped my heart in two. We were engaged to be married, Kelitia! How could he do that to me? Even worse, it was the loss of—"

"I know. You lost your daughter too." Kelitia wrapped her arms around Sara. "You can have more babies, if that's what you want. And think about this. If you had died during childbirth and Willy had lived, do you think he would have grieved over you for even *one* year? He would have gone to that other woman and married her. Willy isn't worth one more of your tears, especially after what he did to you."

Sara had relived the pain of Willy's betrayal so many times it affected her ability to trust anyone. She had inadvertently bumped into the woman whom Willy was seeing behind her back. She had been visiting with Willy's parents and was on her way to her car when three women gathered at the base of the house stairway. "*Lookam, lookam,* that's her, that's her!" one of the women said, nudging the heaviest one in the arm.

As Sara reached the bottom step, the woman had rolled her eyes and hissed loudly, "I told Willy I'd never let no other woman wear his ring. I'd show up at the church to stop any wedding from happening. What he saw in her is a mystery to me!"

Sara had held her head high, ignored the women, and headed straight for her car. Instead of mourning the loss of her fiancé with dignity, she had suffered from the knowledge of his infidelity and deceit. She had endured the death of her dreams for their future and the future of their daughter. One moment, she would be crying; the next, she would feel an inner rage, mostly at herself, for being so naïve, so foolish, so stupid.

Kelitia threw her hands into the air. "Okay, I've had enough of your self-pitying nonsense, Sara John! Come back to earth, right now! What about this Ben? What are you going to do?"

"He invited you to go with us. Said he would be 'doubly blessed' to have your company."

"Sounds like a nice guy, but you're too old for a chaperone."

The phone interrupted Sara's reply. Her eyes widened, and she froze. "I can't answer that," she said.

"Of course you can. You're a mature woman, and you have full control of your faculties. Answer the phone and tell Ben you'd be delighted to have dinner with him."

Sara had the receiver over her ear on the fifth ring.

"Have I succeeded in changing your mind?" Ben asked.

She could hear the smile in his voice. Still she hesitated. "Please, can we do this some other time? . . . I really appreciate your kind invitation, Ben."

"Not at all. I'll call you later this week, and we'll set up another time. I don't intend to give up, Sara. I'll try very hard not to become impatient."

"I give up, Sara!" Kelitia said, heading for the door. "I can't be with you right now. I'm too mad. I'm likely to kill you if I hang around and listen to any more of your pitiful excuses." She stormed out of the house without waiting for a reply.

Sara wept. She wept because she knew Kelitia was right. She had given up living. She lacked courage and had given up living for a man who wasn't worth a second thought. It was time to move on. This was the last Sunday she would spend mourning over the past.

# Chapter 2

"If you had died during childbirth and Willy had lived, do you think he would have grieved over you for even *one* year? He would have gone to that other woman and married her." Kelitia's words echoed in Sara's mind throughout the night and forced her to reevaluate her life. Why had it taken her so long to realize the futility of living in the past? She had placed blame on a stranger and on Willy and indulged in self-pity over losing a baby when thousands of other women all over this continent lost not only their babies, but their toddlers and young children to poverty and disease. There were so many things she could do with her life and talents, with her education; it was up to her to lead the way.

Intermittently, she thought about Ben Moses. She rehearsed the reasons—excuses, really—why she had turned down his invitation for dinner, but none of them made sense. The high opinion he held of her must be scattered in the March dust and have been destroyed by now.

For the next several days, Sara found her attitude change affected everything she did. She was full of vigor and accomplished more at work; she returned home energized and optimistic. Even her stereo appreciated Sara's recognition. The Everly Brothers' song "All I Have to Do Is Dream" was Sara's favorite. Curious about the man who wanted to buy her dinner and get to know her more, she decided to conduct research. Employing the stealthy tactics of a teenager with a crush, she asked around and learned he was an economic adviser to the Sierra Leone government.

It was almost 10:00 p.m. on Thursday when she heard the phone ringing. Hoping it might be Kelitia and ready to patch up their differences, she picked up the phone. "It's about time you called," she said, laughing softly.

"I guess you've been waiting for my call. I'll take that as a good sign, Sara."

"Ben? Is that you? I-I was expecting my sister to call."

"Hmm. I've got to meet this sister of yours. I apologize for taking so long to get back to you. I'm in London. I had to fly here on the spur of the moment to replace a colleague who was scheduled to attend a meeting here and fell ill."

"You're calling me from London?"

"I didn't want you to think I was avoiding you. I'll call again as soon I get back to Freetown. It might be Sunday. Next time, I won't call as late as tonight. I promise."

Waiting for Sunday evening was like waiting for her birthday. Sara was giddy and full of anticipation. Each passing day felt like an eternity. Although she wanted to talk about the long-distance phone call and speculate on its importance, she kept it to herself. Maybe it meant nothing more to Ben Moses than keeping his word. Nevertheless, by the time Sunday arrived and church was over, she rushed home and directly into her house. No more brooding. She was done with that. All day long, she found her eyes wandering to the wall clock, wondering if the phone would ring again and when.

By six forty-five, she had given up. Since cooking was her passion, she set about preparing herself fried fish. No sooner had she begun nibbling when the phone rang.

"Have I caught you at a bad time?" Ben asked.

"No, not at all. I'm just fussing about the kitchen." She gazed at the plate with four slices of fish lying side by side and pushed it aside. "Have you returned from London? You must be tired."

They spoke for well over an hour. Their conversation flowed effortlessly, as though they had known each other for years. They spoke about everything, from the weather pattern in England compared to what it was in their own country to the vagaries of politics and the plight of so many of their countrymen. Ben spoke about his interest in preserving natural resources, and she shared her interest in cooking. She grilled him on the escalating prices of various commodities and the high cost of living that descended like locusts on Sierra Leoneans. They discussed economics and domestic affairs, especially the country's deteriorating infrastructure and inadequate public transportation. No topic was off-limits.

As they conversed, Sara was impressed not only by Ben's intellect, but by how well read he was. Although she wasn't as well apprised as he on international issues, he made her contribution to the conversation seem important. All the while, she thought that this man would be a joy to have around, because he respected her viewpoints as a woman. He treated her as his equal. That earned him high marks. Something about him was just different.

By the end of their conversation, Sara also knew his favorite dish was jollof rice, especially made with chicken. His least favorite was okra. He enjoyed the local Star beer as opposed to imported beers, and ginger beer rather than local *soft drinks* on a hot afternoon.

"Cooking and entertaining are high on my list of favorite pastimes," she said. "And it may surprise you, but I love to cook with firewood."

"Firewood? You're joking. You're not interested in saving the environment?"

"If you mean cleaning up the environment, then I am certainly interested," she said, rather testily. "Are you free for dinner on Wednesday evening?"

"I certainly am. Are you inviting me over to sample your cuisine?"

It was set then. They would have their first opportunity to share each other's company across a table. Sara would have the opportunity to impress someone she already admired, and hopefully, discover whether their affinity for stimulating conversation could continue unabated even when they witnessed each other's body language and facial expressions. *I'm not going to expect miracles*, she decided.

The silence between Sara and Kelitia had stretched like an elastic band since their blow-up over Willy and Ben. It was a silence that spoke louder than their argumentative words. They had never gone so long without speaking. For some reason, though, Sara was hesitant to make the first call, even though the issue weighed heavily on her heart. An entire week had passed. Kelitia had been supportive during the ten years of her grieving and rarely shown even a hint of impatience. She had been right in her assessment of Sara's self-pity indulgence, and she should be thanked.

Still, Sara argued, her date with Ben Moses was something she wanted to experience without advice or judgment. But that being said, she became increasingly remorseful as she began her studies on the subject matter for the following week's Sunday-school lesson. As the teacher of twelve young children, she was expected to walk the walk, not only talk the talk. With forgiveness as the theme, it seemed a rather barbed sign from above that she was derelict of her Christian duties. She should patch things up with Kelitia. By Monday night, she knew she couldn't put it off any longer.

"You may not recognize my voice, but this is your long-lost sister," she said, hoping her attempt at humor would soften any lingering ill feelings.

"I knew you would come to your senses, Sara. You have, haven't you?"

Sara laughed. "Why have I been so worried about losing you? You're still the world's champion chatterbox. How in the world have you kept yourself from calling me this past week? Haven't you been bursting to tell me off a little more?"

"It has nothing to do with telling you off, Sara John. It was just time to give you a little tough love."

"You gave it to me all right, and I want to thank you. It worked. I'm free of the past, and it feels glorious to walk into the future. By the way, a friend of mine asked about you."

"You know I hate playing games, Sara. What friend and why was I a subject of your conversation?"

"Ben—"

"*Benjamin Moses?* That guy you told me about who asked you out to dinner?"

"The very same."

"Tell me you've decided to give him a chance!"

"As a matter of fact, he's coming over for dinner on Wednesday evening."

"Dinner? And you're doing the cooking? Why am I not surprised? I know it's a cliché, but I firmly believe you can win over a guy through his stomach. You'll have him fainting after one of your meals, Sara. He won't stand a chance." Kelitia laughed aloud. "So *that's* why you called me. It wasn't about an apology or your missing me or my incessant advice; you wanted to fill me in on the juicy news!"

"Don't twist my words, Kelitia. I wanted to apologize. Honest."

"Liar. You wanted to indulge in a little girl talk. You're happy. I can hear it in your voice."

Sara laughed with her. "I'm not going to argue with you. You know me too well."

\* \* \*

When Ben rang her doorbell on Wednesday at exactly six thirty, Sara was ready and waiting. She had taken the day off from work to clean the house, set the table with her finest linens and dishes, and prepare jollof rice and chicken stew. Cleaning was one of the times she used her part-time maid; but because she received much pride and joy in cooking, Sara seldom looked for any assistance with meals. While in her kitchen, she deep-fried the cut-up chicken and waited until it was golden brown before she removed the pieces and placed them into a circular enamel plate. She then added into the hot oil the chopped-up onions, whole tomato, tomato paste, hot pepper, garlic powder, and herbs she harvested from the garden; she stirred and allowed the ingredients to cook for a few minutes by adding half a cup of water. She removed some of the burning wood from the fire to reduce the heat. Five minutes before the stew was done, she tasted it by dipping the spoon into the pot and smacking it on the palm of her hand; at this stage she added a pinch of salt and then the pieces of chicken.

Cooking the rice was simple. She had done it so many times. With the soup spoon, she took two scoops of gravy from the stew and added enough water and some more tomato paste. She allowed this to boil for about seven minutes before adding the rice and salt to taste.

She felt surprisingly like a teenager going on her first date and had fussed too long over what to wear. She decided on a simple turquoise linen top and matching skirt that flattered her figure.

"Welcome to my home," she said, standing aside and gesturing for him to enter. "I'm glad you didn't wear a suit. I never thought to mention that." Her stomach fluttered with butterflies when she saw that Ben's eyes were filled with admiration.

"Wow," he said, holding her gently by both shoulders. "The second I met you in church that day, you made a lasting impression. You are beautiful. Love that color on you."

"Thank you, sir. Flattery isn't required, but it *will* get you a bigger dessert!"

Ben laughed and kissed her on the cheeks. "You've got a sense of humor. I like that." He walked directly into her living room and scanned it with interest. "Thanks for having me." Ben beamed as he scanned her living room with great interest. "I can see you like to read . . . What you are playing is groovy."

Sara offered Ben a cold glass of his favorite beer and summoned him to join her at the dining table.

"If this dinner tastes even half as good as it looks and smells, I think I will die and go to heaven tonight." Ben assisted and placed the jollof rice on the table and pulled out her chair.

"Tell me something about yourself," Sara said once they had started to eat.

"Contagious smile . . ."

They both laughed.

"A smile that shows dimples, by the way. I like them," Sara said, lowering her eyes to her plate.

"Then I'll flash them often when I'm with you!" Ben flirted. "This is very possibly the most delicious jollof rice I have ever eaten," he said. "It has the right amount of spices, and I could eat it every day."

"I've had lots of practice," Sara said. "Now, you were about to tell me about you and your family."

"I'm the youngest of three brothers who were brought into this world by Leah and Levi Moses. My father died when I was nine." He paused. "My mother died a year ago."

"You probably already know that I work for the government as an economic adviser. It's a fairly new position established by the president. We need a better system for exporting our natural resources and importing the food our citizens need to live longer and healthier lives."

"You're a fine man, Ben Moses."

He put down his fork and gazed at her intensely. "I want you to know that I have been married before, Sara. I've been divorced for about three years now. My ex-wife lives in England with our son. Ben Jr. is doing well. I saw him while I was in London. He is healthy and strong and going to school. I'm happy about that. He'll have a better future. Now, enough about me; it's your turn."

Sara was stunned by this new revelation and took her time refilling their glasses from a bottle of ice-cold water. "Our Guma water is so refreshing it's such a shame that not everyone in Freetown gets water from the dam. The system is such a failure. If I had the power and the money, I'd dig up and replace the entire pipe network in Freetown. Because of pollution in some areas, it's no wonder that our people suffer from far too many cholera outbreaks."

She was having such a wonderful time with Ben, she found herself chattering almost nonstop like Kelitia. The subject of Ben's ex-wife and son weighed on her mind, but she resolved to ruminate on that later and decide if it made a difference. After all, he was an attractive man in his forties. "I am the only child of Hannah and Solomon John, but they unofficially adopted my sister Kelitia when she was very young," she said. "My father died six years ago, and my mother a year before that. I operate the family auctioneer business, which I inherited from my papa."

"That's what I heard . . . that you're a successful entrepreneur."

"Probably not as successful as you think, but I work hard and enjoy what I do." Fumbling with the cutlery, Sara thought carefully about how much she should reveal of her personal life. "What else would you like to know about me?"

"Everything!"

She cast a quick glance at him and saw that he was watching her closely. Uncomfortable but secretly enjoying the attention, she folded and then unfolded her napkin. "I was engaged to be married several years ago, but my fiancé died in a motor accident three months before our wedding—"

"Oh, my God! I'm sorry, Sara. That must have been a devastating ordeal to go through."

She nodded. "Yes, it was." She stared at her glass of water and thought of the argument with Kelitia. Avoiding Ben's eyes, she put on a bright smile. "It's all in the past. We need to live for today and tomorrow, don't we?" Talking about the miscarriage would serve no good purpose. If their relationship got serious, she would tell him about it. Not now. "Are you ready for dessert? I baked a cake. And how about coffee?"

Later that night, she confessed to herself that Benjamin Moses would make a fine husband. He had all the makings of an outstanding gentleman—charisma, intelligence, stability, and a go-getter attitude.

## Chapter 3

Sara hurried to church on Sunday morning, as she always did. She took her teaching responsibilities at Sunday school seriously, and she looked forward to interacting with the children. At Sunday school, she conducted her class like a regular school session with a scripted curriculum as the guideline for her lessons. There were examinations at the end of the Sunday school year. The children looked forward to their successes and the party that rewarded them for good work.

Thankfully, parents in the surrounding communities allowed their children to participate. Some simply sent them to the church, while others attended as church members. Many parents relished being part of the church community because their children could play and make new friends as well as develop their spirituality. A haven of sorts, the church was a beacon of hope and support to its members and the greater community. The more affluent members bought school uniforms, books, and food, and financially sponsored less fortunate families whose children attended school.

Poverty brought other dilemmas too. Poverty forced parents to give up their children to be unofficially adopted. As a prominent community leader, she was confronted with this issue on a regular basis. It was not uncommon for her to receive letters or visits from family members requesting a discussion of their children's plight. Her heart ached for all of them and for so many others. She often wished she could take a few home with her, but her grief over the loss of her own baby and the man she thought would be the loving father had always prevented her from taking action.

When Nete dropped her daughters off at Sunday school, she was delighted to see Sara.

"Madam, I want to talk to you about my daughters." Nete had a frail skeletal frame and was almost in tears as she pleaded for Sara to provide her financial assistance. Sara saw the anxiety on her face and heard the desperation in her voice and knew what it must be doing to her, to put the welfare of her children first.

"I'll get back to you soon," Sara said.

"*Tenk ma.*" Nete stroked Sara's hand and left the church's compound.

All during the Sunday-school class, Sara eyed the two girls. They enjoyed listening to the lesson and participated eagerly in the discussions. The only outward indication they were poor was their appearance. They were dressed in oversize outfits, similar to those used in a colder climate; the unneeded warmth combined with Sierra Leone's hot sun caused them to perspire nonstop. The clothing came from bales of used apparel shipped from developed countries for the less fortunate in the country.

"Did your mama braid your hair?" Sara asked the girls.

"Yes," they both said.

"She does beautiful work. You look especially pretty today." Sara watched them beam in response to her words.

The motto for the school was *Love one another as God loves us.* Sara scanned the faces of all the children in her class and smiled. They were so eager to learn. "Boys and girls," she said, "let's look at our fingers. Are they the same shape and size?"

"No," the voices in the class exclaimed loudly, after carefully examining them and holding them high in the air.

Sara pointed to an eight-year-old boy. "Pius, tell me something about what you see."

"The middle finger is big and this one is small," he said, while trying to wriggle his pinky. "And this one is very fat." He made a fist and lifted his thumb.

"Do you agree with him?" she asked the class.

"Yes," they all yelled, while wiggling their fingers.

One of the youngest said, "No, no, *le-me tauk, le-me tauk.*"

"Just as our fingers are different, so is every one of you," Sara said. "And nobody's fingers are any better than anyone else's. Right?"

"Yes, Teacher Sara."

"When we have a task to perform, we will get better results if we use all our fingers," she said, hoping they would be able to understand the underlying message she hoped to convey. "I can't pick up a piece of paper with only my thumb. Can you? And I can't lift a book with only my pinky finger. It is the same way when we have important things to do for our family members or for our community; we have to come together. Remember this whenever you look at your hands. United we stand and divided we—"

"Fall!" the children cried out in unison.

Sara nodded. "That's right. We become stronger when we work together. Now, let's play awhile and see how many different ways you can use your fingers." She watched as they played with each other in the classroom. Six boys faked a tug-of-war match, while two undid their buttons. The girls hugged each other and pretended to fix their hair.

When they were all gathered together again, she held up a hand to shush them. "We have much to be thankful for, but sometimes we ask God to hear our special prayer requests. Do you have any today?" A dozen hands waved at her.

"Sal," Sara said, "your hand went up first. What is your prayer request this morning?"

Sal stood and sucked in a deep breath. "Please, Teacher Sara," she said, while swaying from side to side, "I want to pray for God to send food to my house. We ate the last bread this morning, and I'm hungry. Mama says for me to pray for food."

The other kids started chiming in.

"My mama says for me to pray that my papa gets a job."

"My papa says for me to pray for some shoes."

Sara went around the class and wrote down everyone's prayer request. "When we pray and believe in God, he hears and answers our prayers," she said. "Now, I have a prayer request too." She saw the surprise on their faces. "I want to pray for all of you to be successful in your school exams, and personally, I want God to help me make the right decision. Now, let's put our hands together." She waited until all of them had stopped squirming.

"Eyes closed. Think about God and let's pray." She put her own hands together. "Dear Lord, we thank you for today and for every boy and girl in this classroom. We pray for the home each one represents. We pray that you will bless and provide for their parents. Some need food today, and some need shoes and some parents need a job. We believe that you will provide in some miraculous way, as you always do, and we will be grateful. I personally ask that you watch over these children as they study for their exams. Give them the ability to think and to remember. We lay all of our prayer requests at the foot of your cross. This we ask in Jesus' name, amen."

After the church service, Sara drove Nana and Meeta to their home. As she drove, she thought about their parents and the three other siblings, all boys. Life for such families was arduous. The disparity between the rich and the poor in the community was striking. Even though poor families worked twice as hard for the basic necessities, it was difficult for them to make ends meet. Most poor people embarked on petty trading in order to provide food. Feeding their children was their priority.

Nete used all five of her children as peddlers. Walking around with circular trays on their heads, Nana and Meeta and their brothers peddled onions, tomatoes and potatoes, fresh and dried fish, pig's feet, rice, roasted peanuts, and whatever else they could. Singsonging their wares, they roamed the streets calling out, "Dried fish here. *Pamine* here . . . *Res* here!" The boys were responsible for peddling the rice (*res*) as it was heavy. Sara knew that Nete sometimes peddled kerosene, mostly in the evenings; during one of their conversations, she mentioned that to Sara. Kerosene, a by-product of crude oil, was used for lanterns, pan lamps, and igniting firewood and charcoal when there were no plastic carrier bags to do the job. Electricity in some homes was a rare commodity, so kerosene was a highly valued product.

Rock Street, where Nana and Meeta lived, was one of the worst roads in the city. As the name implied, Sara found herself dodging rocks, as well as potholes. Since garbage littered the edges of the road, it was impossible for pedestrians to use the sidewalks. Several times, she had to honk the horn to get them to move. When she finally parked her Mercedes in front of the girls' thatched-roof house, Nete ran out to greet her.

"Any trouble, madam? Any trouble?"

"No trouble," Sara said. "I just thought the girls would enjoy a ride in my car, and I wanted to see you again." She helped the children get out of the car and then drew a sealed envelope from her handbag to hand to Nete.

"A letter, madam? I cannot read . . ." Nete eyed her with suspicion.

"It's not a letter. It's money." Sara pushed the envelope into her hand.

She peeked at the contents. "For what?" Again Nete was hesitant.

"For you and the children."

"Haa! God, he has answered our prayer! *Tenki, tenki*." She fell to the ground and held onto Sara's feet in deep appreciation. As if she were chanting a chorus, she recited *"tenki, tenki, God,"* over and over again. Sara pulled her to her feet.

"Thank you, Teacher Sara. Thank you, Teacher Sara," Nana and Meeta said, wrapping their arms around her.

As she negotiated the potholes and rocks on the road while returning home, Sara watched in the rearview mirror and saw all three of them wave good-bye to her with both hands. Nete continued to dance with the envelope in the air. Their joy filled her heart to overflowing.

Later that evening, Sara thought about them as she sat on her steamy porch. The mosquitoes were managing to escape the tendril of smoke emanating from the mosquito coil burning nearby. They whined relentlessly in her ears and were adept at the bob and weave, no matter how often she waved them away. The mild breeze did nothing to cool things off. She knew she would feel better indoors under the ceiling fan, but from the porch, she could see the moon as it brightly lit up the night sky like an electric bulb and created what seemed like endless patterns on the gigantic leaves of the breadfruit tree.

The pungent smell from the burning coil took her back to the day she had held a three-day-old baby on her lap. She remembered every detail of the trip she had taken with her Papa Solomon, who made frequent trips to the provincial towns to sell various merchandise, including mosquito coils. He had promised to take her on one of his trips on her seventh birthday. She had looked forward to that special day, knowing that not many children born and raised in Freetown were given the opportunity to travel outside the capital city.

A twenty-seat bus was parked in the lot when they arrived at six in the morning. Sara remembered her excitement had been palpable, and she had fidgeted constantly as she waited impatiently for the driver to request passengers to board.

"Ready, ready, ready!" the driver shouted. He counted the number of passengers in the line, and the first twenty were allowed to board. Sara was the very first one, and she climbed the three steps and slid onto the first seat of the front section and scooted over to the window so her father could sit beside her.

Since she could already read fairly well, every word she saw fascinated her. She remembered reading the inscription at the back of a truck driving in front of the bus. "Papa, that sign on the truck says *See Me No More*. What does it mean?"

Solomon had smiled. "It means that when the truck driver steps on the gas pedal, he'll go so fast, he'll be out of the sight of other drivers."

At that very moment, the bus driver had revved the engine, and they had begun their five-hour journey. Sara couldn't keep pace with how quickly they rushed past the houses, trees, and people. She pressed her face against the window so that she wouldn't miss seeing anything. Although she enjoyed the ride, she welcomed the rest stop that came two hours later at the Mile Ninety-One junction. Her papa had told her it was a special spot, the hub, because it led to provincial towns in the northern, southern, western, and eastern regions of their country.

The minute the bus stopped, traders rushed to catch the attention of the tired and hungry passengers, hoping they could make a sale. Sara watched as people swarmed around the bus. She saw several women carrying heavy luggage while toting their babies on their backs. Boys and girls as young as she were selling food items, and drivers of vehicles were purchasing fuel at a filling station.

Every passenger disembarked from the bus and wandered around the already overcrowded area.

"Come on, Sara," her papa said, pushing her in front of him. "Stay close by me and don't wander away," he added. Solomon walked across to a woman selling *akara* balls, a mixture of bananas, rice flour, and sugar, deep-fried in hot oil. The woman, who was sitting in a chair, rose sluggishly and waddled over to where the *akara* snacks were piled onto a tray. She counted a dozen balls, wrapped them up in brown paper, and handed the package to Solomon.

Sara struck up a conversation with her. "Aunty, are you having a baby?" she whispered.

"Sara!" her papa admonished. "You mustn't ask her that question. It's rude."

"*No, no, lef am, sir,*" the lady protested, convincing Solomon she wasn't offended by the question. "Yes," she said, rubbing her stomach. "My name is Mary."

"I wish you well." Solomon had taken money from his pocket after paying for his *akara* snacks and handed it to her. He had hurried Sara in the direction of the bus when they heard a loud and troubling screech. They turned back to see Mary on the dirt ground in a fetal position, caressing her stomach. Before Solomon and Sara could reach her, her colleagues had rushed to her aid and flagged down every passing vehicle. "Stop . . . stop, she is in labor; it's an emergency. She needs to go to the hospital now." Solomon's bus only left after they were satisfied that Mary was safely headed to the hospital.

As they boarded the bus and continued on, both Solomon and Sara couldn't help but worry about Mary and the baby. Three days later, on their return journey, the bus once again stopped at the junction, and Sara had peered eagerly about for Mary. She spotted her immediately. "She has her baby, Papa!" she had said excitedly. She had never held a baby before, and when she asked if she could do so, her papa had shaken his head in discouragement.

"What's the baby's name?" he had asked Mary as he fished some money from his pocket and forced it into her hand.

"Kelitia."

"Please, may I carry baby Kelitia?" Sara had asked again.

"Yes, of course," Mary responded graciously. She pulled a small stool forward and motioned for Sara to sit on it. Then she placed the bundled-up baby on her lap. Sara had fastened her eyes on the baby in awe and thrilled when the chubby fingers had tightened around her own. She was like a living baby-doll.

Before they left, Solomon had given Mary their address. "If you ever come to Freetown, you must visit us," he'd said. "It would greatly please Sara to hold your baby again."

It was only a few years later that their doorbell had rung and Mary had greeted them from their front porch. He had not recognized her at first, but when she handed him the address, he was happy to see her. "My husband died in a truck accident," sobbed Mary uncontrollably. "He died and left me with all these children." Collapsing to her knees, Mary clasped her hands and looked up at Solomon as if he were her last lifeline. "I have two other children. I want you to care for Kelitia. You wish to have her? Adopt her? She'll make a nice sister for your Sara."

Sara smiled now at the memory. Kelitia had been a blessing. She firmly believed God had sent her and her papa to the provinces that particular day. And thankfully, too, her parents had fallen in love with Kelitia as deeply as she had. Their home had been happier with Kelitia in it.

Sara peered up at the moon. Dark clouds had covered its face. It was already eleven o'clock, and she had been lost in memories for far too long. Someday—and she hoped sooner rather than later—she would adopt a baby or two of her own. It was the right thing to do.

She rose from the porch rocker and shuffled indoors. A long and potentially traumatic day awaited her, and morning would come all too soon. She had scheduled two meetings, one with Othneil, the lawyer recommended to her by Ben, and in the afternoon, an important conference with her senior staff.

Hours later, she was still wide-awake. She had too much on her mind to find peace in slumber. She dug behind a couple boxes in her wardrobe and rescued the mini safe she had hidden in one corner. She opened it and rummaged through several papers for the documents she might need for the meeting with Othneil. She

*Smoke in the Kitchen*

placed the documents on the bed, including her birth certificate, her parents' birth and death certificates, and the deed for her house. But when she picked up the deed, dated June 6, 1966, made "in consideration of the grantor Solomon John's natural love for his daughter Sara Mary John," she separated it from the others. If Grandma Corinthia had not informed her of the problem, she would not have known a family dispute affected her ownership of the business.

Sara was thirteen when her grandmother had said, "Sara, please listen to me. When you are old enough to run the business, I hope your cousin Thomas and his sister, Little Becca, will not humbug you." Sara had wondered why she was so concerned about her operating the business when she was still so young and didn't understand anything about it. "I'm just warning you, Sara, time will tell."

Her grandma had introduced the subject with subtlety. It was a weekend when Kelitia had gone to see her mama. Sara had been skipping rope outside when Grandma Corinthia had called her to come into the house. She thought she had gotten into trouble, especially when Grandma Corinthia had asked Sara to go to her bedroom. Her heart was in her throat, and she could feel the tears start. She couldn't see behind her grandma's heavy-set shoulder if she had a whip in her hand. Surprisingly, her grandma had patted the space next to her on the bed. "*Sidom*," she had said. "Have your parents ever mentioned the auctioneer business to you?"

Sara had shaken her head vigorously and never moved her eyes from her grandma's.

Over the next hour, her grandma had related the history of the family business. "I am already seventy-eight, Sara, and my memory could fail me." She had risen from the bed, hobbled to the dresser, and carefully picked up her King James family Bible. Returning to the bed, she had opened it and placed one half on her lap and the other on Sara's. Then she had leafed through several pages, until she reached the section where she had documented every important event in the family.

Sara had used her hands as a cushion between the Bible and her skinny legs.

"This is your Grandpa Aaron on your papa's side," Grandma Corinthia had informed her.

Sara looked up, but her grandma's index finger pointed to the handwritten names. Aaron had two sons: Sampson the elder, and Solomon the younger. Sampson had married Becca and had two children, Thomas and Little Becca. Solomon had married her mama, and they had one child, Sara.

Sara smiled, but felt disappointed when her grandma informed her that her papa had wanted a boy. "Why, Gramma?" she'd asked.

"The business, that's why." Her chewing stick was in her mouth. "The business!" she'd stated again, more emphatically. Intermittently, Grandma Corinthia scrubbed her teeth with the tiny stump in her mouth as she spoke.

"What business?" Sara had asked, more interested than Grandma had thought she would be.

"The shop. That's why your papa wanted a boy. But a woman can sell just as good as a man, and don't let no one tell you they can't."

That's when Sara learned the background to the controversy of the auctioneer mart. According to Grandma Corinthia, the business should have gone to Sampson, but Grandpa Aaron had punished him for his misdeeds by giving it to his younger son. Sampson had stolen from the family and crippled the business, not only because he was an alcoholic, but because he was also a con artist.

Grandpa Aaron's wife had never been happy with the decision, but she had to live with it. Following the decision, Sampson, his wife, and their two children—Thomas and Little Becca—emigrated to Fernando Po.

Then Sara's grandma had turned the page in the Bible over to her own family. "Here are the names of our own family, your mama's side. Please be attentive. These are my family members. *Wen ah die, dis Bible na you yone.*"

Sara had stared up at her and couldn't figure out why she had said the Bible would belong to her when she died. "Gramma, why did you say that? I'm scared."

The woman had assured her not to worry. "My death is not about to happen anytime soon, dear."

The name at the head of the maternal tree was Ruth, Grandma Corinthia's grandma, who married a Joshua Jacobs and had one daughter, Sara. Mama Sara married Sammy Fine, and she had one daughter, Corinthia. Corinthia married Jonas Paul, and she had one daughter, Hannah. Hannah married Solomon John and had one daughter, Sara.

Sara smiled again. "Why is it that all the women of your family had only one child . . . a daughter?" she asked.

"Your mother's uncle, Uncle Jabez, is not a girl! He is the son of Joshua Jacobs, my grandpa. He married two times."

"Great-grandpa Joshua married two times?" Sara asked.

"Yes, unfortunately, he did."

Now, Sara thought about that family history day and realized, for the first time, what her Grandma had meant by *"time will tell."* The letter from Thomas's lawyer was tangible evidence of the future bitterness she had anticipated. Even though the business had nothing to do with the maternal side of Sara's family, Grandma Corinthia had preempted something that would eventually cause another feud, and this time, it would have an effect on Sara's own future.

James Murray, a lawyer, had stated in his letter to her that his client Thomas was contesting the administration of the deed, which should have been administered to a male grandchild, and not to Sara John, who was a female grandchild. She read the deed again

*Smoke in the Kitchen*

and wondered whether her parents had ever known about Grandma Corinthia's discussion with her about the auctioneer mart.

Sara folded the legal documents and placed them into her briefcase. It made no difference whether they knew or not. An important message had been conveyed to her, because Grandma Corinthia expected her to stand tall and speak for all the women on her family tree. That was exactly what she would do. The auctioneer mart was hers legally and otherwise.

The other thing that kept her awake through the night was the lingering memory of the daughter she had lost. Would there be another to inherit the business from her? First things first. She must do everything possible to keep Thomas from conning her into giving it up.

# Chapter 4

**August 1981**

Cooking was Sara's favorite hobby, but entertaining was a close second. When she entertained, she usually cared little about who the guests were, be they young or old. She was just particular that her food was first-class. This time, however, it was a little different. Her intention was to impress Ben Moses. Like smoke in her kitchen, love was in the air, and she enjoyed every inhalation of it.

She and Ben were celebrating the five-month anniversary of their first date. It wasn't surprising to her; she had known from that first time that it would be safe for her to fall in love with him. Every week since then, her feelings for him had grown stronger, and now she was hoping another fine meal would encourage him to express how he felt about her. She wanted more than sweet-sounding words. Three days ago, she had tucked an envelope containing her house key into his jacket pocket as she kissed him good night.

Now that he could enter the house unannounced, he could visit whenever he wanted to. She enjoyed cooking on *three-fireside-stone*, where wood burned relentlessly. She only used her kerosene stove in emergencies, and the gas in extreme emergencies. Moving to the far right-hand side of her kitchen, where she had positioned the *three-fireside-stone*, she swept the ashes from the previous day's cooking into a dustpan and then meticulously arranged

## Smoke in the Kitchen

new firewood into the middle of the stones. Next, she carefully sprinkled kerosene onto the tips of the firewood and then struck the match she had taken from the box mounted on the wall nearby. Red flames leaped from the positioned wood sticks, and she stood back to watch them, satisfied that a good fire would follow. The previous evening, she had marinated beef, pork, and chicken for the stew to go with the jollof rice. Hopefully, Ben would be happy that jollof rice was on the menu.

Sara's kitchen area was huge and contained several cupboards. She had long ago purchased a table and one chair to adorn one corner; both were utilitarian and could be used whenever she wanted to sit while performing certain tasks. After she sliced the onions, tomatoes, and peppers into a bowl, she added fresh spices for the stew. She lifted the cast-iron pot onto the fire and poured a small quantity of vegetable oil into it. The intensity of the burning firewood maintained the heat she needed to cook. She cautioned herself to be sparing with the hot pepper.

For the next hour, she moved about the kitchen, preparing the rice and dessert fruits. All the while, she whistled happy tunes, not minding that she was perspiring profusely. She opened the pot of stew that sat atop the blazing fire, while turning her face away from the steam that engulfed her. She dipped the soup spoon into the stew, tapped it on her palm, and licked the juice. "Hmm," she said, smacking her tongue in reassurance. "Tastes as good as it smells." She watched the melding display of different colors in the boiling pot and knew she was right on target. Everything would be finished on time and to her strict standards of excellence.

At exactly 6:30 p.m., she left the kitchen and headed for the bathroom to shower. By 7:50 p.m., she was dressed in her favorite butter-colored dress that hit just below the knees, knowing it enhanced the tone of her light brown skin and gave Ben a glimpse of her toned legs. With shaking fingers, she opened the clasp of the gold chain that held a circular pendant with a small S in the middle and hooked it behind her neck. The necklace was a gift from Ben on their first date. Tonight was a perfect time to wear it. For the next few minutes, she clock-watched. He was late. Was he coming, or had she been too bold to offer him her key, without discussion of what it might mean?

When she heard the sound of Ben's car, she hurried into the dining room and pretended to be busy with the china. She looked up and smiled at him when he entered the house, using that very key. "Hello, Ben," she said.

"Something smells mighty good," he said, "and the cook is looking beautiful, as usual." He strode directly to her side and kissed her cheek.

"Welcome!" She smiled and touched the pendant on her neck, a subtle reminder that she thought enough of it and him to wear it.

"I am sorry I'm late," he said, looking at his watch when he saw her glance at the wall clock. It was 8:20 p.m. "Aunty Philomena phoned as I headed for the door."

"Who is Aunty Philomena?"

"You'll meet her. She's an interesting woman. Mama's youngest sister."

They sat in the parlor for a short while and enjoyed a glass of wine. "Are you ready to eat?" Sara asked finally, eager for him to taste her food. She grabbed hold of his hand and led him to the dining room. She had covered the table with her best white embroidered tablecloth. The six mahogany chairs glistened from regular polishing efforts. She had placed a vase of roses and jasmine from her garden on the table, and their pungent scent sweetened the air.

"Please have a seat, Ben . . . I'll join you as soon as I carry in our dinner." Sara's voice trailed off as she disappeared through the doors leading to the indoor kitchen area. She returned to the table with two steaming bowls. They were wrapped in two blankets to maintain the heat. When Ben saw her, he leaped to his feet to assist her. His eyes widened when he saw what she had prepared. "I hope you'll enjoy the menu tonight," she said. "I have prepared jollof rice, beef, chicken, and pork stew, tossed salad, and boiled cabbage."

Ben shook his head. "I am one lucky man. Nothing beats home cooking. You have outdone yourself tonight, Sara John. I can't wait to dig in!"

Sara beamed with pleasure. "I hope everything meets your expectations."

"Who's saying grace?"

"You!" Sara motioned to him lovingly.

"Let us pray then." He paused for a moment. "For food, friends, and fellowship," he said, placing emphasis on each word, "we thank thee, oh, Lord."

"Amen," they said in unison.

"Short and sweet," Sara said, smiling at him.

"I don't want the food to get cold." He spooned generous helpings of everything onto his plate.

Sara excused herself, went to the refrigerator, and returned with a bottle of champagne, which she placed on the table unopened. "You may do the honors, and I hope you know how to unscrew the cork without having it fly up to the ceiling! I don't want to lose an eye."

He laughed as he reached for the bottle. "I'll do my best." But his best wasn't quite good enough. As soon as he pushed the cork with his thumb, the froth erupted from the bottle, and the bubbly sprayed everything in its path with uncontrollable force. "I'm so-so . . . sorry!" he exclaimed. Once again, he leaped up from the table while snatching up his napkin to dab at her face and dress. "I'm so sorry, so sorry."

Sara's laughter filled the room, but her delight wasn't matched by his own. "There is no need for you to apologize," she chuckled and gently put a stop to his efforts to clean up the mess. "Let's consider this a fitting endorsement of our relationship. It's rather like the champagne blessing on a new ship!" They both laughed then, and Ben settled back into his chair.

After tasting everything with enthusiasm, he pointed his fork at Sara. "Does someone know how to cook, or is it the bubbly that added to the taste?"

"You figure it out. Can you cook, Ben? Do you prepare your own meals?"

"Me? No way. I've never attempted it. That would mean I'd have to go to market and face the hostile fishmongers, butchers, and all the others."

"You can sweet-talk the fishmongers,"

"I'd rather use that time to do other things—like think about you." He winked as he reached for the meat stew. "May I have a second helping?"

Pleased that all her efforts were succeeding, Sara nodded. "Eat as much as you'd like. If anything is left, I'll send it home with you."

"Now that's an offer I won't refuse. The only person who has cooked jollof rice as well as yours was my mama. Aunt Philomena cooks for me, but her efforts never quite hit the spot. Again, I have to say how very impressed I am with your cooking. This is mmm, mmm good, or as my son would say, 'yummy.'"

Sara smiled at his remarks.

Fanning her face with her napkin, Sara prodded, "From what you've just told me, I have to believe you miss your mama as well as her cooking and that, perhaps, you were a mama's boy. Did she spoil you?"

Ben laughed. "Yes, I suppose she did. When I was growing up, she not only washed and ironed all my clothes; she practically did everything she could lay her hands on. We had a strong bond. She was a loving and nurturing woman. Her greatest desire was for me to do well in school and college. She knew that education is what gives us the most choices as adults."

Sara's parents had loved her, but she remembered them more for the way they disciplined her. Grandma Corinthia was also part of the team that had continuously harped about what was right or wrong. The adage "Do unto others as you would have them do unto you" was repeated often, and it was only later in life that she appreciated this reminder. Even now, she tried to live by those words. But what benefited her even more was the time her grandma had spent teaching her and Kelitia how to cook. They had spent long hours with her in the kitchen and had never regretted them.

If Sara had one lingering disappointment regarding her childhood, it was the way her papa had treated her mama. He had yelled at her and faulted her for any and all reasons; he even hit her on countless occasions. Now she looked at Ben and wondered whether he would ever treat her that way. Because of her past experience with Willy, it was still difficult for her to completely trust men. She wondered, too, if he would ever be unfaithful to her by living a double life. A small corner of her heart was still recovering, and she dreaded the thought of ever being hurt again.

As soon as they had finished eating, Ben assisted her in cleaning up, but not without several time-outs for hugs and kisses. She knew, intuitively, that this gentle man was worthy of her trust, and soon, her laughter regained its spontaneity and strength. She felt at peace with herself and thoroughly enjoyed being in Ben's company. Already her mind was racing to thoughts of what it would be like to cook for him every day and, maybe, to even spoil him a little, as his mama had done.

"Is Kelitia okay, Sara? Is she joining us at the beach tomorrow?" Ben asked once they were through in the kitchen and seated beside each other on the living room sofa.

"Why yes, I believe she is, if that's all right with you."

"Of course, it's all right with me. She's a fine woman. She loves and respects you, so how can I not respect and like her? You're lucky to have such a staunch devotee. We all need someone in our life to love us like that." He entwined his fingers with hers and squeezed hard.

Sara smiled to herself. She felt certain that Kelitia had said something to him about Willy, because soon after their first outing together, Ben had said he wanted her to know he would never misplace her trust. She reached up to kiss his cheek. "I agree with you. Remember the song 'Unforgettable' recorded by Natalie Cole?

I believe the words were something like, 'The greatest thing you'll ever learn is to love and be loved in return.'"

"I agree wholeheartedly, my dear. I've been thinking more and more about love recently and the lack of it in my life. I read something once by a David Viscott that has struck a chord with me." He wrapped his arm around her and pulled her closer. "Especially since the day I met you. It goes like this: 'To love and be loved is to feel the sun from both sides.' I'm feeling the sun, Sara John."

# Chapter 5

**January 1982**

Sara remembered the first time she'd entered Ben's spacious home. It had startled her to see that a single man lived alone in such a beautiful and well-organized space. "My goodness, whatever made you build such a huge home when you're rarely here to enjoy it because of your business travels?" Sara quizzed him.

"I'll tell you all about it while I give you the grand tour," he'd said. "I built this house to accommodate my ex-wife and young son and, of course, any addition to the family. Since she was a foreigner, I wanted to make her comfortable. Obviously, that plan never came to fruition. So here I am."

The house was built with a double garage, which led to a modern, fully equipped kitchen. Also on the first floor, there was a beautifully furnished, full-size dining room, an expansive living room, and a bedroom with an en suite bathroom. There was even an extra room that was supposed to be his son's playroom. Upstairs, there were two more bedrooms, with an adjoining bathroom and a master bedroom. As if this weren't enough, Ben had also built a generator house in the backyard. His brother Chad, who had lived in London, had drawn up the plan, and his mama had supervised the contractor while he was living overseas.

"I was quite devastated when Carol informed me only two months before our move that she had changed her mind. She didn't feel she could live in Sierra Leone. It was too far away from her family, she said. I was more than a little upset. I loved her. I dearly love my son and wanted him near me. I knew we could have a good life here." He had avoided making eye contact with Sara. "I did my best. This was our decision when we got married. She was thrilled when I got this job and started making plans to join me." He paused and then sighed. "I don't hold it against her, Sara. I might feel the same way if I were in her position. What is it they say . . . that sometimes love is blind?"

Sara had merely smiled one of those closed-lip smiles that meant, "I'll hold back any comment on that!"

Later, Ben had gone up to his bedroom and returned with several pictures of his son. "He looks like you," Sara had said.

"Yes, everyone says so." He had smiled at her. "I know one day he'll come home to Sierra Leone. It's just a matter of time. I will be patient."

Now, she entered the house again, with her heart pounding hard enough to be heard. Ben was reciprocating her dinner invitation with one of his own. During the past few months they had continued to have weekly dates and almost daily phone conversations, but the dates were usually at local restaurants or the movie theater. They were finding it increasingly easy to talk with each other about everything that had an impact on their lives and their country, and she always hated to say good-bye at the end of each evening. Being in his home again was special. More intimate. Something to savor and remember. And somehow it seemed appropriate that it was January, the start of a new year.

"Come to the living room, my dear," Ben said. "I have another one of those infamous bottles of champagne waiting for us. This time, I promise not to ruin your lovely dress."

The champagne was cooling in a silver bucket on the coffee table. "You certainly know how to woo a woman, Ben Moses," she said, clasping her hands in front of her.

"No better than you know how to woo a man with that delicious cooking of yours." This time, Ben deftly opened the bottle of expensive Moet champagne and poured the sparkling wine into the two crystal flutes on the tray. Then handing one to her, he raised his own. "To one of the loveliest flowers to ever grace my home," he said. Peering deeply into her eyes, he added, "How would you like to make the arrangement permanent?"

"You say so many wonderful things, Ben, and likening me to one of those perfect roses has my heart all aflutter. I'm not at all sure I understand what you mean by 'permanent,' though." Sara played coy while her heart was racing with the hopes of a proposal.

Ben laughed. "I was trying to be romantic, but I believe this is the time for plain speaking. What I mean is, how does the name Sara Moses sound to you?" He placed his champagne flute on the table and pulled a small square box from his pocket. Flipping it open, he showed her an engagement ring with round and baguette

3.8-carat cut diamonds in a beautiful square shape, with smaller diamonds at each shoulder; it was crafted in sterling silver. "I love you with all my heart and don't feel I can take one more step into the future without you by my side. Will you marry me, Sara? Will you be my wife and share this home with me?"

"Oh, Ben," Sara said as tears stung her eyes. She swallowed a mysterious lump in her throat that had appeared instantaneously with the tears. "I love you too, and I've been praying for this moment. Yes, of course, I will marry you!" She quickly placed her flute on the table next to his before she dropped it. Her hands were shaking like leaves in a rainstorm. Then, throwing her arms around him, she smothered his grinning face with kisses.

*A second engagement*, she thought. *Would a wedding take place this time?* Pushing aside any doubts, she raised her face to peer into Ben's eyes. The tears finally spilled and streamed down her cheeks. "Are you s-sure about this?" she asked. "Y-you don't want to take back your proposal? You w-won't regret making it when tomorrow comes?"

"I'm more sure about wanting you in my life than I've been about anything in a long, long time," Ben said. "Now, let's get this ring on your finger and let's stop those tears." He kissed her. "Don't find things to worry about, Sara. Everything will be just fine. We're perfect for each other."

*Is he a mind reader?* Sara thought. *Does he know me so well already?* She held out her left hand and tried to still its trembling.

Ben removed the ring from the case and kissed it before sliding it onto her finger. Then he kissed her, pouring all his feelings for her into its sweetness. She reciprocated in kind. How wonderful it was to finally express her full emotions without fear. "I love you, Ben Moses," she said again.

"I can never hear that too often," he said. "Now, I don't know about you, but I'm hungry." He held her hand and led her to the dining room. Another bouquet of flowers adorned the table. There were two lighted candles on the table. "There. You have to admit this is a romantic setting. We can gaze into each other's eyes over our meal. I've already confessed to you that I don't know how to cook. Our dinner is being catered. Sit here and be patient. I intend to wait on you myself."

He left the room and returned with a huge silver platter arranged with sirloin steaks, broiled mushroom caps, roasted potatoes, and baby carrots. It was an artistic display that appealed to the eyes. The aroma was stimulating, and she was eager to enjoy every morsel. Suddenly she had a ravenous appetite, which was contrary to everything she had ever heard and read about feeling hopelessly in love. Supposedly, love diminished the appetite, because the brain was so intoxicated with the overstimulation of chemicals that were activated. She was experiencing the racing heart and the feeling of walking on cloud nine, but she couldn't wait to share Ben's special meal with him. "My goodness, Ben," she exclaimed, "you've outdone yourself. You are going to have me thoroughly spoiled."

"I fully intend to pamper you, as I know you will me, my dear. I had intended to have the catering staff from the hotel here to serve us, but decided I'd rather be alone with you. I also gave my houseboy an early dismissal." He placed the tray on the table to the left of his place setting and then seated himself. A bottle of wine was already open and ready to be poured.

All during the meal, they smiled at each other. Sara was so happy; she thought her heart would surely burst. "This is the happiest day of my life," she said, and meant it. She held up her ring finger often and admired Ben's choice.

"Do you like it?" he asked. "I've had it in my dresser drawer for about three months, waiting for the right time and the right moment."

For some inexplicable reason, another rush of fear gripped her. It ran from the innermost part of her and ended up in goose bumps on her arms. In a few months, she would be moving out of her house and into Ben's. For forty-three years, she had either lived with her parents or by herself in the same house. What would she bring with her, and what would she leave behind? Would her many items of mostly sentimental value fit into Ben's organized space and blend with the quality of his furnishings? Maybe she needed more time. No, the earlier they settled into their new life, the better it would be for both of them. They needed each other.

Ben interrupted her rampant thoughts. "I can feel your mind at work, Sara. Are you thinking about the date for our marriage?"

*Smoke in the Kitchen*

"To tell you the truth, Ben, I can't think straight about anything right now," she said. "My mind can't wrap around what has just happened." She ate several mouthfuls of her dinner and sipped her wine. "We have plenty of time."

As Sara drove home very late that evening, she compared Ben's proposal to the one she'd received from Willy. Ten years ago, her parents had influenced her decision to go through the traditional *Krio* engagement procedure called *put stop*. As their only daughter, her parents had so looked forward to a proposal, an engagement, and a wedding, that they had taken charge of everything and treated her as though she were a teenager.

In keeping with their culture and tradition, she and Willy were expected to put a stop to any clandestine affairs after they had made their commitment to each other. As it turned out, however, Willy had instead moved full steam ahead, embracing the adventures of bachelorhood; he had never been committed to her. Despite the tragedy that had ensued, Sara had to smile over the elaborate game played by both families. Fifteen minutes before Willy's relatives and friends were expected to arrive at her home, her parents, grandmother, and other relatives and friends had assembled in their parlor to wait.

Sara replayed the details of her engagement to Willy West in her head. Instead of planning a wedding for two individuals, her mother had told her that it was, rather, a marriage of two families. Both her parents and Willy's had agreed on a date for the engagement or "put stop" ceremony. This was unlike the romantic proposals seen in movies when the man gets on one knee and asks his usually unsuspecting girlfriend to marry him. No, the Sierra Leone put stop was a fun community event that sought to test the resolve of the suitor's family. The entire goal of this affair was for the groom's family to secure a resounding "yes" from the bride's family: "Yes, our daughter will marry your son."

Equipped with the dowry, the designated spokesman and several other members of the groom's family set out to make their case for marrying the bride. Sara remembered how excited she was and how much she struggled to calm the fluttery feeling in her stomach. She remembered the first knock at their door and how her family playfully rejected the Wests' first attempt "to pick a beautiful rose from the Johns' garden." This beautiful rose was Sara, and her family was not about to let Willy's family pluck her that easily.

After several more tries, the smooth-talking spokesman got Sara's family to open the door. The West family was on a mission to find the correct rose and to get the John family to part with it. Rather than show them just one rose, the Johns decided to parade several roses in an attempt to distract Willy's family. All of this was done in good fun amid exhilarating laughter.

Hiding in Sara's bedroom, with their ears pressed to the door, the ladies enjoyed the banter coming from the living room. "Okay! It's our turn soon," Kelitia whispered as she reviewed the order in which the roses would be revealed. Almost like catwalk models, the ladies started to come out one by one. The first rose came out to a collective oohing and aahing, but the shy six-year-old was rejected by Willy's family for being a young rosebud. Unlike the rosebud, the next rose drew much admiration. She was Sara's eighty-year-old great-aunt; but sadly, the West family rejected her as well. The parade of roses ended with Sara, beautifully adorned with gold jewelry and simple makeup; she wore a kabaslot, the traditional garb worn by a newly engaged woman. Cheers erupted, and rising to their feet, the West family happily declared, "This is our rose! This is our awesome rose!"

Having identified the rose, the West family spokesman handed the dowry, which was in a raffia basket called a shuku basket, to Sara's mother. She quickly retreated to the bedroom to examine its contents. Sara, her grandma, Kelitia, and the other ladies gathered around. In the basket were a pocket Bible, a gold engagement ring, safety pins, needles, coins, a spool of thread, a package of kola nuts, a container of grains of rice, a bolt of fabric, and a bottle of sherry.

"Each of these items symbolizes the realities of life, Sara," her mama had said. "It means that in your home you will find happiness and enjoy laughter and wealth. You'll also encounter challenges and shed a few tears in difficult times."

All Sara could think about, however, was her love for Willy and how much she wanted to be his wife and mother to their children.

After much jubilation, eating, drinking, and dancing, the West family members didn't only receive a gift from the John family, but they had also received the assurance that the parents of the bride had agreed for Willy to marry Sara.

By the time she had relived that remarkable evening, Sara had reached her home. She parked her car in the garage and rushed into the house. She was eager to examine her engagement ring once more. None of the past mattered to her. Nothing except that her beloved parents would not be present at her marriage and have the opportunity to know and love Ben as she did. Confident that the future would bring the elusive happiness she had longed to enjoy for ten long years, she strolled through every room of her dear house and took a visual inventory of what she owned and could not live without. She imagined where each piece could be placed in Ben's home—a home that would soon be hers as well.

Once again, she thought of her two engagements—one formal and traditional, which involved every member of the extended families and many friends, and the one that had taken place only hours ago . . . an informal ceremony with only she and Ben in attendance. It had been more personal and heartfelt, more endearing and memorable. A ceremony that she would cherish forever. Her first engagement had ended with no wedding. It had been instigated because she was pregnant with Willy's child, and her father had coerced him to marry her and make their child legitimate.

Although there had been no pronouncements, no families or friends present, no African raffia gift basket, no cloak of tradition to enfold the ceremony, and no knock on the door in search of a rose tonight, Ben's proposal had been founded on love and commitment.

## Smoke in the Kitchen

Sara danced about the living room and kissed the ring on her finger. Then she stopped and peered at her reflection in the wall mirror. "I only have four months," she said aloud. "Then Sara John will become Sara Moses."

It was a prospect that brought back the tears, once again from pure joy.

## Chapter 6

Early Monday morning, Sara phoned Kelitia. "What time will you be home from work? I have to see you."

"Is there a problem, Sara?"

"Nothing that can't be solved, but I need to discuss it with you in person."

"You know my antennae have shot up with a remark like that. I have the day off, so why don't you come over right away?"

Sara hurried into the bathroom to wash her face and brush her teeth. While waiting to shower, she glanced out the window. How she would miss this view of the bougainvilleas and other flowers when she moved to Ben's house. She had tended them for decades. She leaned with her elbows on the windowsill and watched the activities of the neighbor's children as they left their washhouse, with towels wrapped around their wet skin. In the makeshift backyard kitchen, their mother poured cocoa into six enamel cups and then added sugar, powdered milk, and hot water. Each child picked up a cup and a slice of buttered bread. Sara had observed this ritual countless times over the years, enjoying the growth of each child. She had fed them herself on many occasions, knowing it was a help to their mother. She would miss them.

Chastising herself for wasting time daydreaming, she then returned to her bedroom to finish dressing. In the process, she became distracted once again and picked up the notebook and pen she'd used the evening before to begin her moving list. Now she scribbled a second list of things she needed to discuss with Kelitia regarding her wedding.

- Wedding dress and accessories
- Notify maid of honor and bridesmaids; choose dresses for them
- Discuss wedding with the pastor
- Reserve the church
- Prepare list of guests
- Select and mail invitations
- Reserve cars
- Reserve reception location and details
- Reserve caterer; make food selection
- Flowers and decorations
- Party
- Select DJ; discuss music choices
- Uncle Jabez

At eight thirty, Sara phoned her secretary. "I won't be in before lunch today, Ruth. I have an unexpected meeting with my sister."

Five minutes later, she headed for Kelitia's. She lived with her mama, Mary, and three other siblings in a three-bedroom apartment at the bottom of a two-story concrete house west of the city. By the time she arrived, Kelitia was already waiting for her on the veranda. She held the wedding notebook in her left hand to conceal her engagement ring until she was ready for the big reveal.

"You took long enough to get here, Sara! What's so important it couldn't wait?" Kelitia was still lazing in an ankle-length *Hug Me* shirt. "Did you break up with Ben? Is your cousin Thomas causing even more ruckus about the mart?"

Sara didn't respond, but held out her left hand and wiggled it.

"Oh, my stars, you're *engaged*! Sara, when did this happen? Why didn't you call me the second that gorgeous ring slid onto your finger?"

"It may shock you to know that some things are best enjoyed in private, little sister." Sara fingered the ring and showed it to Kelitia again. "Isn't it the most beautiful ring you've ever seen? I was stunned when Ben presented it. I had no idea he was ready to propose. I'm thrilled, of course."

"Well, you should be! That diamond is as big as a rock. I bet he bought this in London. You deserve it. I'm so happy for you." Kelitia hugged her tightly. "When is the wedding date?"

"In four months."

Sara opened her notebook. "I'm here to go over the list of all the things we need to do before the wedding. You'll help me, won't you? Needless to say, I'm more than a little uneasy about tackling such a huge event on my own. I've never missed Mama as much as I do right now."

*Smoke in the Kitchen*

Kelitia hugged her again. "Of course, you miss her. Every bride wants her mama to lend her expertise at a time like this. I'm the next best thing you have, and I'll help in every way I can. Now, let's see that list of yours." She studied it and then laughed. "Were you up all night writing this?"

"Did I leave something out?"

"Not that I can tell. Are you going to rent your family home?"

"I'm not sure. Suddenly I find myself incapable of making any decisions at all, even the most simple. I've been remembering the many years I've lived in that same house and wondering how I can make the transition to Ben's home. I'm so eager for you to see it, Kelitia. It's big enough for three families!" She played with her ring again. "Ben had roses and champagne and a wonderful catered dinner for us to enjoy by candlelight. It was romantic and . . . memorable. I will treasure the evening for the rest of my life."

Kelitia clasped her hands and brought them to her chin. "I wish I could have been a little mouse in the corner to enjoy it with you. Lucky you, to have found the love of your life!"

Sara beamed. "He feels the same way about me. Maybe I had to go through ten years of turmoil in order to recognize what real love is all about. We respect each other. And I trust him. He is so different, Kelitia . . . he is different!"

"I'm going to call that man right now and congratulate him on being so smart! Do you have his phone number?"

Minutes later, Kelitia hung up the phone and turned to her sister. "He's happy as a kid at a candy store! He said we should plan the wedding of your dreams and not worry about the cost. He wants to pay for everything."

Sara shook her head. "That won't happen if I have anything to say about it!"

"Don't protest too much, Sara," Kelitia said. "Save your arguments for something more important. Maybe you can divide expenses exactly in half. That's fair. Now, I see Uncle Jabez's name on your list. Is it your intention to have him give you away during the ceremony? Do you think he's up to it? He's got to be at least seventy-five years old."

Sara shrugged. "I know, but he's my only surviving blood relative of that generation. He's Mama's uncle. I took Ben to meet him not long after we started to date, but we'll need to drive out next weekend to see him again. I want to tell him in person about my engagement."

A retired bus conductor, Uncle Jabez had worked in the Road Transport Department for most of his life. Ever since his wife died, Sara had cared for him. She prepared his food and arranged for her houseboy to clean his house and do his laundry once a week.

Driving to Uncle Jabez's house in No. 2, a village west of Freetown, she felt as if they were going on a safari. Though wild animals were absent from the vicinity, there were dogs and cats in abundance, in addition to sundry goats, sheep, and pigs straying aimlessly on the sides of the road. She teased Ben as he dodged several and had to slam on his brakes when a cat being chased by a dog darted across the road.

"I can't imagine how alert you are when you drive here on your own, Sara," he said. "I may have to hire a chauffeur when you make future trips," he teased.

Her uncle's corrugated sheet metal house was hot enough to bake a loaf of bread. The heat was often so unbearable for him, most days he retreated to his hammock under two adjacent avocado pear trees until late at night before finally returning to his bed to sleep.

As soon as Ben parked his Land Rover, Uncle Jabez rushed to meet them. "Bra Ben, how you do?" He offered his hand in greeting, bowing slightly. "Sara, how you do? Come, come. Sit down."

"I'm all right, Uncle. How are you?" Sara took Ben's hand and followed her uncle, cringing when the indoor heat blasted them upon entry.

"Fine. Fine. Any news?" Uncle Jabez gestured to the settee and three other armchairs in his little parlor.

"Yes, I have good news, Uncle. Ben and I are getting married. We became engaged last weekend. See my ring?" She held out her hand for him to see.

*"Watin! mek ah sidom for listen de good news."* He pulled out a straight-backed chair next to the table opposite them and moved the kerosene lantern to one side of the table. After seating himself, he examined the ring and laughed aloud, chattering excitedly in Krio.

Sara poked Ben and smiled when she saw all twelve of her uncle's tobacco-stained teeth. "He's happy for us," she said. "I'm going to tell him we've agreed that he should walk me down the aisle."

She reached out to touch the gnarled hand of her uncle. "You're my only senior relative, Uncle. I want you to participate in our wedding. Will you take the place of my papa and walk me down the aisle?" She watched as he reamed the charred tobacco from his pipe into an ashtray on the table.

He methodically refilled the pipe with fresh tobacco from his pouch and then lit it. Like the smoke from the fireside of her kitchen, his pipe smoke filled the small parlor. He coughed several times and puffed on the pipe, not immediately answering her.

Unexpectedly, he turned to Ben. In halting English, he explained that Sara's road had been rugged at times. He knew that, with their level of maturity, they would make a great couple. He blessed their relationship and wished them good luck and God's blessings. "Bra Ben, you get good woman *weh sabi cook.*"

Ben laughed and patted Jabez's back. "I have already experienced her cooking, Uncle, and I wholeheartedly agree with you. I can testify to her expertise in the kitchen. I'm a lucky man."

"Be happy. I keep on praying." Uncle Jabez nodded, satisfied that he had spoken well on behalf of Sara's deceased parents.

"Thank you very much, Uncle," Ben said. "Everything will be fine."

"By God's grace." Jabez then turned toward Sara. "How is this handsome old man to dress?"

"I'm not sure yet, Uncle, but you mustn't worry about it. I will take care of everything. It will be my pleasure."

"My sweet, sweet Sara."

Sara felt her eyes mist over at his words. "I am so happy," she said.

"I want us to drink to your health and this good news," Uncle Jabez said. He pushed himself to his feet, shuffled to his adjoining bedroom, and returned with three bottles of warm Star beer. Then he reached for two glasses from a cupboard next to the table. Ben assisted him to open the bottles and poured two of them out into two glasses; Uncle Jabez then drank his beer straight from the bottle. "Cheers to my niece, Sara, to her *intended*, Benjamin, and to this man, Jabez Joshua Jacobs, JJJ."

Sara lifted her glass and clinked his bottle. "To your good health, Uncle. Thank you."

"It be my honor and duty, me *yone yone* Sara."

A few days later, Sara accompanied Ben on a visit to his Aunty Philomena. She had looked forward to meeting her, after learning that she often prepared Ben's food. Since the woman was almost the same age as her Uncle Jabez, she was hoping the two of them would get along.

Once again Ben maneuvered his way driving along the equally treacherous streets that led to the east end of the city, where she lived. What should have been a twenty-minute trip took far longer, due to heavy traffic, vehicular as well as human.

When they finally stopped in front of her house, Sara remained seated to peer intently at Philomena's house. The structure, of stained-green concrete, was small in size but seemed perfectly adequate for an elderly woman. When they approached the entrance, she saw an oblong welcome mat placed at the bottom of the steps. It was an appropriate way to ensure the dust from the street didn't enter the house. Ben knocked on the mahogany door exactly five times. *Is he looking for a rose?* Sara wondered.

A rather tall and lanky woman, wearing an ankle-length house dress, appeared at the door almost immediately. She welcomed them with smiles, but her eyes peered closely at Sara, evaluating her from her newly coiffed hair to her beige, short-sleeved suit and brown-leather handbag that matched her three-inch-high heels, which Sara had purposely selected because of Ben's height.

Ben embraced his aunt. "Aunty, this is Sara, my wife-to-be, and Sara, meet my Aunty Philomena, my mama's youngest sister."

"It's a great pleasure to meet you, ma." Sara extended her hand thinking that Aunt Philomina wasn't at all what she had imagined.

"So, this is the lady you told me you intend to marry, Ben. Nice to know you, Miss . . ."

"Her name is Sara John, Aunty." Ben ushered Sara into the house. "Aunty Eva, how nice that you're here too. Sara, meet Aunty's favorite cousin."

"It is a pleasure to meet you too, ma." Sara shook her hand, while estimating she had to be in her mid-sixties.

Ben gestured toward two chairs near the entrance door. "Let's sit here," he said, winking so that only she got the message that they were on display and being judged by the two women. Sara quietly observed them and wondered why they were frowning.

Philomena sat comfortably by the double window, which overlooked the activities in the street. "Who are your people?" she asked bluntly.

Sara smiled to herself. Now the cross-examination would begin. Ben's aunt needed to know if she were worthy of marrying her nephew. "Solomon and Hannah John, ma," she said graciously.

"John. You mean the auctioneer John people?"

"That's right, Aunty," Ben said. "Sara's father owned and operated the business and then left it to Sara in his will. She runs it now. Both her parents have passed away, and she is the only heir."

Philomena fidgeted with the *Daily Mail* newspaper and reached for her reading glasses, which were on the end table next to her chair. She narrowed her eyes and peered closely at Sara. "Your grandma was Corinthia; I remember her."

"Yes," Sara said.

"Humph! Were you the lady who had that mishap when your intended died? About ten years ago, wasn't it, Eva?"

Like a bomb, the unexpected question shook Sara to her very core. She struggled to remain seated, because she wanted to pace the floor and defend herself. Thankfully, she had discussed her baby with Ben. "Yes, ma."

"Where is the child?"

Sara felt the trickle of perspiration run down her back. News traveled fast in a small town, and memories were long. "I suffered a miscarriage," she said, whispering the still-painful words.

Philomena cast a quick glance at Eva, who shrugged. "So, Ben, you two don't want me to do anything at your wedding?"

"Aunty, we've decided on a small, intimate wedding for only a few family members and friends. We are taking care of everything.

Sara's adopted sister is the manager of the hotel where the event will take place."

"Hotel? That's a waste of money, Ben. You got that big, big house, so why don't you use it? Makes more sense to me!"

"We've made all the arrangements, Aunty. Sara and I both work and have limited time to spend on arrangements. Neither of us have parents, and we're both old enough to know what is best for us."

"Humph," she sighed. "I shut up."

Eva mimicked her sigh and smoothed the fabric of her dress in a gesture of defeat.

"Sara," Philomena said, in a more authoritative tone of voice, "it will be your duty to look after Ben as well as you look after yourself. Did he tell you his mama died a year ago, and that I am his second mama? I cook his food." She sighed audibly again and peered at a framed photograph of Ben's mother she had mounted on the wall. "I promised his mama I would always take care of him."

Eva gazed at the photograph too and sighed even louder. "Cousin Leah may be gone, but she will never be forgotten."

Ben squeezed Sara's hand. She squeezed back. "I'll do my best to see that Ben is happy, ma."

"What about children? How many do you intend to have?" Philomena cocked her head to ensure she would hear the reply. "Or can't you have any more?"

Eva lifted her chin and gazed directly at Sara.

Sara smiled, but didn't respond. She wished she could fan her face. It felt hot, and another surge of heat had enveloped her entire body. She fully understood why the woman had asked such a question; it wasn't as if she were in her twenties. But the question was too personal. When Ben made no move to rescue her, she rose from her chair.

"It was such a pleasure meeting both of you. Aunty Philomena, Ben speaks of you often with love and respect. You mean a great deal to him. Please know that you will always be welcome in our home. I hope you will visit often. You, too, Aunty Eva." She turned to Ben, who was staring at her with his mouth agape. "We will need to leave now, Ben, as I have an important meeting this evening and mustn't be late."

Without asking permission, she reached for the doorknob and pulled open the door. Stepping out onto the porch, she waited for Ben to say his good-byes and then headed for his car. As soon as they were on their way, her fury erupted. "Why didn't you say something, Ben? It is no one's business how many children I have, or if I choose to have any at all! That is between you and me. I did not find that interrogation pleasant, and especially not the references to my past pain. I . . . I found that remark intrusive. And mostly, I'm disappointed that you didn't offer your support to me."

"I am not marrying my aunty or her cousin, Sara. I am marrying you—the woman I love," he said, defending himself. He tried to lighten the mood by attempting to draw her close as he drove.

Sara tried to remove his arm, but he resisted. She tried again.

Suddenly, their vehicle was in the ditch.

"Oh, my God, Ben! Are you trying to get us killed?"

Ben grimaced. "We're still alive. We're not even injured. It was your shouting and resistance to my attempt at pacifying you that caused me to lose focus on this despicable road. You're getting yourself worked up unnecessarily, Sara. Take a deep breath."

Two robust-looking men ran toward Ben's car. "Sir, need help? Need help?"

"Yes, yes," he said, climbing out of the vehicle. "Could you help me get the vehicle back onto the road?"

Still upset, Sara said nothing and didn't bother to get out. She sat in the car with pinched lips, nursing her anger and staring straight ahead through the windshield while the three men lifted and pushed the vehicle back onto the road. She noticed that Ben rewarded each of the men with money for their assistance.

When he climbed onto the seat beside her, he reached out to pat her hand. "I love you, Sara. I'm upset that you're upset. What anyone says or thinks doesn't matter. I should have said something to Aunty, but she would have been hurt and offended. She is of the old generation. She sees her duty to her sister and to me being usurped by a beautiful, much younger woman. She's probably jealous." He smiled at her. "Who wouldn't be? She thinks she'll be on the sideline."

Ben's attempt at pacifying her worked like a charm; Sara couldn't hide her smile. Cooks were always competitive, even within a family. Her own mama and grandma had sparred often over whose dish was superior. Nevertheless, would her happiness be marred if Ben's family members didn't respect her? "I want so much for them to like and admire me," she said.

"They will. Give them time. Right now, everything is new and upsetting to them." Ben was quiet for the next mile as he focused on his driving. Then he reached out to hold her hand once more. "You should know, Sara, about a year ago, Aunty worked hard to persuade me that the daughter of one of her friends was the perfect woman for me to marry. I disagreed and refused to meet the lady."

"So she resents me because I'm the one you chose," Sara concluded. Now she understood what the future held for her.

# Chapter 7

**May 1982**

A week before the wedding, Sara toured the hotel with Kelitia and Ben. After going over the wedding setup with the manager, the three of them decided to have dinner at the hotel's Bamboo restaurant. "You can see that everything is under control, Sara," Kelitia said. "I've worked several hours with the restaurant manager. The decorations and flowers have been handled. An abundant menu is being designed specifically for your wedding, and you can trust that it will not only be delicious but also plentiful and displayed elegantly. Your guests are in for a treat; they'll enjoy every morsel. You have nothing to worry about."

"I'm pleased with everything I've seen, Kelitia," Sara said, "and your assurances lessen my concern, but in the back of my mind, I'm fretting that something will go wrong."

Ben patted her hand. "Then we'll laugh about it, Sara. From what I've heard about weddings, there are always a few glitches. That's to be expected. If your major concern is whether Aunty Philomena will find fault . . . you know she will. Let's agree ahead of time that we'll let her complain and then laugh it off."

"I know you're right," Sara said, "but saying that's what we'll do is not the same as what happens in actuality."

"This is no time for pessimism, Sara," Kelitia said. "I'll take care of Aunty Philomena. I deal with difficult customers all day long who always find something to complain about. I know how to smooth things over. I'll seek her advice. She'll like feeling important. If I can do some little thing her way, she'll have something to talk about all evening. How does that sound?"

Sara clapped her hands and blew her a kiss. "You always have the right solutions, little sister. I'll not spend one more minute worrying about Aunty."

On the second Saturday in May, at one in the afternoon, Sara took her vows. The sun shone brightly, and not a single rain cloud marred the light blue sky. Fortunately, it was neither too hot nor too muggy for that time of year, and the generous sea breezes did what they could to cool the already beautiful day. Because of Sara's past, no one expected an over-the-top, glamorous wedding. For that reason and others, she chose not to marry in her local church. Instead, she selected a small seaside village church in Torkeh, a stone's throw from one of the seaside resorts and about twenty miles from Freetown. The brown masonry, cone-roofed church building was just large enough to accommodate the thirty invited guests, comprised of several relatives and closest friends.

About a dozen white tourists on vacation at the beach saw the wedding party arrive and soon slipped into the back of the sanctuary to see how a Sierra Leone wedding was conducted. Later, Kelitia announced her approval of their presence. "They added a little color to the proceedings, Sara. From where I stood next to you, I thought the church sanctuary looked rather like a piano keyboard, you know, with black keys and white keys."

As Sara waited at the back of the church with Uncle Jabez, her round face sparkled with the natural beauty that came with being happy. She had little need for make-up. Her skin was smooth and soft, and her radiant smile and the glitter in her eyes provided all the embellishment required for such an important event. Her champagne, strapless wedding gown warmed the darkness of her skin. The matching short-sleeved jacket was adorned with yellow sequins, and the amber stones in her earrings and necklace coordinated beautifully.

Uncle Jabez adjusted the knot on his red tie and smoothed the sleeves of his fawn-colored suit that Sara had arranged to be made by one of the finest tailors in town. He winked at her and offered his arm just as the organ started to play. Together, they strolled, feet stepping in unison, up the aisle to the front of the church, where Ben waited with a wide smile. When the pastor said, "Who gives this woman to be married to this man?" he lifted his chin and stated, "I do," in a clear voice.

When the pastor asked whether anyone could present a reason why the couple should not be lawfully married, Sara held her breath, waiting to hear the raspy voice of a certain aunty raised in protest. The butterflies in her stomach flitted about at will, and she could feel her knees wobble. The wait seemed interminable, but only silence reached her ears. She glanced at Ben from the sides of her eyes, and he appeared calm and relaxed.

Finally, with the absence of a response, the ceremony continued, and Sara regained her composure. It went too quickly. What she savored most was the moment Ben took her hands and peered deeply into her eyes to speak his personal vow.

"I, Benjamin Moses, take you, Sara John, to be my wife, my life partner and closest friend, my only and dearest love. I look forward to growing old with you and to learning more about you with each passing day. I will support you in all your endeavors, laugh with you in the good times, and comfort you in times of sorrow. On this special day, I give you my heart, my hand, and my unconditional love. In the presence of God, our families, and friends, I offer my solemn vow to be your faithful partner, no matter what obstacles come our way. I will love you without reservation and always be open and honest with you. That is my promise, Sara, for as long as we both shall live."

Tears stung her eyes, and she could barely speak above a whisper as she made her promises to this remarkable man. Ben meant every word of his heartfelt vow, and she understood that his choice of words was meant to erase her lingering doubts that he would become as unfaithful to her as Willy had been. She trusted him. This was the beginning of the rest of her life, and she looked forward to it with joy.

As she hurried back down the aisle on the arm of her husband, she welcomed the applause of their invited guests and the uninvited onlookers. Her eyes fell on those of two women in the second pew. Aunty Philomena and her cousin Eva were whispering and glowering at her. She tightened her grip on Ben's arm and smiled up at him. "I love you, Mr. Moses."

"I love you too, Mrs. Moses," he said. "I am the luckiest man in the world."

\* \* \*

By the time the wedding party reached the reception, the DJs had already set up their system to supply background music, and a familiar song was playing as they entered the reserved room. Seven beautifully decorated tables had been arranged around the head table, which itself was set for six. Kelitia had ensured the hotel's finest china, glassware, and linens would be used, and everything sparkled.

The master of ceremonies announced the arrival of the bride and groom. Sara paused at the entrance to take in the magnificence with teary eyes. "Oh, Ben, can you believe this!" she enthused. "Where is Kelitia? She has outdone herself. I must thank her."

"A beautiful setting for a beautiful bride," Ben said. "It is as it should be."

He guided her to the head table as a soloist from Sara's Sunday school sang "Guide Me, Lord," one of her favorite hymns. Bougainvilleas arched overhead and filled the room with fragrance. Other arrangements throughout the room and on every table created a colorful indoor garden that only Mother Nature could supply during the May season. Every flower was indigenous to Sierra Leone, just as Sara had wanted.

As custom dictated, the family members of both sides welcomed each other. First, Uncle Jabez welcomed Ben in the traditional way, with the glass-of-water ceremony. With his glass in hand, he rose from his chair and lifted it high. "Men are not short-winded, but I am to be brief. Mr. Ben Moses, I welcome you into the John family as a son, not a nephew-in-law." He offered Ben the water, and then Sara. Both sipped from the rim, and then he took a sip himself. Satisfied that he had handled his role with sincerity and skill, he acknowledged the guests and took his seat.

Sara leaned closer to Uncle Jabez and kissed his cheek. "Thank you," she mouthed.

Aunty Philomena rose from her chair and raised her glass of water. "Ben, I have said what I needed to say when you introduced Sara to me. So, Sara, I welcome you into our family. If you and Ben really love each other, take a sip of this water to symbolize that love." Sara sipped, Ben sipped, and then Philomena sipped. She reveled in the applause that followed her welcome speech and bobbed rhythmically to the sounds of the local talking drums—*gumbay*—as she posed as the bridegroom's surrogate mother. Lifting the glass higher into the air, she was joined by her cousin Eva.

The only toast to the bride and groom was given by Ben's cousin, Josh Moses. "I will take full credit for getting these two to the altar," he said, patting his own shoulder in personal congratulations. "I was the fellow who invited Ben to attend church with me, and I was the one who introduced him to Sara that very day. Obviously, it was a smart move on my part. I wish them my best."

There was considerable laughter and applause.

Ben rose from his chair and shook hands with Josh. "I will not argue with my cousin over taking credit where credit is due. I was looking for a soul mate after my mother's untimely death, and Sara was an answer to my prayers. I will give myself credit, however, for recognizing that fact and for taking whatever measures were necessary to convince her that I could be her soul mate too. I am a happy man." He leaned over and planted a firm kiss on Sara's lips.

The DJ's song choices were a hit with guests. Uncle Jabez was even inspired to dance with his niece, the bride. Whenever African tunes filled the room, the women leaped to their feet, wiggled, and shook their hips to the rhythm; the men followed and danced in admiration.

The reception was to end at ten o'clock. Five minutes before then, Sara waved her arms to get everyone's attention and tapped on her champagne glass for reinforcement. "Once again, Ben and I wish to thank you for celebrating this auspicious occasion with us. We treasure every minute of it, and you have made it all the more special for us by your presence. I especially want to thank Kelitia for her untiring assistance in planning this event. She is totally responsible for our dinner, the decorations, the flower arrangements, and for seeing that everything ran so smoothly, and that all of you had a good time."

She was about to move away from the microphone when she stopped to smile directly at a pinch-lipped elderly woman who was openly glaring at her. "I cannot forget to thank a very special woman in my husband's life—his beloved Aunty Philomena. After his dear mother passed away, Aunty took it upon herself to care for him with a most attentive motherly love. Her affections and selflessness will always be appreciated. And I must share something with you. Kelitia informed me that our delicious wedding cake was inspired by one of Aunty's personal recipes. Ben and I will value her generosity for years to come."

Sara watched as Philomena's eyes widened considerably and then crinkled with the appearance of the first semblance of a smile she had seen on her well-weathered face.

# Chapter 8

**October 1982**

Five months into their marriage, Sara had her first serious disagreement with Ben. They had decided, because of their age, they would not use any form of birth control in order to ensure they could quickly fill the extra bedrooms in their spacious home. Both of them felt strongly that children were a blessing and that, more than furniture or paintings, they were what made a house a home. But whether those children were biological or not became an issue.

Unbeknown to Ben, Sara had made monthly trips to her gynecologist and obstetrician. She was concerned that her late-month miscarriage of Willy's daughter and her age might greatly affect her ability to conceive. When five months passed and she wasn't pregnant, she had called for another appointment and a more thorough examination. Now, Dr. Kate Zed had called her in to discuss the results.

The waiting room was filled with women of all ages. Some were in various stages of their pregnancies, while others were elderly women with menopausal complaints. She listened to them chatter with each other and smiled, without discussing her own problem. She didn't want their advice or admonitions. While leafing through several issues of expired women's magazines from the table next to her, she tried to squelch her uneasiness. There was no sense in worrying about something that might not be an issue.

"Mrs. Moses?" the office nurse said from the doorway. "Follow me, please." She led her to an area where she went through the routine of weighing in and having her blood pressure checked. "The doctor will be with you soon," she said, leaving her in a small cubicle that afforded privacy for both exams and consultations.

Sara noticed a folder on the desk by her side. It had her name on it, and she wished she had the nerve to open it. Instead, she snapped open and shut the catch on her handbag several times to keep her trembling fingers occupied. Finally, the door to the room opened and Dr. Zed entered. She was wearing her white coat and had a stethoscope draped around her neck. She smiled and sat facing Sara.

"Hello, Sara. I know you're eager to discuss the results of your last exam, so we won't spend any time with idle talk this morning." She opened the folder and pushed a few X-rays and other documents around the desk for easier viewing. "For the most part, you're very healthy. We've already discussed that age can be a concern for some women who wish to conceive, especially if they're having premenopausal symptoms. This doesn't seem to be a problem for you. However, I did find something that may be preventing you from becoming pregnant."

"Oh." Sara sucked in her cheek and began chewing on the inner skin. She wouldn't be able to have a child for Ben. She was being punished. Literally frozen in place, she stared at Dr. Zed with widened eyes.

"The X-rays I took of your uterus showed that you have several submucosal fibroids," the doctor said. "These are little tumors that bulge into the inner cavity of your uterus. Depending upon where they are in the uterus, they can sometimes prevent or impair fertility by blocking."

"Tumors?" Sara could barely think of what she had read in one women's magazine. The very thought of cancer struck fear into her heart.

"No, no, we have no evidence that fibroids ever become cancerous. They are completely benign." Dr. Zed leaned forward. "We know now that certain fibroids can grow quite large during a pregnancy, because they feed on estrogen. In some cases, they can cause a miscarriage, and then scarring can ensue that blocks the fallopian tubes."

Sara felt her fingers tremble and clasped them tightly together. "Is . . . is that why I lost my baby daughter? Is that what you're saying?"

"We can't know for sure, Sara. This is what we do know about fibroids. A heredity factor is involved. If your mother had them, your risks are greater. I'm not slamming the door on your ever becoming pregnant again. I just want you to understand it may be more difficult for you. Medical science hasn't developed to the point where we know exactly what to do with these things."

When Sara didn't reply, Dr. Zed patted her hand. "Are you sometimes in pain? You've never told me if you suffer from abdominal discomfort around the time of ovulation."

Sara shook her head. "I've had pains off and on over the years, but nothing I couldn't handle. I should have told you. Maybe we could have done something to prevent this." She felt the stinging of tears and blinked rapidly several times to stem their flow. "So, what's going to happen now? Will you have to operate?"

"Unless they grow in size or cause complications, we don't remove them. In fact, we don't do anything. You learn to live with them, and let us know if they cause undue pain or excessive bleeding. Did your mother suffer from uterine fibroids?"

Sara shrugged. "I wouldn't even know, nor would she. It's not something she would have discussed with me. I asked her once why I didn't have any brothers or sisters, and she said God only gave her one child."

Sara gazed at her doctor with greater appreciation. She always took the time to explain things. Kelitia had introduced her to Dr. Zed after her previous gynecologist of fifteen years had relocated. Dr. Zed's husband was a lecturer at the university. They had stayed at the Funkia Hotel when they were house hunting, and Kelitia had introduced them to a real estate agent.

"As I've already said, this condition is often hereditary, Sara. It's possible your mother had fibroids and couldn't conceive a second time."

"I'm not aware that my mother ever visited a gynecologist. Few women did in her days. They typically used a midwife." Sara felt

*Smoke in the Kitchen*

the sting of tears again and brushed them away with the back of her fingers. "Tell me, Dr. Zed, will I ever have a child?"

"That's something I can't say, Sara. It's possible, but it's just as possible that you will not."

A nurse poked her head into the examining room. "I think we've got an emergency, Dr. Zed. Mrs. Dufka is in the waiting room, and she unexpectedly went into labor."

Dr. Zed rose from her chair. "Everything will be fine, Sara. You're not to worry one minute about the fibroids, unless you develop complications."

All the way home, Sara thought about her family. She visualized the family tree in Grandma Corinthia's Bible. Every woman on her mother's side of the family had given birth to one daughter. She was the last of the line. Her miscarriage may have cost her the only chance she'd have to continue the family line.

After parking her car, Sara entered the house with dragging feet. For a long time, she stood in the dining area of the house that had become her home. She climbed the stairs and entered the first spare bedroom. She had imagined it as the nursery of her daughter, while conceding she might give birth to another son for Ben. Now it would remain empty—a guest bedroom. Unless . . .

When Ben returned from his business trip to Ghana later that evening, she was waiting with a late dinner. Preparing the meal had occupied her mind and kept her hands busy. She wasn't looking forward to telling him what she'd learned from Dr. Zed, but it was a conversation she couldn't postpone. It meant too much to her.

While Ben ate, she sipped on a glass of wine. She asked a dozen questions about the purpose and success of his trip and forced herself to remain focused on his replies, even though her mind continuously wandered to the subject matter she most wished to discuss.

"Enough about me," Ben said. "How have you filled the three days I've been away from you? Every hour, I wished you were by my side. I hope the day comes when we can travel on some of my official trips."

"Yeah . . ." she said.

"What's wrong, my dear? You're not smiling, and you look like you're in mourning. Is it the business? That cousin of yours? Has he—?"

"No, no, it's not Thomas. The lawyer is handling everything for now. No . . . it's something else. Something even more important . . . at least to me." Sara peered wistfully into Ben's eyes. Would he understand? Would he support her? Would he be as enthusiastic about her proposal as she was?

In the next fifteen minutes, she summarized her meetings with Dr. Zed and the results of the exams and X-rays. "I was devastated, Ben, for both of us. You know how very much I want children with you, and you've said you want to be a father of more children than the son you already have . . ." She broke off when a tear slipped down her cheek.

Ben reached out to gently wipe it away with his finger. "From what you've said, I don't believe the door is shut. It sounds to me like we must simply practice patience and enjoy ourselves in the process."

"You aren't fully understanding the problem, Ben!" Sara pushed his hand away. "My great-grandma had one daughter, that daughter had one daughter, and my mama had one daughter."

"So . . . what does that have to do with you? You worry unnecessarily."

"It says a great deal!"

"About what?"

"I have lost the only chance I had, Ben! I lost *my* daughter!" Sara buried her face into her hands.

Ben rose from his chair and sat by her side. "Sara, it's not like you to indulge in self-pity. The doctor did not close the door on your having more children."

Sara peered at him through tear-filled eyes. "She said fibroids are hereditary. She said it was possible that my fibroids caused my late-term miscarriage and that these same fibroids may be prohibiting my ability to conceive. I can't ignore the fact that my mother and grandmother may have suffered from the same malady."

"That's a lot of maybes, Sara, and imagining trouble where there may be none won't make you feel any better. What does Dr. Zed suggest you do?"

"I have to see her again in six weeks."

"Then that is exactly what you will do. Don't lose hope, my darling. We love each other. For now, that's enough."

"It's not enough for me, Ben."

"Let's wait and see, Sara."

Sara rose from her chair and walked to the window. She couldn't put off the purpose of her dialogue with Ben. Turning, she wrapped her arms around her chest to hide her shaking hands. "I would like you to agree to our adopting a couple children."

Ben stared at her without comment.

Sara followed behind him like his shadow as he headed to the refrigerator.

"We have a fifty-fifty chance of producing our own children, Sara. That spells hope in my vocabulary. I am asking you to wait, Sara. Let's discuss all our options at a better time."

*Smoke in the Kitchen*

He patted her shoulder and headed for the dining room. Almost through the doorway, he stopped. "And by the way, we also need to discuss your use of firewood to cook. The government wants to crack down on excessive use of our natural resources, and it wouldn't look good in the community for me to have smoke coming from our kitchen as a sign of not adhering to government regulation."

Sara bit back her retort. This was no time to create unnecessary antagonism.

## Chapter 9

**March 1983**

Sara was sitting in the lawn chair reminiscing about her life with Ben and the three problems that were causing some tension between them when she heard a voice behind her.

"I can't believe my eyes! Sara Moses is actually relaxing in her yard?"

Sara turned with a start. "Kelitia, you scared me. I didn't even hear your footsteps. Is it later than I think, or did you get off work early?"

"It's late afternoon, sister. Have you been out here napping? Aren't you feeling well?"

"No, no. I'm just relaxing. Thinking about things. Pull up a chair and sit with me."

Kelitia peered more closely at her. "Exactly what things are you thinking about? You look worried." She handed Sara an invitation addressed to Mr. and Mrs. Benjamin Moses.

"I've been seeing Dr. Kate Zed over the past few months, and the news isn't good."

"News about what?" Kelitia pulled up another chair and sank into it.

"Last October, she informed me that I have several fibroid tumors in my uterus."

"Tumors! Sara . . . that's terrible! What does it mean? Do you need to be operated on?"

"No. No treatment either. But I have only a 50 percent chance of becoming pregnant."

"Oh, Sara, I'm so sorry. But, fifty-fifty . . . there's hope then. That's good, isn't it?"

"I don't have your optimism. Especially with all the other pressures on me. She says tension can worsen the situation. Nothing has happened over the past several months."

"What does Ben say?"

"There's hope."

"There you are then. That's what you need to do. Hope."

Sara stared into space while shaking her head. "Think about it, Kelitia. The women on Mama's side have each given birth to only one child—a daughter. I miscarried that baby girl. Ben says that doesn't mean I'm doomed."

"I agree with him. Surely you don't think you are! Hope and faith go hand in hand."

Sara looked back at the house and then lowered her voice. "Ben isn't distraught at the possibility we may never have children of our own, Kelitia. He says we'll wait and be patient. He won't listen to other alternatives. I—I'm beginning to wonder if I will carry this burden to my grave. He already has a son."

"Oh, my goodness, Sara, I'm sure that's not true. He's probably just trying to stay calm and strong. Deep down, it can't be easy for him either. He loves you so much!"

"When I first learned about my fibroids, I suggested we adopt one or two children. He wouldn't discuss it." Sara leaned her head against the back of the chair. Suddenly she felt quite exhausted.

"Give yourself some time. You've been married less than a year."

"Almost a year!"

"If you want children so badly, my nieces and nephews are available." Kelitia laughed and reached out to touch Sara's arm. "Why don't you read the invitation in your lap?"

Sara opened the envelope, pulled out the invitation, and scanned it quickly. "I know you're trying to lift my spirits with your humor," she said, "but I want to do my part in providing a quality life for a couple orphaned or abandoned children. I don't want to uproot any from their parents."

"That's easier said than done."

"I've been thinking about it for several months now. Everywhere I drive, I see poor children on the streets. I want to help those in the most need . . . even if Ben won't agree to letting me adopt any legally." She wiped a few tears from her eyes. "I may not be able to get my little Moses any other way."

Kelitia could feel Sara's desperation and was sad she couldn't bring her any real comfort. "Please, Sara. Don't give up. Try to find solutions to your problems and focus on the solutions."

Sara sat up straight. "You're right. So many children out there have no parents—no one to provide even a loaf of bread and no one to send them to school. Do you know that fewer than 20 percent of our children are in school and most of their parents are illiterate? They need someone with a voice strong enough to be heard—strong enough to insist that eyes be opened to this problem in our country. Poverty and disease kill families. Education should be mandatory."

"If it weren't for your family taking me in, I wouldn't be where I am today, so I understand, Sara." Kelitia perched on the edge of her chair. "My mother was a trader, and I would have followed in her footsteps if it weren't for you. Because of your kind heart, I'm educated and hold a great position at the hotel—one that allows me to help my mother and siblings. They have a decent home and are educated."

"That's what I want for all Sierra Leonean children. It's probably a dream that will never come to fruition, but maybe it can happen, one child at a time." Sara sighed. "Far too many children don't have the opportunity, and some ne'er-do-well husbands live double lives—some even abandon their wives and children."

"Hmm," Kelitia sighed. "Push for the adoption, then. You'll make a great mother. Ben will support whatever decision you make. I'll say it again—that man loves you!"

Sara opened the envelope and pulled out the invitation. "We're invited to the grand opening of a new restaurant in your hotel next Sunday? Ben won't be traveling next week. We'll be happy to attend." She pushed herself out of the chair. "Would you like to stay and eat with us?"

"No, I won't be able to this time. Say good-bye to that husband of yours for me. I thought I saw his car drive into the garage just now." Kelitia gingerly negotiated the pebbles in the yard in her high-heeled shoes.

On the way back to the house, Sara stopped to look over her flower and vegetable garden. In the same way she took care in the preparation of her meals in the kitchen, she and her gardener had spent months trying to re-create her former garden. They had tilled and made compost for the soil, and then planted seeds and nursery plants. They had also transplanted several of her favorite bushes and flowers from her home. She observed, with satisfaction, the tomatoes, cucumbers, lettuce, hot peppers, and greens that had already germinated and were producing a voluminous crop. She leaned over to pull out a few weeds and realized she was purposely killing time in order to put off facing Ben.

Which was ridiculous. She loved her husband, and he wasn't a monster. They just didn't see eye to eye on a few things. In particular, those that meant the most to her. But marriage wasn't just a ceremony. It represented the blending of two individuals with different backgrounds and experiences and two sometimes widely divergent ways of dealing with issues. She thought of the plans that were germinating in her mind . . . solutions to two of her three problems.

Gathering an armful of vegetables, she headed for her outdoor kitchen. Within the next few minutes, she had a good fire going.

"I thought I saw Kelitia with you when I arrived a few minutes ago," Ben said from the doorway of the kitchen. He leaned against the frame and watched her.

"Oh, hello," Sara said. "She stopped by to bring us an invitation to the grand opening of a new restaurant in her hotel Sunday night. I said we'd be happy to attend. That's all right, isn't it?" She peered up at him, suddenly feeling anxious about presuming something without discussing it first. Could he tell she wasn't being entirely open with him?

"Of course it is." He brushed the perspiration from her forehead. "Don't you think it's a little hot to be out here cooking? Why don't you want to come in and cook? I spent a great deal of money to equip this kitchen with the finest appliances."

Sara busied herself stirring the soup, adding several handfuls of ingredients to the pot.

"Did you hear me, or are you purposely ignoring me?" Ben sighed. "Sara, we've discussed this so many times. I thought you had agreed to come out here only for emergencies, power cut or shortage of gas."

She whirled and glared at him. "Honestly, Ben, why is this such a big issue with you? You enjoy every single meal I put on the table."

"That isn't the point! The meals you prepare indoors are every bit as delicious as the ones you prepare out here."

"That's not true, and you know it. The firewood makes the food taste better. You know it is much more convenient to use the charcoal pot to roast fish, meat, and pepper chicken—or do you want me to smoke up the house? Your business is to eat what I cook."

"And I will continue to eat what you cook and enjoy every morsel. Why are you being so stubborn about this? You are, like many others, contributing to the destruction of the forests, and the government is trying to preserve them. You should know better."

"Oh, Ben, please. Don't be so dramatic."

"Look around you, Sara. It's hot and uncomfortable. The place is . . . antiquated."

## Smoke in the Kitchen

"My kitchen is always clean and well kept."

"I didn't say it wasn't clean. I said it was antiquated and full of smoke!" Ben threw his hands in the air. "You know what, Sara? I give up. You're just too defiant. You don't listen." Ben left the kitchen and headed back to the house.

Sara continued with her cooking, mentally stewing. Ben was being unfair. She had uprooted her entire past to replant her life into Ben's space. Her shrubs and transplanted flowers were thriving, but she wasn't. And why? Because he wasn't listening to her! She wanted to adopt children and to continue cooking in her outdoor kitchen. Was that asking too much? Modern kitchens made the long-established methods of cooking appear outdated and cumbersome, but there was far more to cooking than merely putting ingredients into a pot or an oven. It was bound up in traditions handed down from previous generations.

She removed the lid to stir the soup with a long-handled wooden spoon. She stroked the back of the spoon against the palm of her hand and then licked it to taste the juice. "Mmm, that's good," she said aloud. "Only firewood gives the soup such a unique smoky taste and aroma." While she stirred, she thought of other reasons why her method of cooking was superior. Regular power outages and continual shortages of gas and kerosene frustrated housewives. The bundles of firewood she shoved between those firestones were always available, and they never failed her.

Fanning the fire, she could hear her grandma's voice in her head like she always did whenever she was in the kitchen. "Sara, don't touch the firewood. It will burn you. Just fan the fire." She had given her a little metal sheet to use as a fan. When she was old enough, her grandma showed her how to crush various items using the mortar and pestle. She also showed her how to crush pepper and onions on the flat stone called pepper stone using a grinder called the *pepper-stone pikin*. It had taken her weeks to learn how to use them properly.

Once again, she thought of how she might never have a daughter of her own to teach these skills and traditional values and pass on her recipes to. "It's important to know how to cook well, Sara," her grandma had said on many occasions. "Good cooking settles many an argument, because the way to a man's heart is through his stomach. And knowing how to prepare and stoke a good fire is necessary for the preparation of every meal. It can't be too hot or too cool. One will overcook and one will undercook." Now that she was married, she knew her grandma was right. Even if Ben hated her method of cooking, he loved whatever she put on the table.

Her eyes wandered to the neatly stacked pile of firewood in the storage compartment adjoining the cooking area in the kitchen. Most of the truck drivers who peddled wood knew her well because she would purchase such a large quantity from them. Only when Ben was away from home, of course. The flatbed trucks had dozens of wooden poles secured into a fenced compound to support the bundles of firewood precariously stacked as high as possible. She thought of the last visit from her regular supplier.

"Good afternoon, Aunty Sara," Cano had greeted her while climbing down from his truck. Cano was the eldest of six children and had dropped out of school at the age of ten to help his papa in the woodcutting business. The robust, smart man was now the head of the woodcutters, and had known Sara since they were children in the same elementary school.

"How you do, Cano? How's business?"

"Business is bad. How body? How pa Ben?"

"We are fine, thank you."

Cano had instructed the boy to cart the usual consignment of thirty bundles of firewood into the kitchen storage.

"Only four sticks in one bundle?" Sara had noticed the reduction in the size of each bundle of firewood. "There were six sticks in each bundle only two months ago, and now only four?"

"Costs go up."

"But you woodcutters make a lot of money, don't you?"

*"Ah . . . Aunty, no to so. Too much control na the forest now. We get for bribe and the amounts go up and the bribing money don go up."*

His teenage apprentice had removed his gray T-shirt and wrapped it around his neck before grabbing two bundles of firewood at a time. Either the weight of the firewood or his style of walking made the boy sway his bony hips from side to side, and his half pants danced as he moved as if they were waving good-bye.

"Aunty, can we talk?"

"What about, Cano?" Sara knew she was his confidant, because unlike Ben, she had always accommodated everyone.

"The unfairness is growing worse with each passing week. The forest rangers give special treatment to timber producers. Nobody cares about firewood men like me. We have families to feed and less money for big bribes. I have two wives and twelve children."

"Have you spoken with the other woodcutters?"

"Yes, but I want your opinion."

"What's good for the goose is good for the gander, Cano. If the government wants to restrict the number of trees the foresters chop down, the rules should apply to everyone. You should take your grievances to the relevant government agency." Suddenly she remembered Ben's adamant statements about her personal destruction of the forests by using firewood and how her insistence upon cooking with firewood was an embarrassment to him. She wondered if the government were proposing the creation of laws to save the forest. It was a topic she wouldn't want to discuss with him. Not yet anyway.

*Smoke in the Kitchen*

"Aunty, you talk things straight. Anyway, we asked for a meeting with the big bosses."

"Tell me what happens after your meeting."

"*Tenki. tenki,* Aunty."

She knew she had a great deal of homework to do. There could be no worthwhile discussion with Ben without an equal storehouse of information. She needed to learn all about the forest-preservation initiative, or her arguments would fall on deaf ears.

## Chapter 10

While they ate dinner, Ben talked about changes in the government offices. "The director of the department resigned today."

"Why?" Sara asked as she cut her meat into smaller pieces.

"He was offered an international position that will have him moving to London."

"His family must be looking forward to that."

"Yes, his twin boys are almost ready for college, and this will give him the opportunity to consider more choices. He'll receive a substantial increase in pay too." Ben helped himself to a second serving of everything.

"Speaking of children, shall I go ahead and begin the adoption process?"

"What adoption process?"

Sara carefully placed her soupspoon on the plate under the bowl and looked at him. "Have you forgotten so soon? The process required for us to legally adopt the children. You said we could—"

"I said we would talk about it when we were a bit more settled."

"But we *are* settled! It's been five months since we last talked about it. Five more months have passed without anything happening."

"Children need the right environment." Ben glanced around the room.

"If this isn't *right*, how do you define *right*?"

"I don't mean a big house or lots of furniture—"

Sara laughed. "Listen to yourself. If we had our own children, you would still be away from home on business trips. We live in a nice house, you have a well-paid job, and I run a successful business. We can hire more help; we need to raise a couple of children who simply need lots of love, good food, and nurturing. What more do we need? What more would they need?"

"Sara," Ben said, pushing his plate away from him, "there is so much going on right now. Don't you think you are rushing into the adoption process? I don't understand you. There is still a chance we could have our own children. Why don't we take a step back and put first things first? Stop obsessing on this notion that you are infertile."

Sara felt her body grow hot and struggled to control her emotions. This was no time to break into tears. "Ben, I am approaching my mid-forties. I don't have time to step back. I'm not a man, who may think he can produce offspring until he's one step from the grave. I'm convinced I have lost my only opportunity to conceive naturally, and that's not easy for me to accept. I-I don't expect you to fully understand how I feel. You already have a son! I have . . . nothing."

Ben rose from the table. "Once again, you throw my son at me in this discussion. My son lives in London with his mother. I rarely get to see him. Do you honestly think I wouldn't like to have more children to see and hug and love and teach on a daily basis? You know what? There is no point in talking with you about this. You have made up your mind, and to hell with what I think or want. I'm going to bed. I've had enough of this."

After Ben had stormed out of the dining room, Sara stared at his empty chair. This time, her mother's words came to mind. "Don't let the sun go down on your anger, Sara. In Ephesians 4: 26, you will find those words of wisdom." She remembered the many times her parents had argued vociferously over subjects that had seemed silly to her and how quickly they had made up. "That's how I maintain a good relationship with your papa. He's a difficult man, far from being perfect, but I need to compromise for the sake of peace. Someday, when you are married, you will understand. Women are not always right, although we like to believe we are."

As she placed the leftover food in the refrigerator, Sara thought about this. So far, she appeared to be losing the battle. Her method for acquiring children and her quest for cooking with firewood were creating a palpable strain in her marriage. What did she have to gain by continuing with such persistence? Flexibility and compromise must become more than vocabulary words if she wanted a future with her husband. And she did. She would practice patience, bide her time, see what nature brought to her life—and in the meantime, thoroughly research both the forestry and adoption problems.

## Chapter 11

Although Sara had usually entertained the Sunday schoolchildren in her church once a year with an annual Christmas party, she decided she couldn't wait that long to invite them to her new home. She got the idea of celebrating during the Easter holiday instead after seeing how much the neighborhood children enjoyed chatting with her and Ben on their after-dinner walks.

"I know you're growing weary of hearing me talk so much about my grandma," she said to Ben on one of these evening strolls, "but she instilled in me the importance of providing for those less fortunate. I promised I would bring honor to her memory and our family by living my life in such a way that it reflected that worthwhile virtue. I can't remember if I ever told you of the annual Christmas parties I held for the children in my church."

She had glanced sideways at him to see how well he was accepting her recitation. "I've been hoping you will share in my determination to carry on that tradition, Ben. What would you say to our having an Easter party instead of my usual Christmas party? I thought we could invite not only the children from our church, but these neighborhood children as well. And their parents, of course."

"I suppose you've already settled on a date," Ben said, smiling at her and squeezing her hand.

"I thought April 2, the Saturday before Easter, would be perfect," she said, "since both Good Friday and Easter Monday are national holidays. I am sure inviting them would bring joy to their hearts. I'll ask some of the mothers to contribute by helping me cook."

"There is adequate space in the yard if the kitchen is too small for all of you."

"Maybe. We'll see," she said. "Thank you, Ben. You're a wonderful husband. You can also invite some of the people in your office . . . they are welcome to come."

"Now that's a great idea, Mrs. Moses."

Over the years, the parties held in Sara's much smaller house had never dampened the enthusiasm or enjoyment. Now she looked forward to decorating their much bigger house and, especially, to cooking.

"I'll arrange for transportation from the church's compound for those who need it," Ben said, surprising her with the offer.

Sara wasted no time in sending out invitations to their neighbors and to those in Ben's office. She informed the pastor of the change from a Christmas party to an Easter party. She also requested him to extend the invitation to the children and their parents and to any others he felt would like to attend.

## Smoke in the Kitchen

In the early hours of the morning of the party, several of her neighbors appeared at the door. "I feel honored to be part of this cooking," Joela said, wrapping her *lappa* tightly around her waist. "I'm already in the Easter mood. It's such a joyous time of the year. Now you have to tell us what to do."

Several others chimed in, and Sara welcomed them all. "We're going to cook, cook, and cook some more, ladies," she said. "I want all my guests to enjoy themselves, especially the children."

The women followed Sara through the house and across the yard, marveling at how well she had organized everything. She had long tables set up and piled high with vegetables and fruits, tubs of fresh fish and shrimp on ice, chicken and meats, bowls, platters, serving utensils, and pots and pans. She showed them the four sets of *three-fireside-stones* in the yard that were ready to be used.

Cano was already busy stacking more than two dozen bundles of firewood into the compartment nearby. "You need me, Aunty?" he asked jokingly. "Why don't I assist the ladies with the cleaning of those pots you've got out in the yard?" He pointed toward six huge three-legged, cast-iron cooking pots that would be used for the stews, the jollof rice, and plain white rice.

"Thank you, Cano, Party or not, you are definitely one of my most valuable helpers. *You na oos pikin,* go clean to your heart's content." She gave assignments to each of her other volunteers. "Ben and I invited eighty guests," she said, "but we must prepare enough food for at least a hundred."

"Or more! You know all sorts of gate-crashers are bound to show up, Aunty," Recha said. "Your invited guests will invite their friends."

"We are all guilty of doing that, every one of us," Jene said, laughing along with her. "A week ago, I was already in bed when my friend stopped by and dragged me out to a party. I didn't know a soul there, but had a wonderful time. What are you planning to serve, Aunty?" She eyed the overloaded tables.

"I thought we'd focus on the usual suspects and mix in a few special surprises," Sara said. "I've got all the ingredients for jollof rice, chicken and meat stew, smoked chicken and roast meat, pepper chicken, fried chicken, couscous, fish and meatballs, and baked fish. We should have cakes, rice and banana bread, and special sweets for the children. If any of you have suggestions, I am open to receiving them. This party is for you and your children as well."

After providing her own recipes for several dishes and getting suggestions from them, she assigned the various women to be in charge of preparing specific dishes, and soon they were busy cooking rice, prepping vegetables for the stews, and seasoning the chicken. Two hours passed, and they chatted amicably while they worked.

Ben arrived from the front of the house and waved at the women from across the yard. He set about putting up beverage tables with a couple of workers. "Good morning, good morning," he called. "I see Sara has already put you to work. Thank you for helping her."

"Good morning, Uncle Ben," the ladies greeted him in unison, beaming in response to his smiles. "He's a fine man," one of them said enthusiastically.

"Good morning, Cano," Ben said when his eyes fell on him.

"Good morning, sir." Cano stood in the cooking area. Although he had supplied thirty bundles of firewood earlier in the week, Sara had requested additional wood for the marathon Easter holiday undertaking.

"Cano," Ben added unexpectedly, walking toward him, "if our people keep killing the trees, our forests will soon be depleted. For your information, the government is planning a strong environmental-preservation program, and—"

Jene clamped a hand over her mouth and whispered to the women closest to her, "Why did he say that? What does he mean?"

"Ask him," Joela whispered back.

"Uncle Ben, what do you mean by 'killing the trees'?" Jene asked.

"Can't you see how many dead trees are lying on the ground?" Ben lifted one of the bundles and pointed at the stack of them near the fireside.

"When they are placed into the fire, they will come alive again, sir," Mary said, grinning.

Several women laughed at her humor.

Cano gazed directly at Ben and smiled. "Killing trees? I collect some of the wood from the already felled trees on the forest floor. Rather than letting them rot or start a forest fire, my friends and I put them to good use."

"Yes, Pa, and it is even a worse situation for the poor in our country. How would they cook if they don't use firewood? They would suffer."

Sara stood with her hands on her hips and glared a silent message with her eyes, hoping Ben would get out of the way.

Cano nodded. "Those who cut timber have friends in the government, sir. They don't treat us firewood people right. They are making our lives even more difficult lately and charging fees we cannot pay. They already make more money than we do, and now they ask for bribes."

Ben eyed Sara and stubbornly lifted his chin, as though to say he would not be silenced. "Timber is used to build houses and to make furniture. The industry supports many workers."

"Most poor people use firewood," Jene added. "What would they do without it? Is the government going to supply them with kerosene stoves or gas cookers? If not, how will they eat?"

"That's true," Sara said, unable to keep her mouth closed any longer. "No firewood, no food, no health, no strength, no means to build sleeping or seating places. Besides that, cooking with firewood is an important part of our culture."

"My uncle, who works for a timber company in Panguma, says that Sierra Leone timber is first-class," Jene said, "but it is being sold to foreigners, and some foreign companies want to buy the sole rights to the timber in particular forests."

Joela took a scoop of salt and sprinkled it over the dozens of barracuda chunks that were in a large container. While marinating the fish, she yelled out, "Wait, wait, wait, we shouldn't forget . . ."

"Forget what?" Jene asked.

"All our houses were built with posts and rafter. Where do they come from?"

"Oh, yes . . . our parents used to purchase them from the wharf. We get them from the forest as well," Jene added.

Everyone stopped working to listen to the conversation.

Cano seemed to become warm at the opportunity to speak of his concerns. "But foreigners have a stronger voice than Sierra Leoneans because they have the money, but this is our land." He shook his head and turned away, mumbling, "Something must be done to preserve our rights to make a living. Who in the government is going to speak on our behalf?"

"All right, everyone, enough of this discussion!" Sara said, shooing Ben away with a stern look. "It's Easter and a time for frivolity and joy. We have so much more cooking to do, and if we don't get to it, our guests will arrive before we finish."

"These onions make me shed tears," Damia said, turning her tearstained face from the dozens of onions she was slicing.

The women laughed, and soon they were enthusiastically occupied with the cooking assignments they had set out to accomplish. One after the other, filled bowls and trays of finished dishes lined the tables, and the aroma of roasting chicken and other meats permeated the air.

Sara bustled about teaching and demonstrating how to prepare and cook the huge quantities of food required for each entrée, and when she was sure the cooking was on schedule, she went indoors to check on the decorations one more time. She and Ben had spent several hours the night before blowing up balloons, cutting flowers from the garden, and making arrangements for every room. Now their aromas perfumed the air. They had hung the balloons and colorful streamers of ribbon across the windows. Then they had spent another couple hours filling fiber baskets with pencils and mini notepads, small toys, toffee, and sweet biscuits to present to each child attending the party. Ben had even bought tennis balls in several colors for the boys. Sara had filled another large basket with hair ribbons and clips for the girls. And in each basket, Sara had placed a colored picture of the Resurrection so that they would remember what was special about this particular holiday.

## Smoke in the Kitchen

Right when she had returned to the house, the doorbell rang. Sara looked at her watch. "It's Martha!" she exclaimed and rushed to welcome her. Martha had been her friend since their childhood days. After earning her nursing certification, she had left Sierra Leone to specialize in public health in England. During their phone conversations, Martha had said she was traveling to Freetown and would attend Sara's party; she would arrive early enough to assist in the preparations.

Sara pulled open the door and threw her arms around her friend. "Oh, Martha, my dear! Welcome! Thank you for coming. The party wouldn't be half as fun without you. You look fabulous!" She openly admired Martha's cream and brown tie-dyed pantsuit and her new cream-colored high heels.

Martha laughed. "Sara, you haven't changed one bit. You're still vibrant and beautiful. Marriage has been good for you. I'm looking forward to meeting the man who's made you know life is worth living." She stepped farther into house and peeked into the living room. "Your new home is huge, and I can see your special touches everywhere."

Sara took her on a tour, and they paused in the kitchen. "Don't say a word!" she said. "We're doing everything in the outdoor. You know this is what we've been used to; people come out to assist whenever there is large cooking going on. I've got several friends and neighbors out there helping me. We're preparing everything. You know me. I don't know when to stop."

Martha laughed again. "You'll never change. You and your grandma were always cooking and feeding the neighbors. And I'm not one bit surprised her legacy continues."

Right then, Ben entered the kitchen from the back door. "Ben," Sara said, "meet Martha, my best friend in the whole world. Martha, meet my dear husband, Ben."

Martha offered her hand. "I have heard so much about you, Ben. All good things, by the way."

Ben smiled warmly. "Sara has told me a great deal about you too, and I am happy to finally put a face to the name. You are a special person in her life, and that makes you special to me too."

"Well," Martha said, winking at Sara, "with talk like that, how can I possibly judge you as being less than perfect? You'd better not let me down!"

Ben laughed. "Perfect I am not. I will warn you of that right now. But I do love this wife of mine."

Sara moved Martha toward the door. "There is a lot of cooking going on outside. Come meet some of my other friends."

"You all look so busy, I hate to disturb you," Martha said, pondering where she would fit in what seemed like a well-oiled production line. "Everything smells delicious. What are you cooking? Mmm, that's one of my favorite dishes." Martha lifted lids on pots and sampled the jollof rice and the stew. Then she noticed the chicken on the grill. "Oh, how I miss roast beef en peppeh chicken, on the charcoal fire of course—" She spoke to each of the women and commented on the ingredients of certain recipes. She told short stories of how she had learned to prepare some of the local foods. "I can't wait to eat some of these delicacies. It's been such a long time for me."

Back in the house, Martha looked at Sara. "I was surprised to see Ben so busy out there. He's not your ordinary husband, my dear."

"Ben's been looking forward to this party," Sara said. "Thanks for your compliments." Sara moved closer to Martha and in a whisper said, "His ex-wife didn't want to leave London for a life in Sierra Leone. She lives there with their young son. They never lived in this house." Sara looked about the dining room. "This is the first time we have hosted a party together and the first time Ben's been involved in the preparations for one. He's been an enormous help. A few of his work colleagues are coming with their children. He wants everything to be perfect."

"Well, in my humble opinion, everything is beautiful, and trust me, no one is going to leave here hungry or complaining about the quality of your food. By the way, how's Kelitia? I didn't see her out there."

"She's been attending a conference for hotel managers in Austria. She has just been promoted to assistant general manager of the Funkia Hotel."

"Good for her. She's done well for herself." Martha fondled several hair ribbons from the huge basket on a side chair in the dining room. "I am so looking forward to helping you entertain the children. It's generous and kind of you to do this every year. Ben is a lucky man to have a wife like you. Now, I suppose, you'll have children of your own. You'll spoil them rotten, and if you don't, I will!"

The doorbell rang, interrupting Sara's reply.

"That's the taxi driver. I told him to return for me in two hours. I'll be back an hour before the party starts to help you lay out the food."

Sara followed her to the door and hugged her one more time. As she watched her enter the taxi and drive away, she thought about her last words and felt the now-familiar pang in the depths of her heart. *I suppose you'll have children of your own.*

If God is willing, she thought. Otherwise . . . well, she wouldn't think about that right now. In only a few more hours, the house and yard would be filled with the laughter of the children of other mothers.

# Chapter 12

**April 2, 1983, Easter Saturday**

Martha arrived early to help Sara as promised, and she brought with her a shopping bag full of cream biscuits, ginger nuts, and foil-wrapped Easter chocolate sweets. "I thought a few sweets from London would make your dessert table even more festive," she said. "They were easy to pack. Now, let me assist in laying out the food. Do you want some of it brought into the house? I think your dining room table would be perfect for the desserts. What do you think? Some may prefer to sit indoors."

"You are such a great friend, Martha. I'll let you set up the dessert table however you think it will best serve our guests. Maybe we should keep some outdoors, though, in order to cut down on traffic coming in and out of the house."

"You're right, as always." Martha set about carrying in the trays of sweets the neighbor ladies and Sara had prepared and arranged them in a decorative manner on the dining room table. She placed a few palm leaves on the tablecloth and then entwined some of the colorful ribbons Sara had purchased around the platters. The display was centered with a tall vase of fresh white and red hibiscus, lilies, and roses.

By four o'clock, the guests started to arrive. Most were mamas with children between the ages of one and twelve. They were visibly excited, and Sara welcomed them with open arms. Ben had created a pathway from the front of the house to their backyard by tying balloons to the fence posts. He had insisted upon having kites around, since they were symbolic of the Resurrection. When the children saw these and all the tables laden with massive platters of food and the aromas of the different types of food prepared in her yard, their wide smiles turned into loud admiration. They danced among the tables and eyed everything, eager for permission to taste a little of everything. The traditional fasting of some Christians during the Lent period had ended on Friday night, and most were eager to go back to their regular eating and drinking habits. Sara watched them with great pleasure, knowing that for the majority, this would be their only Easter party and very likely one of the most memorable events in their lives. The children and their mothers were well-dressed, some in their party clothes, others in colorful Africana outfits.

Sara watched as Ben handed out the balls to some of the young boys and kites to a few of the older boys and girls. Their eyes grew even bigger, and they didn't have to be urged to select their favorite colors.

Within the hour, Sara and Ben's home was filled with excited guests. After a brief welcome and introduction, the guests fell into groups of men, women, and children. The boys set up an informal soccer game, and the girls happily played the popular game of *akra*. The children also played *Hide-and-Seek* and *Catch Me If You Can*; Sara watched them wistfully. As little faces popped out from behind tree trunks and various sections of the house, she smiled and laughed with them.

Sara joined a group of women discussing the Easter celebrations. Most were centered on their church activities. "I always look forward to Palm Sunday," Jene said. "Last Sunday, our congregation formed a procession and marched through the streets in our area behind a huge cross made of freshly cut palm branches all the way to the church sanctuary. The choir led the way in their royal blue robes, and we sang hymns and gave witness of our faith. It is such a joyous experience to think of Jesus riding into Jerusalem on a donkey and having people line his pathway with palm leaves."

Joela nodded. "For me, I love the Easter sunrise service, when we meet outside the church before dawn to signify Jesus' resurrection. We watch the sun rise, and then go into the church for a jubilant service of worship and praise. In fact, tomorrow we have the inductions of new members during the service."

"Sometimes the masquerade crowds are too rowdy on Easter Monday," Mary said. "I know it's a part of our culture to have these masqueraders in their masks dancing and cavorting throughout the city, but sometimes the competition between the Paddle and Bloody Mary societies frightens me. When you hear the name Bloody Mary, you know it means terror. At least for me, it does. I'm not saying I don't enjoy the costumes, the singing and dancing, but I don't enjoy when things get violent."

"I love Easter so much . . . it gives me a spirit of renewal of life," Martha butted in.

Sara listened with one ear as she and Martha replenished the food on the tables from the pots in the yard.

At nine, when it was time for them to leave, no one was ready. The children begged to be allowed to stay longer. Sara motioned to Martha and a few of the mothers to help her distribute Easter goody bags. Finally, when the children had celebrated to their satisfaction, they were more willing to go home.

Several adults who had arrived without children stayed until midnight, enjoying the food, music, and dancing. When Sara and Ben waved the last couples good night, they were surprised to see that several of the women had cleared off the tables and washed the dishes.

Martha had decided to spend the night at Sara and Ben's so she could help Sara clean up and use the opportunity to reminisce. With little to do, they found the comfort of the sofa in the living room and chatted about their parents and grandparents, and their former escapades as teenagers and young women. "It's amazing how much we learn to appreciate our parents as we age," Martha said. "When we were young, we thought they didn't love us, because they disciplined us strictly."

"I know. As teenagers we had the notion they were mistreating us if they ever said no to our demands."

"They did well for you, Sara. They sent you to college."

"The first one in the family. It was an honor and also a huge responsibility. One I wasn't particularly eager to take on at the time." Sara sighed. "Now I'm so grateful."

"You are your own boss. Maybe that wouldn't have come about if you had married early. By the way, whatever became of your cousins, Thomas and Little Becca, and their parents? I haven't heard you mention them lately. If I remember correctly, they hated your family. Are they still hostile toward you?"

"Hostile is a good word for it! Thomas, Little Becca, and their parents emigrated to Fernando Po—that's where their mama came from—and we lost touch. I heard their parents had both passed away. I heard that Thomas has been going back and forth between here and there and Little Becca is married. Now Thomas is taking over from where his papa left off. All the same bitterness and hostility seems to be in his blood. I didn't tell you this, but I understand he's been searching official records to see whether he could find any evidence of fraud in order to claim the auctioneer business for himself. He is challenging our grandpa's will."

When Martha gasped, Sara warmed to the subject. "Papa deeded that business to me in his will. He inherited it fair and square from his father and then spent all his savings to get the crippled business back on its feet."

"Is Thomas out of his mind? Does he honestly believe he has a leg to stand on?" Martha's voice rose with her fury.

"He'll find out soon enough. Right now, I have handed it over to my lawyer. We have to wait until we learn exactly what so-called evidence Thomas has to stake his claim. I'm trying not to let it worry me, but it's always in the back of my mind. I don't know what I'd do if this drags on. I've grown to thoroughly enjoy my business, my staff, and the good things we do for the community. Plus, it's a good feeling to know I'm contributing financially to our family . . . what there is of it."

"Are you ladies still up?" Ben asked, coming into the room. "It's already two o'clock in the morning. Aren't you exhausted after such a long day?"

"Please join us," Sara said, rising from the sofa to hug him. "Did you enjoy the party?"

"How could I not? Our guests were having a wonderful time. You did a superb job, my dear. You and all those ladies catered a feast that will go down in Freetown history. And you, Martha, thank you for all your help. Hope you had a good time."

"You are always welcome . . . it was a great party," Martha said. "You have a beautiful home, and you and your wife entertained us so well."

"You did me proud, Ben. Thank you so much for all your hard work. I couldn't believe it when you hired a special DJ. Why didn't you tell me you'd hired him to entertain?" Sara punched Ben playfully on the arm.

"Because I wanted to surprise you. What is an Easter party without surprises? The music was good. Everyone was on their feet dancing, the food was good, company great, and music, again superb. Guests were happy. Now *that's* a party!"

"It was the best one I've ever had," Sara said.

Massaging Sara's shoulders, Ben grinned at Martha. "Did you hear your friend? In her subtle way, she's really saying she has a man in her life now, one who is supportive and strong and whose masculine touch made a significant difference."

"Must you men brag every time you pitch in and help out?" Martha teased.

Ben laughed. "It's in our DNA."

"I'm going to let you do all the bragging you want, because I had dozens of women tell me I was the luckiest woman alive," Sara said. "They were shocked by how much work you were doing all day long to assist with the preparations."

"Well, there you go. And with that firm endorsement, I'm going to bid you both a fond good night and be off to bed. I'll see you in the morning."

"I'm going to come with you," Sara said. "If you get up before I do, you know where the kitchen is, Martha. I've got the coffeepot all ready on the counter. You just have to plug it in."

"Don't worry about me. I'll be fine."

Although they were both exhausted, Sara prayed with Ben before climbing into bed. "Ben," she said, "did you notice how happy the children were? I've never heard so much laughter. Their joy filled me with such satisfaction."

"I agree with you. It was a party they will never forget."

"It was important to me that they remembered the reason for Easter."

Sara reached over and turned off the lamp next to their bed. When her eyes adjusted to the dark, she turned over onto her side. "Ben," she asked, her voice soft and slightly tremulous, "I watched you with the children tonight. You seemed to be so happy . . . so in your element. Would you agree now to our adopting a child . . . two at the most?"

Ben was silent for such a long time, she was certain he had already fallen asleep.

"Okay, Sara, you're right." He turned toward her and gathered her into his arms. "Thank you for being patient with me. It's taken me awhile to think about what this will mean. I'm afraid I was being selfish. I wanted you all to myself for a while."

"Oh, Ben, Ben, . . ." Sara felt the tears well up in her eyes and then roll unchecked down her cheeks. "Thank you with all my heart. You . . . you won't be sorry about this. Our children will provide us with far more blessings than we will ever bestow on them. You'll see."

"How do we go about this? Have you looked into it? We can't just drive down the street and pick up a couple who look as though they need parents."

Sara swallowed the lump in her throat. "No, we must ensure the adoption process is legal and binding. My only criteria is that they be orphaned or abandoned—"

"Adoption? You want to legally adopt them . . . not just bring them into our house?"

"Yes. I want them to be ours in every way . . . as though we had conceived and given birth to them. They will be our heirs."

Again, Ben was silent. "All right. How soon would you like this to take place?"

"As soon as possible. I learned about a place here in town . . . a children's center. The Freetown Children's Center, that's what it's called."

"I've never heard about the organization. Are they new?"

"Sort of. I've checked out a couple others, but the adoption procedure from this one is straightforward." Sara twisted out of his arms and switched on the light again, hopping out of bed and rushing to the dresser. She pulled open the drawer, withdrew a folder, and returned to the bed. "I already have the application forms, Ben. Do you want to read them?"

"I don't suppose we could wait until after church? I can't say until 'tomorrow' because it's already Easter Sunday." He yawned. "We're going to church, aren't we?"

"Of course. We'll sign them after church."

An hour later, Sara was still wide-awake as the prospect of becoming a mother milled around in her head. She thought of all the Easters to come. She thought of how she would teach her daughter how to cook, the same way she'd learned from her mother and grandmother. She thought of how she would never forget her first Easter party in her new home and of how maybe, just maybe, the party and her cooking had influenced her husband.

## Chapter 13

With her eyes still shut, Sara pulled the blanket over her ears. For some reason, she felt chilly, which was preposterous, considering the time of year. When she heard an unusual sound, she finally opened her eyes and peered across the bedroom. The multicolored window curtain was flapping in a strong wind like an unbalanced kite. "Strong wind!" she whispered aloud. She popped out of bed and dashed to the window to shut it. On the way, she stepped over the adoption papers that had fluttered off the dresser top and onto the floor.

Falling to her knees, she hurriedly gathered them up, along with several photographs she had taken out of the drawer to show to Martha. Just as she was about to rise, Ben came to the doorway.

"What are you doing on the floor? Some new kind of exercise?"

"That's not funny, Ben." Sara chuckled, finally rising. "The wind blew the adoption papers all over the carpet. I was picking them up. Where's Martha, by the way? Is she up yet?"

"She's already downstairs having her coffee. You'd better hurry, or we'll miss the Easter service. I'll wait downstairs and chat with Martha some more."

Sara rushed through her shower and dressed in her best Sunday outfit. By the time she reached the kitchen, she was out of breath.

"I'm so sorry," she said. "I couldn't sleep last night, I had so much to think about. By the time I finally dozed off, it was already morning." She patted Ben's cheek and smiled into his eyes.

"No one's clock-watching, Sara," Martha said. "You're entitled to sleep in all day if you need the rest. How you managed to put in a full day at your business and then do all the shopping and cooking for so many people is beyond my comprehension. How did you keep all the ingredients straight for so many dishes?"

"Practice," Sara said. "And I cheat. I write lists and more lists and then actually use them."

Martha laughed. "You have more patience than I do, my friend. I would have to hire a caterer or go crazy. And my kitchen would have been such a mess, you'd never find half of what was needed for any preparation."

Ben took a mug from the cupboard and poured Sara her morning brew. "You gals had better watch the clock. We need to leave here in about forty minutes if we intend to sit inside the church this morning. You'll want a seat close enough to see some of your new Sunday schoolchildren. They are receiving certificates today?"

Sara nodded. "Yes. They were so excited last evening. Both of the boys told me they had new white shirts and pants for the occasion."

## Smoke in the Kitchen

Sara peered out the kitchen window. "I can't remember when we've had such weather so early in the season. Usually we don't get this much rain until about June or July."

"I've got the umbrellas by the front door," Ben said. "The streets are likely flooded and will be harder to traverse. Maybe we should leave even earlier."

Sara sat with them at the table. "You've probably forgotten what the weather is like here, Martha. It used to be rather predictable, but for the past few years, we've been experiencing storms in the dry season, and the rainy season is supposed to be starting in another month."

"The humidity I do remember. It's like living in a sauna." Martha sipped her coffee. "It seems that everything in the world is changing, and not always for the better."

"Part of the reason our weather pattern is changing is because we're losing so many trees," Ben said. "Depletion of our forests has affected the environment, and that influences the climate. They go hand in hand."

Sara glanced at him and decided to steer the subject away from his forestry issues. "Living with so many trees has its advantages, but it also has disadvantages. Sometimes the squawking of the birds makes me lose my concentration!" Sara made a growling sound.

"Some of those birds have lived here longer than I have," Ben said. "Some don't reside here year-round, of course. They visit because of the overripe mangoes and the fruit on other trees. Can't blame them for that."

"Have you changed your profession?" Martha teased.

"What do you mean?"

"You sound like a bird-watcher." Martha peered at Sara over the rim of her coffee mug. "Are you a light sleeper? Do you wake up at the crack of dawn with the chirping outside your windows?"

Ben threw back his head and laughed. "Light sleeper?" he repeated. "A few weeks after we were married, our neighbors were drumming, clapping, and shouting obscenities for what seemed like hours one night and—"

"How awful!" Martha sounded appalled.

"The point is that Sara slept right through the noise."

"I'd rather have a flock of birds chirping than neighbors creating a commotion!" Martha said.

"The next morning, the neighbor apologized. He said they had created the hubbub to get rid of a bird called a *korkor*, evidently associated with witchcraft. They said whenever this bird is seen or heard at night, someone dies. Sighting the bird in the vicinity of your house is regarded as a bad omen."

"I didn't hear much of that when I was young. You know, we lived where there were no trees. So everyone's sleep is disrupted in the process?"

"Everyone's sleep but Sara's," Ben said, leaning forward to pat her hand. "She slept right through the night. I haven't heard a repeat performance from our neighbors since that night."

"Maybe you've been sleeping through the commotion as well," Sara said, smiling at him and winking at Martha.

"Despite that little gibe, I will treat you ladies to breakfast this morning." Ben went to the refrigerator and pulled out an already arranged plate of fresh fruit and placed it on the table. In the center of the plate, he had a jar of clotted cream and strawberry jam; he also took out some fresh English scones a friend of his brought from England. "I was up bright and early this morning. You can see how busy I've been."

Both Sara and Martha reached for a scone at the same time. "For such a magnificent gesture, you have earned the Husband of the Year trophy," Sara said.

An hour later, she squeezed into a pew at the Ebenezer Methodist Church beside Ben and Martha and gazed with joy at the beauty of the bunting decorating the front of the sanctuary. Members of the choir sang "Christ the Lord Is Risen Today, Alleluia" as they moved up the aisle to the choir stall. For the next two hours, everyone in the congregation sang lustily and listened to the retelling of the Easter story. The service culminated in the singing of the well-known hymn "Christ Arose" by Robert Lowry.

> Up from the grave He arose,
> With a mighty triumph o'er His foes,
> He arose a Victor from the dark domain,
> And He lives forever, with His saints to reign.
> He arose! He arose!
> Hallelujah! Christ arose!

"Now, ladies," Ben said as they made their way back to the car afterward, "we're going to relax the rest of the day. After working so hard yesterday, we all deserve to be waited upon. We'll enjoy someone else's cooking, although I'm sure it won't in any way compare to what Sara could produce if we gave her the opportunity."

"I counted on having leftovers," Sara said, "but with the extra people at our party, there is nothing left worthy of an Easter lunch."

"Then it's a good thing we have another option." Ben drove slowly as he navigated the potholed street, dodging several puddles that had grown to become dangerous-looking pools. "It has been my longtime dream that someday we'll have beautifully paved streets that will treat the tires kindly," he admitted. "It'll probably not happen in my lifetime, but I'll continue to hope anyway."

Sara chuckled. "We'd just find something else to complain about."

*Smoke in the Kitchen*

"I swear it would be so much easier driving in the first world than here. There would be footpaths for pedestrians, dogs and cats would be locked in their homes, and pigs, goats, and sheep would be out on the farm where they belong. Here, everyone and everything wander about at will, with no boundaries, and drivers are expected to contend with them."

"Better goats than children," Sara said. "I confess to having narrowly missed children on several occasions when they dashed across the road without looking for cars. I lose a year of my life each time. Of course, they kick their ball in the streets, not because they don't have nearby fields; it has become a habit."

"How about all those who carry heavy water buckets on their heads, or all the children with walking mini-supermarkets balanced precariously on their heads?" Martha added. "They maunder dangerously close to the road. I can't drive myself. I have to take a taxi or hire a driver if I have some place to go."

"Talking about pedestrians creating mayhem for drivers . . . how about the masqueraders up ahead of us?" Ben honked the horn several times and was forced to stop and watch a group of them dancing and cavorting in the middle of the road. "I don't want to kill their enjoyment of the holiday, but they should be confined to other areas." They closed the car windows as several came close to their vehicle.

"Some of the dancers pickpocket and cunningly distract drivers while their cohort grabs items from the cars. The police have never been able to catch these thieves," Martha complained.

"Talking about police, you remember when we were in school, Martha, the city policemen would visit our schools to teach us the Highway Code? We had to recite the code in unison. 'Look left, look right, look left again, before you cross the road.' I guess they don't do that anymore."

"I was so scared the first time that happened," Martha said, laughing. "The policeman was tall and lanky, and I was intimidated by his navy blue uniform. I loved the silver buttons on the front of the jacket, though." She got distracted at the masked revelers passing by. "Not to change the subject, but I thought we'd never get out of the church after the service. Everyone who attended your party had to comment on how wonderful it was."

"Especially the children," Sara said. "They were so happy. I noticed that several of the girls were wearing their hair ribbons." She turned to whisper in Ben's ear. "May I tell Martha about the adoption?"

He nodded. "Sure, why not. She's your best friend."

Suddenly the rain stopped and the clouds parted, revealing the blue sky behind. "Look! A rainbow!" Sara pointed out through the windshield. "It's a sign that this is going to be a great afternoon."

They had arrived at the hotel, and Kelitia, her mama, and her siblings rushed out of the entrance to greet them. "Happy Easter!" the children cried. With all the hugs and happy chatter and then the sumptuous Easter lunch—which included roast pork, barracuda, and tasty fried shrimp—taking center place in their conversation,

## Smoke in the Kitchen

Sara didn't have the opportunity to speak about the children she and Ben hoped to adopt. She kept the secret close to her heart and looked at him often during the meal, admiring his way with both the children and adults. He would make a fine father.

Surprisingly, after the unexpected storm, the weather turned out to be quite the opposite—blazingly hot. The heat was no surprise, however; they were used to it. As they drove along, on their way home, they eyed the holiday activities.

"I heard you telling Sara that you've moved back to Freetown for good," Ben said, peering over his shoulder at Martha in the backseat. "Where do you plan to live? Have you found a place yet?"

"I'm going to live on the top floor of the two-story family house; my brother lives on the bottom floor," she said. "He has three children, all under ten years old, so they can use my help. I sent him some money to fix up the top floor for me. You remember my brother, don't you, Sara?"

"Yes, I do. It will be fun to renew our friendship."

"You can drop me off at his place instead of taking me back to your house."

"You're not imposing. Stay in our guestroom for another couple days. We have so much more to talk about."

An hour later, Sara handed Martha a refreshing ginger beer. "We still have electric power and a working refrigerator, so our drinks are cold."

"Mmm, you can't beat a ginger beer on a day like this. In England, it's tea, tea, tea." Martha sipped the drink and then placed it on a coaster placed conveniently on a side table near the sofa. "You said that Ben is part of the government. He's an economic adviser?"

"Yes. He travels quite a bit. I miss him, but we are able to keep in touch with phone calls."

Sara related how she and Ben had met and about their traditional wedding. She told her about Ben's former marriage and of the son he had in London. Then she shared her special news. "After months of trying to conceive, Ben agreed we could adopt a couple children. I am beyond happy. I have wanted children of my own for years—ever since Willy died in that car accident and I lost my baby daughter."

Martha heaved a long sigh and rubbed her upper arms nervously. "I-I've never shared something with you before now, Sara, but I can't keep it to myself any longer." She reached for her handbag and pulled out an envelope and a handkerchief. Dabbing at her moist eyes, she waved Sara away. "No, no, I'll be all right. Holidays make me especially sad. You'll know why in a minute." She withdrew some photographs from the envelope and handed them to Sara.

Sara examined them closely. They showed Martha and a young white man. A few others showed a baby. "Who is this handsome guy, and whose baby is this?"

"The man is Adam. We started dating the day I entered nursing school."

"And the baby? He's beautiful, by the way."

Suddenly Martha broke into tears. She sobbed so loudly, she couldn't speak.

Sara rushed to her side and gathered her into her arms. "What's wrong, my dear? Why are you suffering?"

"Because . . . because I'm still mourning the loss of . . . my only child. My precious baby s-son. The . . . the baby in the pictures is mine, Sara."

"You gave birth to a son? When? I never knew." Sara's breath caught in her throat. Memories of her own daughter rushed to mind. There was no greater pain than losing a child.

Martha nodded. Hesitatingly and with her eyes radiating the depth of her despair, she related what had happened. "Like any two people in love, Adam and I shared in each other's passion. He took me everywhere in London, showing me all the famous and historical sites. We went on river cruises, to amusement parks, to Madame Tussauds Wax Museum, to see the London Bridge, to the zoo, and the Tower of London. We even watched the changing of the guards on several occasions. We thoroughly enjoyed each other's company and hated to be apart for even an hour. I-I didn't know I was pregnant until I was almost five months along. I was so naïve about those things."

Martha dabbed at her eyes again and sighed deeply. "Anyway, when I told Adam we were going to have a baby, he was f-furious. He was angry with me and at himself. Abortion wasn't an option." She blew her nose and sucked in another deep breath before continuing. "He categorically refused to marry me. He . . . he said he was about to enter his second year of college and wasn't going to quit to support a f-family. He handed me some money and said I should . . . I should give the baby away for adoption."

"Oh, Martha, my dear. I am so sorry. So sorry." Sara wiped away her own tears with the back of her hand. "What did you do then?"

"I never heard from him after that day. I-I tried to reach him several times up to the week of birth, but he wouldn't respond to my calls or messages. I realized I was on my own. The sudden and total rejection was a painful blow to my heart, even more so because of my predicament. I was in school myself. I-I was in a foreign country. I didn't know very many people. I realized I had no other choice but to . . . to give up my son for . . . for adoption." Martha choked back more sobs and stared vacantly across the room. "When I made up my mind to come back here, I started searching for him, Sara, but I've had no luck. It's not that I want to take him back. I know it wouldn't be fair for me to suddenly show up on the doorstep of his new home and announce who I am. I-I just want to know that he found a nice home and that his parents love him. Is that asking too much?"

"Of course not, my dear."

"When you mentioned that you and Ben were planning to adopt, it . . . well, it seemed as if my entire world had collapsed once again. I don't know where my child is, Sara, and the continuous wondering and worrying is so difficult to live with. I don't know who adopted him. I hope his parents are as fine as you and Ben."

"I can't offer you any great words of advice, Martha, because it took me ten years to come to terms with my own grief. All I can say is that Ben brought me hope and love again, and I know there is someone special out there for you too. We will both pray that you have the opportunity to at least see your child someday soon . . . to put your heart at ease. My daughter died, so that hope has never been there for me. But, my dear friend, there are so many orphans in our country needing our love. Have you thought of adopting a child yourself?"

Martha shook her head. "I don't know if I could. Maybe. We'll see. Right now, I'm just thankful I finally shared my grief with you. Having your understanding and your shoulder to cry on means everything to me."

"That's what friends are for." Sara smiled through her tears.

"Now, enough of this sad talk. It's time for you to go find Ben. I'm going to take a short walk outside and then go to my room. Thank you for being such a great listener."

Sara found Ben in his study poring over government documents. She sat on the chair next to his desk and told him about Martha's heartbreaking story.

"Is she sure the father is that college student?"

"Of course, she is. He was the only one she dated for several months. He abandoned her and his child and went off to college. Education is important, but it is possible to achieve it while working to support your wife and child. Too many men seem to enjoy the process of impregnating a woman and then run like jackrabbits from their responsibility. Is there anything we can do to help Martha, Ben? Do you know of any way to trace an adoption in England? All she wants to know is that her child was, indeed, adopted and that he is being cared for by those who love him."

"I don't know the system personally, but I'll ask a couple of friends. By the way, I've read the adoption documents you gave me last night. I even filled out the application forms. They are all ready for our signatures."

"Thank you, sweetheart. How was I ever so lucky to have someone like you come into my life?"

"It's not a matter of luck," he said, smiling up at her. "You were God's gift to me. But I do want to offer something from the male point of view before we end this conversation. You talk about your grief and your friend's grief. Men can suffer too, Sara. Do you think it has been easy for me to have my son withheld from me by his mother? I don't see him enough or spend nearly enough time

with him. There isn't a day that goes by but that I wish he were here in our home. Thank God I am able to travel to England from time to time on business so I have the opportunity to see him."
He stared across the room, as though envisioning himself there. "I didn't tell you before now, because we were so busy with other things, but I received a letter from Ben Jr.'s mother this week at the office. She has evidently remarried and may be moving to France. I don't know how that will affect my relationship with him in the future." He handed Sara the forms he'd signed. "They are ready for your signature now. You can take them to the adoption agency on Tuesday."

Although Sara was thrilled with the prospect of moving forward with her plans, she was touched by Ben's revelation. As she browsed through the forms, she couldn't divorce the fact from her mind that Ben, too, had painful personal issues.

Ben looked up from his desk as she was about to leave the room. "I'm sure Martha will be fine now that she's returned home. You're here, she'll be in familiar surroundings, and she may meet someone who will help her look to the future. None of us can relive our pasts, Sara. We have to deal with them the best we can. Some things are best forgotten."

"Martha will never forget the child she had to give up, Ben. When you have carried a child in your belly for nine long months, it becomes a part of who you are. A mother's love begins with inception." As Sara left the study, she was surprised that Ben was still thinking of Martha.

## Chapter 14

**April 5, 1983**

Tuesday morning, Sara drove straight to the Freetown Children's Center. She recognized the concrete fence, took a right turn at the first corner, and then saw the two-story building housing the facility. As she approached the black wrought iron gates manned by a security guard, she felt her heartbeat accelerate. Today was the first step to finding the children God wanted her to raise as her own. After months of prayer, she had finally come to terms with knowing she wouldn't conceive Ben's child. But the two of them had love in abundance, and parenthood had little to do with the hours spent in the delivery room of a hospital.

The security guard, who was attired in a light-green jacket and bottle-green pants, strode toward her car with his hand up to stop her. He interviewed her briefly to know why she wanted to gain entrance to the center before he opened the gates and waved her through. She found an empty space in the visitors' parking lot and followed the directions to the matron's office. The receptionist introduced herself and then escorted her to the waiting area, composed of six upright chairs and a coffee table. "The matron will be with you in a few minutes," she said. "Please make yourself comfortable."

Sara glanced about the waiting room. She was its only occupant. Feeling nervous, she fidgeted on her chair and finally leafed through the pile of magazines strewn atop the table. She selected one called *Africa* and scanned through the pages until something captured her attention. She then rummaged through her purse for a notepad and a pen and hurriedly scribbled questions she had about the deforestation issue and how it affected the lives of firewood users and cutters. The article was a godsend because it enlightened her on an issue that was very close to Ben's heart.

Fifteen minutes later, a door at the far side of the room opened, and a woman smiled at her. "Mrs. Moses? Please come into my office. I am Madeline Brown, matron of this center."

Sara followed her into her office and took a chair in front of her desk. She had spoken with her previously on the phone, but this was the first time they had met in person. Mrs. Brown, who was in her mid-fifties, had chubby cheeks on a decidedly round face. When she smiled, the first thing Sara noticed was the gold tooth that matched the frames of her round spectacles. "I'm so pleased that you could see me so early this morning," she said.

"It's a pleasure for me to meet you, Mrs. Moses. I have known about your family for many years. I suppose everyone in Freetown is familiar with the auctioneer mart, at least by name. I have been there many times myself."

Sara removed the application forms from the envelope she carried and handed them to the matron. "I have read and reread them several times to ensure that all the sections have been properly completed. If there is anything else you need to know, please don't hesitate to contact me."

"I'll submit them to the board members before the day is over."

"How long will the adoption process take?"

"Usually between two and four months."

"That long?" Sara couldn't withhold her disappointment. "I don't understand why so many weeks are required. Is it because you have so many other parents making adoption requests?" She peered over her shoulder, as though looking for a long line of applicants.

"No, it's just that we are determined to make the adoptions legal. None of our adoptive parents would be happy to have the children suddenly taken out of their homes. I placed your request on the fast track, because you have requested two children and, if possible, siblings. We don't have many who are willing to take older children, let alone two. Most want babies."

"My husband and I thought very carefully about what was best for our children, not only ourselves. Older children will be able to adjust better to our busy lives." Sara paused for a moment and leaned forward to confide, "If you had them available today, no one would be happier than the two of us."

The matron nodded. "I cannot begin to tell you how kind and generous you are to take a couple of orphaned children into your home. We struggle to provide not only shelter, but medical care, clothing, food, and schooling for all those who come to us. Half of our budget comes from donors, and we fall short most of the time.

The children seem to thrive on the meager services we provide, but the individual love from those they can count on for the rest of their lives cannot compare."

Mrs. Brown moved several objects on her desk. Finally, she looked up again. "We are a poor country." She sighed. "Only a third of our people are literate, and only a third have access to medical care. There is so much to do with so little money and wholly inadequate resources. Some days, all we can do is to pray for a miracle."

Sara placed her hand over the matron's. "I will do whatever I can to help you. I have a couple other important issues on my plate right now, but within the next few months, I will know how I can assist you with your mission. We must all do more to provide our children with a better life. Since Ben is in the government, perhaps we can find a way to get the message out to the rest of the world that we need help."

"Your kindness warms my heart, Mrs. Moses. Do you have any questions about the adoption process?"

"I understand the process. I've never been a mother before, and I worry that I may be too set in my ways, but it is amazing how motherhood comes naturally."

"You'll do fine. You have a big heart. I hear people discuss the issue of whether parents are only those who conceive and give birth to their offspring, but all you have to do is look around to know the answer to that. In every country of the world and in wealthy, educated families as well, children are essentially abandoned by those birth parents through neglect. Is it nature or nurture that makes a woman a mother? I'd say nurture every time. What children want most is to know they are loved and wanted."

When Sara left the children's center, she didn't know if she should shout with glee or cry from overwhelming sorrow. With so much abject poverty in outlying villages resulting in thousands of starving, lonely, sick, and abandoned children, how could she rejoice in becoming the mother of only two? Her heart ached for them.

As soon as she entered the auctioneer mart, Sara was hustled straight into her office for a meeting. She and her general manager spent two hours poring over every detail of the report she had ordered after receiving an accusatory letter from a Mrs. Salma White, who claimed the business had discriminated against her. She asserted that the furniture items she'd brought to the mart were in good condition, but the sales staff had refused to purchase them.

According to the sales assistant, Mrs. White had not fulfilled the requirements of authenticity. There was no signature from her husband on the verification form. Instead, she had allowed her brother, James Murray, an attorney, to sign the document. "What this report states is that this is the first allegation of discrimination we've ever received," Sara said, frowning. "In the past, we had occasional problems arise when family members in the midst of a squabble or divorce tried to sell items without the other member's permission or knowledge, which is why I initiated this new policy a year ago. It ensures both parties are made responsible for their actions."

"That's right," her general manager, Edmund Coster, said. "But according to Mrs. White, she fulfilled the requirements of our new policy. In the absence of a receipt with the signatures of both parties involved, a lawyer is allowed to sign. When we conducted our own investigation into her allegation of discrimination, we learned that she had moved out of her marital home while her husband was out of town on official duties. She wanted to receive the cash for the sale before he returned. Mrs. White was unhappy with our decision not to accept the purchase of her furniture until her husband was apprised of the situation."

Sara stuffed the document into a folder and pushed it toward Coster. "Turn the matter over to our own lawyer. Our policy is clear, and Mrs. White's brother has no authority to change it willy-nilly simply because his sister wants to cash in while her husband is out of town. Lawyers are not above the law either. He knew what he was doing was collusion."

Back in her own office, Sara thought about how greedy some people could be. And selfish. She was fortunate to have someone so selfless in her life. Ben had such high moral fortitude; he would never step over the line in order to receive unearned favors. She had nothing but respect for him. Once again, she thought of how lucky their children would be to have him for their father.

While she worked, she breathed a prayer. *There are many people in the world without a voice, Lord. Give me the courage to speak for them.*

## Chapter 15

Two days later, Sara heard a knock at her office door. "Mrs. Moses, have you got a minute?" Jeremiah, one of the clerical assistants at the Family Auctioneer Mart, stuck his head around the door. He had a huge smile on his face, and his dark eyes twinkled.

"With that smile, how can I resist, Jeremiah? Come in. I'll make time." Sara had a close working relationship with every member of her staff. They felt free to come to her with any of their problems, and she listened with patience and appropriate concern. Some even requested personal loans from either the company or her, and she usually granted them. No one had ever reneged on repaying the debt. "Do you have a problem with your college registration?"

"No, no, Mrs. Moses, I have good news for you."

"You've already been accepted?"

"Not yet. I'll inform you the minute that happens. Because you spoke to your contact and your contact spoke to the registrar, I'm certain I'll be admitted. I'm not worried."

"So, what do you want me to do for you this time?"

"Believe it or not, nothing!" Jeremiah's smile broadened. "I have something important to tell you. Something that affects you personally."

Sara sat straighter in her chair. "I'm all ears. Why don't you be seated?" She gestured toward the chair in front of her desk. The phone rang, and she spoke quietly for the next few minutes. "Now," she said when she had hung up, "what do you have to tell me?"

"My aunty said you are a nice person—"

"And your aunty is someone I know? A customer?"

Jeremiah shook his head. "Not a customer. My aunt is Madeline Brown. She's the matron of the Freetown Children's Center."

Sara's eyes widened. "I just met with her a couple days ago. She's your aunt?"

"Yes, Mrs. Moses, and I lived with her for ten years. I visited her yesterday. Aunty has great respect for you. She said she met with you and you're a very nice lady. I agreed with her."

"She said that?"

"And more. She said, 'I'm going to let Mrs. Moses have Esther and Joseph, Jeremiah. Although I've only met her one time, her sincerity has impressed me. She will make a fine mother for them.' I know those children, Mrs. Moses."

"Tell me about them." Sara listened giddily to catch every word Jeremiah spoke. Her eyes lit up, and she leaned over her desk.

Jeremiah inched forward on his chair. "They were abandoned by their mother several years ago."

"Abandoned by their mother?" Sara buzzed her secretary not to put through any calls to her. "Tell me everything you know."

"Yes, Mrs. Moses. I was living with my aunty next door when it happened."

"How long ago was this?" Sara closed the file in front of her and pushed it to one corner of her desk so she wouldn't be distracted.

"Maybe four or five years ago."

"You were staying with your aunt at the time?"

"Yes. The children were abandoned on Grandma Abigail's front porch. She was the next-door neighbor and a good friend of Aunt Mad. We both arrived at the house at the same time when we heard the scream for help." Jeremiah stroked his chin as he recalled the episode. "I'll never forget seeing those children lying so helplessly on that concrete porch. They had only a thin piece of cloth spread out under them. I cried. Grandma Abigail wept too. We didn't know what to do."

Sara felt a lump rise in her throat and perched her cheeks on her knuckles as she braced herself for the unpleasant history of the children she hoped would call her Mommy.

"Grandma Abigail called for Uncle Chris, a strong hand in the neighborhood. He called the police. I was there from the beginning to the end."

"It must have been a difficult experience for the children. How old were they at the time?"

"I think Esther was about four and Joseph was a couple years younger. He couldn't even speak well and could barely walk, he was so weak."

"The poor, dear baby. What happened then? Did your aunt take them to the center? How did you know the mother abandoned them?"

"Let me start from the beginning. Grandma Abigail heard someone knock on her front door. She peeked out the window and saw the profile of a young woman. She immediately opened her door and found no one there. She heard footsteps crunching on the fallen leaves. That's when she saw the children and screamed, but she did no longer saw the mother. The police came to the conclusion that no one else would do that except the mother."

"But why did the woman come to Grandma Abigail? Why not to someone else?"

"That I can't tell you. Grandma Abigail was dumbfounded to see the two toddlers sleeping on her porch. A carrier bag containing their clothes, biscuits, and a small bottle of water was next to them. When she screamed, '*Jikrumaria! Ebosio,* Lord, have mercy!' the children woke up and started to cry.

"'*Way you mama?*' Grandma Abigail asked Esther. The girl had no answer. She just continued to cry out, 'Ma-ma. Ma-ma?' Joseph was too young to know what was happening."

Sara found it difficult to hide her emotions as Jeremiah continued with his narration. Would these precious siblings be her children? She wanted to meet them.

"Grandma Abigail picked up Joseph and tried to get him to stop his crying. My aunt carried Esther, and they went into the house. '*Wey you mama?*' Aunt Mad asked them several times. '*Ah-ah-nor-no,*' Esther said. She didn't know. She was so scared. She couldn't tell them where she lived or the names of anyone or the name of a village. Nothing. They tried to feed them with bread and tea. Joseph ate a little bit. When the police arrived, Esther wailed again. Each time she did, Joseph followed suit. One of the officers examined the porch and the surrounding area and found nothing. When the police told her she would have to go to the station to make a statement, Grandma Abigail was furious. She told him that she was not leaving her house. Her statement would have to be taken 'right there and then.'"

"Good for her," Sara said. "Makes no sense to have her make a trip to the station."

"She told the policeman to have a heart. The children's mother had abandoned them, and he shouldn't add to their traumatic situation. The officer was upset, but my aunt tried to pacify him. More and more people gathered in front of the house to get a glimpse of what was going on. Someone out in the crowd even asked whether Grandma Abigail had died. She was a well-known woman in the area. When the officer informed his superior officer, he was instructed to take a statement from Grandma Abigail and leave the children with her while they investigated. The investigation went on for some time. As there was no system set up for abandoned children, Grandma Abigail opted to care for them. Esther and Joseph became her responsibility. Her own children, my aunt, and some other neighbors and friends assisted her."

Jeremiah crossed his arms over his chest and finally sat more comfortably in the chair. "I've known Esther and Joseph since that day, Mrs. Moses."

Sara nodded, but spent some time thinking about the story. "I don't understand exactly why you have told me this, Jeremiah," she said. "My heart aches for the children, as it does for all abandoned and orphaned children, but it sounds as though they already have a happy home."

"Not any longer, Mrs. Moses. Grandma Abigail became ill and died three months ago. Her funeral was packed full, because she had helped so many people. By this time, my aunt had become involved with the Freetown Children's Center, and she took Esther and Joseph there. The children are confused and sad."

Sara felt tears stinging her eyes. Were these children to become hers? First they were abandoned by their own mother and then by the woman they considered a second mother, albeit by death. "You say that your aunt mentioned me as their potential mother?" she asked, clearing her throat and reaching for her handkerchief.

"Yes, Mrs. Moses. She will work hard to see that the board agrees to let you have the children. I want you to have them too, ma'am. It will be good for them. I know from personal experience how kind you are. If you want to adopt children, I feel strongly that Esther and Joseph will bring you joy." He rose from the chair and left Sara's office.

For the next half hour, Sara paced back and forth behind closed doors. She couldn't get the picture of the two children out of her mind. If everything happened for a reason, then she would have to believe that God led her to Mrs. Brown and the center, because she was related to her employee Jeremiah and they both had personal knowledge of the children she was meant to adopt. Life had so many twists and turns. But things happened for a reason.

Her attention was divided when she picked up the file folder from her desk and shouldered her handbag. She would be patient and wait to hear from Mrs. Brown. If she hadn't received a call in a week, she would call her.

The following Monday and for the rest of her workweek, Sara spent her lunch breaks in the public library. Admittedly, she needed to get enough information about activities in the forest. While the application forms were being processed at the center, she would use her time investigating her second family problem. The adoption of the children was her priority, but research into the deforestation issue was equally as important and somewhat urgent. Before she could present logical arguments for maintaining her use of firewood for cooking, she needed to understand its relationship to the environment. She couldn't understand why the use of firewood should be lumped into the same conversations as those iterating the destruction of the forests and what this meant to Sierra Leone's future.

Sara patiently combed through the reference section of the library for whatever she could obtain to assist her with the information she needed. She was definitely on a fishing expedition. The topic was multifaceted, and the historical facts she unearthed were dumbfounding. She realized that our colonial masters were the pioneers of deforestation because in 1896, when the Europeans decided to move in and settle down in Africa, the British took charge of Sierra Leone; they expanded the boundaries to what currently exist in the country, Freetown, and the provincial towns. Their intention was to generate and protect revenues. As a result, they formed and instituted a means whereby the country's natural resources could be exploited for exportation as a key objective of the Sierra Leone colonial government. In 1912 a forestry department was established, with a focus on European-style commercial timber harvesting. One of the actions of the forestry department in 1916 was the establishment of a forest reserve in the Freetown Peninsula Mountains.

Taking copious notes, Sara found herself more interested in the history of forestry than she had anticipated. Sierra Leone's first forestry law was passed in 1912, and for the next seventy years, it was the main law relating to forestry activities in the country. Several amendments were made to the law between 1929 and 1941. Deforestation was also an issue in other West African countries. A century ago, West Africa had some 193,000 square miles of coastal rainforest extending from Guinea to Cameroon, but decades of relentless logging, combined with road building, mining, and subsistent activities such as the collection of fuelwood and agricultural clearing, left the region vulnerable.

Firewood was one of the earliest trade forest products in Freetown, prior to the establishment of the Freetown settlement in the seventeenth century. This activity had gone on for centuries. It was also observed that in 1908, the tree species Aniosophyllea laurina was sold in the local Freetown market as posts, and these posts were used for scaffolding and construction of houses. Charcoal, a wood-based product, had been in existence for hundreds of years between 1450 and 1700. The historical form of charcoal production was conducted by blacksmiths for their own use. At the start of the colonial era, timber was the first product that generated revenues.

The research she did became overwhelming. Packing up her voluminous pile of notes and stuffing them into her briefcase, Sara left the library and returned to her office. The historical facts left her with adequate knowledge of how it all started and how it would only get worse if no steps were taken to change the way in which Sierra Leone's natural resources were used. Something had to be done. The government had the most blame, for not formulating policies to arrest the situation relating to the rapid depletion of the forest. At this stage the door was left wide-open for foreign companies to log at will. Because of her own preference for cooking with firewood, she decided she needed to become an advocate for the woodcutters.

Sara collated the information, which was no different from writing a thesis. She chose the benefits of small business as her thesis for her college degree because she was familiar with the subject. This subject she now embarked on was foreign to her, and she didn't know where to begin. She called Ruth, her secretary, into her office. She often picked Ruth's brain when she had a particularly thorny decision to make. By now, she had typed up all her library notes and was familiar with the subject matter. "I've been thinking about this national problem for a long time and have come to the conclusion that I must become personally active in the environmental movement, Ruth," she said. "It's very young, not only in our country, but throughout the world, but I see it becoming an issue for every country. Populations are growing, industries are expanding, and the use of cars and fuels will only grow considerably."

She peered at the solemn Ruth and then laughed. "You know me well enough to know I have a personal investment in this issue. I love to cook, and I choose to cook using firewood. I buy it from a woodcutter who is being pushed by timber bosses to pay increasingly hefty bribes in order to fell trees for the firewood to sell to people like me. Cano has twelve children. If he can't sell the firewood, his children will starve. I'm sure there are hundreds of Canos out there."

Sara looked over the typed notes on her desk. "I couldn't get the idea out of my mind that we need a catchy slogan that can be remembered and used over and over again. If soft drink and beer companies can use slogans, so can we. Which of these two slogans do you consider more appropriate?" Sara pulled a paper from a folder and read: *"Cook with firewood and still save our forests*, or *Replant and keep our forests green."*

"Both are appropriate, Mrs. Moses, but I prefer the first one."

"I'm not so sure." Sara paced her office while tapping her left palm with the pencil in her hand. "I prefer the second. Not everyone in the country cooks with firewood, whereas everyone uses wood-based products. Look around the room. What do you see?"

Ruth turned her head from left to right and then nodded. "I see what you mean. The pencil in your hand is made of wood." She pointed to the chairs on the opposite side of her desk and continued, "Those three chairs are wooden chairs. All the office furniture and bookcases are made of wood."

"Yes. And think of our homes. The doors, window frames, plywood under roofs, floors, even cooking utensils are made of wood. All of these products are derived from the trees that come from our forests."

"I don't see how we can get around continuing with this practice, or whatever you want to call it," Ruth said. "What's the option? The majority of our citizens could never afford to buy imported vinyl furniture. And don't forget that wood is used to make paper, books, newspapers, and magazines. Even linoleum is made from a wood product. We can't do without using trees from our forests."

Sara stood by the window and crossed her arms over her chest. "I am amazed that we get practically everything from trees. They've provided us with beauty, shade, oxygen, clean air and water, fruit, nuts, and wood products such as paper, furniture, and housing. Many have surprised me." She moved to her desk and flipped through the typed notes. "My goal would be to remind the *powers that be* that the trees are not only used by those who cook but by everyone."

"I see why you chose the second slogan, but I don't know what any of us can do to replant the forests. The rights are essentially owned by big industry loggers, who ship most of their harvest overseas. They hire local workers to do this, but pay them a pittance."

"It's not going to be easy, Ruth. Education is essential, for all our citizens, not just those who can read and write. That will be our challenge."

As Sara required a professional opinion, nowhere could she get this except at the university. She drove up the mountain, where she engaged in a very fruitful discussion with the head of the economics department, Professor Samuel, and Professor Gaia from the agricultural economics department at Njala college. This college was over one hundred miles from Freetown. She hadn't discussed her project with Ben yet because she wanted to be thorough. She needed well-thought-out arguments—ones that couldn't be refuted.

The more she learned, the more she realized the complexity of the topic. There were lots of opinions, but few solutions. She was a solution-oriented person. Discussion without action couldn't achieve anything. Any important issue requires action. Since Ben was an economic adviser for the government, she wanted to present him with an initiative that was both logical and workable.

Although she struggled with the research, by the end of the week she would have compiled some form of a report. Her intention was to form a reforestation organization made up of people from the grassroots up; she would include people in the timber industry, local citizens interested in environmental issues who had money and clout, and representatives from villages. A prominent member of her league would be Cano.

The following Friday when she returned to her office, she had three phone messages. In order of priority, she dialed the number for the Freetown Children's Center. With shaking hands and a heart pounding like a drum, she waited for the matron to answer. "Good morning, Mrs. Brown. This is Sara Moses returning your call."

"Hello, Mrs. Moses. Thank you for getting back to me so promptly. I believe I have some good news for you. We've set a date for your interview. Would you and your husband be able to make it for the interview next Tuesday morning at ten o'clock?"

Sara swallowed hard and stroked her neck to get the lump in her throat to move so she could reply. "Yes, of course. We'll be there promptly at ten o'clock. Should we bring anything with us?"

"Everything's in the letter on its way to you. It will explain the purpose and procedure of our meeting. By the way, I'm required to send an inspector to your home shortly after the interview. It's just a matter of formality. There should be no problem."

"Thank you, Mrs. Brown. This is wonderful news for Ben and me." Sara wanted to ask about Esther and Joseph, but bit her tongue to keep the question to herself. She didn't want to get Jeremiah in trouble if he had spoken too soon and against the rules.

Unable to work, Sara left her office early, feeling decidedly upbeat. Her plan had been to tell Ben about her deforestation research over dinner. Now she felt that dinner should be elevated to something more special. Good news deserved fine dining.

Ben was surprised when he arrived home. "What's going on?" he asked, standing by the dining area in the house. "Something smells extraordinary. Are we expecting guests for dinner and you didn't tell me?"

"The dinner is just for the two of us, because I love you," Sara said, taking his briefcase from him and helping him remove his suit jacket. "I'm celebrating you as my husband tonight."

"What is it you need, a new car?" Ben grinned.

Sara laughed. "You are too suspicious. Can't a wife do anything nice without having a reason?"

"Some wives, maybe. Mine? No." Ben glanced at the table and saw that it was beautifully set. His eyes showed bewilderment when he saw the platter of krio salad artfully arranged with roast meat and roast chicken on a silver tray. "What is all this about, may I ask again?"

"Wait and see!"

"What time did you get home?"

"Early enough to prepare our dinner."

After the meal, Sara excused herself and returned to the table with a folder. She placed it near Ben. "I've been very busy working on a special project—"

"I was right! You need money. Not so?"

"Just wait until I finish. It's a project that I hope will earn your approval. I've been working for a couple of weeks on the formation of an association to be known as the Reforestation Association."

Ben stared at her in bewilderment. He opened the file and peered at the title of the top document. "When you decide to do something, you don't go halfway, do you? The thickness of this file represents a lot of hours."

"I've studied everything I could find in print about the history of the forest, the pioneers of deforestation, the importance of poles, firewood, timber, and charcoal. I understand the problems now,

Ben. I believe I know even more than some of the people in the government. Too many of them are looking for a quick solution that will end up costing us dearly. I want to get all users of forest products involved, including those in the villages who have been doing things the same way for generations. The association will provide information to educate everyone of his or her social responsibility to preserve our forests."

Sara showed him the pages that listed similar associations in other parts of the world. "The Reforestation Association would also hold regular meetings with members of the community. The importance of rehabilitating our forest areas is important to our future. By emphasizing the replanting of trees, they will live into perpetuity. The rules will apply not only to people who must have firewood in order to survive, but to timber companies who, until this time, have been allowed to come in and cut down every tree in vast areas."

"Well," Ben said, "to say I am stunned is woefully inadequate. I'm literally at a loss for words. How in the world . . . ? When did you do . . . ? Is this really something you want to do? You really want to work with the community and the government on this? How did you come up with this idea?"

"I'm not as altruistic as it seems, Ben. I want people to continue cooking with firewood. For my part, you have not been silent about voicing your complaints, although you certainly enjoy the food I prepare out there. Literally hundreds of thousands of people in Sierra Leone cook the same way. They have to. They don't have an option. Few have modern facilities in their kitchen like we have in this house. I wanted to research the situation and come up with a solution that would not only please you, but other government officials dealing with this problem. You know, deforestation is not only the result of firewood cutting, Ben. Most of it is due to timber producing, bushfires, storms, farming, mining, and logging activities. Most, if not all, of the wood used for firewood comes from already felled or unhealthy trees."

"This is not going to be an easy task, Sara. It's going to take considerable time to organize. I'll give you whatever assistance you need, but the issue of deforestation is interrelated with the economic, political, and social issues in the country."

"I know." She spent the next hour discussing some of her strategies with him, picking his brain regarding the socioeconomic aspects of the issues.

When she brought the coffee to the table, she felt her excitement elevate. Now she would be able to tell Ben the most important news . . . the news she'd been eager to share all week, ever since Jeremiah had visited her office. "Ben, I have more good news."

"Ah . . . just as I thought. Here comes the real reason we're dining."

Sara laughed. "You know me too well. This has been an incredible two weeks. I know who our children are. Their names are Esther and Joseph." For the next several minutes, she related the story as told to her by Jeremiah. "I spoke with the matron of the children's center this morning. We are to have our required interview next Tuesday morning. She said it would speed up the process for us."

"Sara . . . I worry that you are putting the cart before the horse. Jeremiah is not on the staff of the center. He may have misinterpreted what he heard from his aunt, who has found you to be a nice person. Everyone who meets you feels you are a nice person. I don't want to discourage you, but let's wait before we have our hearts set on these two particular children. If the matron suggests two others, it wouldn't be fair to them to feel you are disappointed."

Sara sipped her coffee before responding. "You're right once again, Ben. When you spoke of disappointment, I immediately thought of the words of Thomas Hardy, the English novelist and poet. He said the sudden disappointment of a hope leaves a scar that the ultimate fulfillment of that hope never entirely removes."

Long after she had turned off their bedroom light, Sara lay awake and thought of those words. She already had a few scars from disappointments. She had no desire to add another one.

## Chapter 16

**April 1983**

Monday morning, Sara worked diligently at her desk, but kept one eye on the door of her office while waiting for her assistant to bring in the mail. The word had spread quickly throughout the office that she and her husband had applied at the Freetown Children's Center to adopt a child. Several had poked their heads into her office to wish her luck. She wasn't ready to talk about it, though. So many things could go wrong. What if . . . ? She shuffled papers around on her desk trying to stay busy, but her mind wandered, continuously thinking of the children Jeremiah had described.

"Your interview will be a mere formality, Mrs. Moses," Jeremiah assured her. "Aunt Madeline wants you to have those children. Besides, I put in a good word for you."

When the letter finally arrived, Sara closed the door of her office and read it quietly several times. As the matron had intimated over the phone, the letter specified the various documents she and Ben needed to take to the interview. Later that evening, when she discussed the letter with Ben, she expressed her concerns.

"Why when there are so many children who are orphaned or abandoned, is it necessary for us to produce evidence of our financial status? We are certainly in a much better situation to adopt a child or two. And why do they need medical records? Can't they tell by simply looking at us that we are able-bodied? These associations copycat some of the requirements from overseas agencies." She paced the floor, becoming more distressed. Every request seemed like a high brick wall that could not be surmounted.

"You're getting all worked up over nothing, Sara," Ben said. "Come sit down." He took her hand. "Now, take a deep breath. We will supply whatever they need and then answer all their questions as honestly and thoroughly as we can. It's their responsibility to ensure that prospective parents aren't seeking children for any other reasons. I'm glad they're being so scrupulous about the process. We will benefit, and so will the children."

"Your ability to be so reasonable shames me, Ben. I need your strength. I've got my heart so tied up in knots I can't think about anything but what I want. You're right, of course. We need this process to be legal and binding and aboveboard. I'll go get whatever documents are required. I'm glad we're both well organized. It won't take long at all."

By nine thirty the next morning, she and Ben entered the center and found their way to the waiting room outside the matron's office. Sara noticed additional furniture in the waiting room; there were two three-seat sofas added to the six straight-backed chairs. Another couple occupied one of the sofas and smiled at them. The husband rose to shake Ben's hand. "Sam Fisher," he said. "This is my wife, Diana. Guess you're here about an adoption too."

"Yeah," Ben said, nodding at the woman. "It's a pleasure to meet you. Ben Moses and my wife, Sara." He pulled her closer.

They had barely finished their introductions to each other when the matron's secretary opened the door. "I'm so sorry about the delay, Mr. and Mrs. Fisher. Your interview is being delayed because one of the members of the board hasn't arrived yet. It shouldn't be more than fifteen minutes or so." She noticed Sara and Ben and smiled. "Your appointment may be slightly delayed also."

Sara cast a quick glance at her watch. They were early, but this unexpected setback was already wreaking havoc with her nerves. While Ben spoke with the Fishers, she moved across the waiting room and read the captions at the bottom of the framed photographs arranged on the white wall. The largest and most prominent was of Grandma Abigail Smart, the founder. The black and white photograph showed a pleasant-looking woman in her late seventies, with pure white hair parted in the middle and falling in two plaits over her ears. The pose emphasized the kindness shining in the direct gaze of her dark eyes. Sara looked at her little mouth and imagined the lips parting to shout *"Jikrumaria!"* when she caught sight of the two young children on her porch. Sara smiled to herself and wished she'd had the opportunity to meet the woman. She reminded her of her own grandmother.

There were a half dozen other photographs of children in various settings. She examined each closely, wondering if any of them were Esther and Joseph. She glanced at Ben and saw that he was still chatting amiably with the Fishers. She moved closer and took a seat, listening to their conversation. "So, you have applied to adopt a baby?" she asked, smiling at Diana Fisher.

"Well, between birth and two years old," she said. "I want to have the experience of caring for a baby or toddler, since I can't have children of my own. How about you?"

"We are looking to adopt older children; we hope for two of them, and preferably siblings if possible." She almost mentioned Esther and Joseph and bit her tongue to hold back her chatter.

Diana's eyes widened. "*Two* older children? That's a handful."

"We look forward to whatever comes," Sara said.

Right then, the matron's secretary returned. "We're ready for you now, Mr. and Mrs. Fisher. The members of the board will see you now."

"Good luck," Sara said, placing her hand on Diana's arm. When they had left the room, she turned to Ben. "I hope they get their baby," she whispered to Ben. "I can't imagine why they wouldn't."

Ben just nodded as he pulled a document from his briefcase. "I really need to read this economic report, Sara," he said. "Since we may have to wait awhile, I'd like to make use of the time."

"I understand. Go right ahead." Sara shut her eyes and daydreamed about her life with the children. Would they be frightened and lonely for their old lives and familiar people? Would they like her food and their rooms? And she needed to buy children's books and new clothes and get them enrolled in school and . . .

She turned toward Ben to discuss how they would go about this, but he was still reading. Finally, after fidgeting for several minutes and finding no interesting magazines to read, she said, "The interview is going to take longer than we had anticipated. We won't get out of here before noon."

"Do you have anything more important to do?"

"Not really," Sara responded.

She flipped through the pages of an outdated women's magazine and found an article titled "You and Your Children." Fully engrossed in it, she didn't hear the matron's secretary enter the room.

"The board is ready to see you now," she said.

The secretary escorted them past Mrs. Brown's office, down the hallway to a larger room that looked like a dining hall. Minutes later, Sara and Ben sat across the table from the matron, Madeline Brown, with the board's membership comprising three women and three men surrounding the table. Sara recognized the chairman as a renowned pediatrician at the children's hospital. She had never met him personally, but had read about him in the newspapers on frequent occasions. She trusted his judgment. The two other male members consisted of a child psychologist and a school superintendent. The female members included a registered nurse, a businesswoman from London with a financial and personal commitment to the organization, and the matron herself.

In the makeshift boardroom, Sara observed the plates, cups, and dishes neatly stacked on a long counter at one end of the room. The brown enamel folding chairs had seen their best days long ago. Forcing herself to relax, she breathed a prayer for the ability to accept whatever was decided and then reached for Ben's hand under the table. He squeezed it, and she turned to smile nervously at him.

Mrs. Brown opened a folder placed directly in front of her at the conference table. "I have apprised the members of the board of your interest in adopting two older children, Mr. and Mrs. Moses. Before we begin the interview, I want to iterate that the Freetown Children's Center is a nonprofit organization formed specifically to provide not only shelter, but clothing, food, education, and medical care for the children placed in our custody. These are children who have been either orphaned or abandoned and would be living on the streets if it weren't for our facility. Obviously, we can care for only a very small number of children. We don't have room or the finances for any more. You can't be an informed citizen of our country and not know there are many such children in Sierra Leone needing homes and parents to love them. We do our best to find homes for as many as we can, but our hands are often tied by the bureaucracy of our supporters."

She peered over the rims of her reading glasses at the chairman. "Thank you for the information you've submitted to us. You may begin the questioning, Dr. Emmitt," she said.

Sara noticed that each member of the board had a copy of their application and the supporting documents they had submitted upon arrival at the center. Mrs. Brown's secretary must have made copies for them.

"How long have you been married?" Chairman Emmitt asked, directing his first question at Ben.

"It will be a year next month," Ben said.

"So, you haven't even celebrated your first wedding anniversary?" He paused for a moment to look at them both. "Why do you want to adopt children?"

Ben and Sara looked at each other, but again, the chairman turned to Ben for a response.

"My wife and I have discussed the responsibility involved in having two children and feel we're more than ready, sir. Perhaps you'd like to know how I met Sara. It was in church. She has been a Sunday schoolteacher for many years. They love her as though she were a second mother to them. It was her concern and generosity toward the needs of these children that made me fall in love with her."

The chairman removed his glasses and placed them on the table. The other members listened intently as Ben spoke.

Ben said, "Every year, Sara organizes a special party for the Sunday schoolchildren and their parents and presents them with

## Smoke in the Kitchen

gifts. Just this month, she invited over a hundred children and parents to our home for an Easter celebration. She cooks meals to take to the homes of the poor and provides money to help pay bills. I have never known a woman so generous. As parents, we will instill this virtue in our children and ensure they never forget their humble beginnings and the importance of sharing what they have with others."

The chairman picked up his glasses and hooked them over his ears. "You speak like a lawyer representing a client, Mr. Moses. Your wife couldn't ask for a better recommendation than that."

Everybody laughed.

"We could use someone with your wife's experience, concern, and generosity in this institution. Perhaps we should entice her to join our board."

"I would be pleased to assist you in any way I can," Sara said. She felt Ben's eyes on her and knew he was thinking about her commitment to form the Reforestation Association. How would she have time to do that, raise two children, run the auctioneer mart, continue to teach Sunday school, *and* take on another responsibility? Somehow she would manage.

The psychologist ruffled the papers in his folder. "Would you be able to recognize the signs of a disturbed child, Mrs. Moses? Our children come from a background where they've been abused, neglected, or abandoned. They often have sleep difficulties, may cry often, and show other signs of fear. Sometimes this apprehension translates into other problems."

Sara folded her hands on the tabletop. "First of all, Ben and I intend to shower our children with all the love and attention they have lacked. It will be unconditional love, regardless of what problems they may exhibit. Once they know we will always be there for them, I am confident many such predicaments will diminish and even disappear. We will keep an open dialogue and work to learn and understand what the children are thinking . . . what their concerns are. If we find it necessary, we will seek assistance. The mental health of our children is important to their physical, social, psychological, and spiritual growth. We know that."

"How would you handle self-destructive behavior?"

Ben looked at Sara, but she followed up from where she'd left off.

"First, we would have to observe and decide whether the behavior was typical of children their age. A certain amount of rebellion against rules is healthy and to be expected. If our children were to display a consistent anger or deviousness, aggression against each other or their schoolmates, or uncalled-for rebelliousness, we would first discuss whether it was due to low self-esteem or lack of self-control."

Ben leaned forward. "I believe we both understand the need to be role models of proper behavior and to set rules that must be followed as part of a structured plan. We also understand the difference between discipline and punishment. Discipline is necessary when raising children. It must be principled and consistent and explained. I firmly believe that becoming a disciplined person ensures better success in life and in the workplace in the future. Punishment should be used when it's necessary."

Sara nodded. "Misbehavior must be addressed, but I know I would focus on praising good behavior and offering constant encouragement to do what is best."

"Thank you." The psychologist gestured toward the others. "I don't have any more questions."

The businesswoman looked up and frowned. "You two appear to be busy people. Mr. Moses, you travel a great deal. Mrs. Moses, you own and operate a big business. How do you expect to keep up with these responsibilities while raising children?"

"Initially, I will depend upon my very experienced staff to take over for me," Sara said. "I intend to work flexible hours until the children are enrolled in school and feel comfortable in their new home. I will work to develop a routine. Also, I will hire qualified help. Most working parents do have help. They successfully combine parenthood with their jobs and do it quite well."

After everyone had the opportunity to voice a few questions, the matron returned their original documents to them. "Do you have any questions?" she asked.

"Just a few," Sara said. "Do you have specific children in mind for us? How soon will we be able to bring them home, and during the adoption process, are we allowed to legally change their family name to ours?"

Madeline Brown hesitated. "Yes, we have someone in mind. We will need time to discuss this case before we can make any comments. As I mentioned before, we are required to make a home visit first. If and when the process takes place, adoptive parents are allowed to give the children their own family names."

Several minutes later, Sara heaved a long sigh of relief as she sat beside Ben in his car. "I feel better, don't you? I think the board members were satisfied with our answers to their questions. Still, I can't help but wonder if—"

"Sara, Sara, Sara, when will you stop your needless worrying?" Ben said, interrupting her. "Of course, we passed inspection. They will find our home more than adequate. I want to be the first to congratulate you. Within days, not months, you will welcome your children into our home. You will be Mother Moses. My only concern now is that you will not be disappointed."

"That will never happen, Ben. My eyes are wide-open." Sara peered out the windshield to think about how her life would change yet again. "I never really believed in miracles," she whispered. "Now God has granted me two of them. He brought you into my life and, soon, two wonderful children. The moment I hold them in my arms, their lives will be interwoven with mine forever."

## Chapter 17

Two days later, Sara was in her office earlier than usual sorting through the previous day's mail and writing a detailed to-do list. She examined the list of items for the next auction sale and made notes for discussion with her sales manager. Completely absorbed in her work, she was startled to the point of dropping her pen when the buzzing of her desk phone sounded.

"Mrs. Moses, the matron of the children's center is on the phone," her assistant said.

Sara quickly grabbed the phone from the cradle and pressed the talk button. "Mrs. Brown? Sara Moses speaking." She placed a hand over her heart to quiet its pounding.

"Good morning, Mrs. Moses. I'm sorry to bother you, but I was sure you would find my news a welcome interruption."

She paused just long enough for Sara to clamp a hand over her mouth to keep from an excited scream. Dare she hope?

"You and your husband impressed the board members with the honesty of your replies. They have approved your application for the adoption of two children. I haven't mentioned it before this, but I have already begun the paperwork for two very special children I know you will learn to love. They are a brother and sister and have spent the past four years in the home of our founder, Abigail Smart.

Esther is eight years old, and her brother, Joseph, is six. They are lovely children and will thrive in your home. If you have time today, would you like to stop by the center and meet them?"

Gasping, Sara transferred the receiver to her other ear. "Oh, yes, Mrs. Brown, I would love that! The children sound wonderful. I-I cannot thank you enough for all your help. This is the happiest news I've heard in, well, a very long time. I am thrilled. I can't wait to tell my husband. May he come with me? What time would be best for you?"

"Any time that's convenient for you is fine. I'm always here. I won't tell the children you are to become their parents yet, just in case something should happen between now and the time the formal papers are signed. You understand the necessity for such caution."

"Of course. We mustn't have their hopes raised and then deflated. They've gone through so much already. Will you hold for a minute while I check my calendar?" Sara traced the day's events with her finger and then pressed the button for Ruth to confirm she had nothing scheduled that wasn't listed. "I would be able to meet with you around two o'clock. Will that be all right?"

"That's fine. I'll expect you and your husband then. By the way, Mrs. Moses, other than informing your husband, this information about the adoption of Esther and Joseph should remain confidential."

*Smoke in the Kitchen*

"I understand legalities. I'll discuss it with no one. Thank you again, Mrs. Brown." After replacing the phone, she whispered, "Thank you, Lord. Thank you for this blessing." She picked up the phone again and dialed Ben. His secretary informed her he was in a meeting but she would have him call her the minute he was free.

Numb and with her mind in turmoil, she didn't notice as the lunch hour came and went. Idly, she jotted several more things on her to-do list. She wanted to shop for new bedding and other items for young children. Over and over again, she thought about what it would mean to hear the word Mama spoken by the lips of her own children. It was beyond thrilling to contemplate. Then apprehension took over. Was love enough? What did she know about nurturing children in a way that would encourage the growth of their esteem? Loath to dwell on the subject for fear she would have second thoughts, she kept one eye on the wall clock until it was close to one fifteen. Ben hadn't returned her call. Should she bother him again? No, she wouldn't be a pest. Finally, when she could take no more of the internal pressure, she snatched up her handbag and marched out, taking no notice of the faces of her staff as they peered wide-eyed at her unusual behavior.

She reached the Freetown Children's Center fifteen minutes later than her scheduled meeting with the matron. Traffic had worked against her determination to be timely. When she shook hands with the matron, however, she relaxed with the warmth of her greeting. They chatted as if they had been friends all their lives. "Once again, I apologize for Ben's not being here with me," she said. "He will be very disappointed. When the government is holding meetings, the 'do not disturb' sign is out."

"Don't apologize, Mrs. Moses. It was a last-minute plan on my part. Now, let's get on with the purpose of your being here. I know you are eager to meet Esther and Joseph. They were abandoned by their mother four years ago. Our founder, Mrs. Smart, found them on her porch and took them in. When Mrs. Smart passed away recently, these children were devastated. I have known them both all these years. They are well-mannered and dear to my heart. That's why I am so eager to place them in a home where they will be loved for the rest of their lives."

She picked up the receiver on her desk and spoke quietly. Not two minutes later, the door to her office opened, and a young woman entered holding the hands of a young girl and an even younger boy. "Mrs. Moses, this is Esther and her brother, Joseph. Children, this is Mrs. Moses. She is a very good friend to everyone at the center."

"Good afternoon, Esther and Joseph," Sara said, holding out a hand to each of them. They shook it as though they were years older.

"Good afternoon, ma," they said in turn, their voices soft and polite. Their eyes widened as they looked her over with undisguised curiosity.

Esther wore what seemed to be a permanent smile. It warmed the darkness of her eyes. Although her hair had been cut very short, it suited her round face. The slightly too small bright yellow cotton pinafore hugged her thin body and ended slightly above her knees, exposing her long thin legs. Joseph's smile was shy. He had the same round face, and the spaces of two missing front teeth became visible the wider his smile grew. He wore khaki shorts and a brown short-sleeved shirt that had been recently pressed.

Sara leaned over to embrace them. "My goodness," she said, "you are the most beautiful children I've ever met. Come sit with me on the matron's sofa so we can talk." When they were seated, one on each side of her, she smiled again. "Now, tell me about yourselves. How old are you? Do you like living here? What are your favorite subjects in school? Can you read? Do you like books?"

Esther laughed aloud, and her eyes sparkled. "I am almost nine years old. Well, eight really, but I will be nine soon. My brother Joseph is six." Their ages were estimated as there were no documents to determine their age. "My brother is shy and doesn't talk so much. We like it here, because everyone is very nice, but we . . . we miss our Grandma Abigail." She cast a quick glance at Mrs. Brown to see if she had misspoken.

The matron nodded to encourage her to continue.

"I can already read, but Joseph is just learning. I love books, but I don't have any of my own. I get books from the school. I also like math."

Sara looked at Joseph and saw him peering up at her with a heart-shattering grin. "What do you like to play, Joseph?"

The boy fiddled with his fingers. Stuttering, Joseph said, "I like to play football; we play football a lot in school. I play hide-and-seek sometimes. We don't have many toys to play with."

Mrs. Brown held out her hands. "Time to return to your lessons, children. Mrs. Moses has to leave now."

"Good-bye," Esther said.

After they had left the room, the matron gave Sara more background information. "Despite our thorough investigation, we were never able to locate the mother; I don't know whether we ever will. Enough time has elapsed that we see no problems in performing a legal adoption. Mrs. Smart never formally adopted them, so they essentially didn't have her family name. You will be able to give them your own."

Although Sara knew most of the story, which meshed with the version provided by Jeremiah, she did not mention this fact or him. Now that she had faces to go with their names, her motherly instincts grew stronger. Hopefully, she could translate the methods used by her own mother and grandmother into ones suitable for her own children in a new age and time.

"Even though the board has approved the adoption, we will still need to conduct an inspection of your home—that's routine, nothing major," the matron said. "I'm sure the report will be favorable and we can proceed very quickly with the adoption process. It should take no longer than a week or so."

Sara was about to leave and had her hand on the doorknob and the door slightly ajar, when the matron touched her arm. "Mrs. Moses, I feel compelled to tell you this." She lowered her voice and pushed the door shut. "Although the board approved the adoption of Esther and Joseph, you should know that the decision wasn't unanimous. One board member objected. The reasons stated weren't viewed as significant by the others." She didn't offer the name of the objector or the reasons given.

Disconcerted by the admission, Sara wrung her hands. "I-I'm surprised to hear this, Mrs. Brown. I-I don't understand how anyone would raise objections to our caring for those two innocent souls. Mr. Moses and I are financially capable and able to care for even four children, let alone two. We are well thought of in the community."

"All that is important is that you will be granted the right to adopt. You mustn't trouble yourself over nothing."

"Thank you again, Mrs. Brown," Sara said. "I'm grateful to you for sharing this information and for allowing me to meet the children today. Don't worry; it will remain confidential. My husband is the only one I will tell, and he will keep it to himself."

"Everything will be just fine, dear. I will talk with you again very soon."

Without giving work a second thought, Sara headed straight home. On the way, she replayed the conversation with the matron over and over in her mind. She mentally profiled everyone who was present at the interview. She couldn't single out anyone who seemed hesitant or overtly critical. Every member had sounded encouraging. What should have been a joyous day had been dampened with a smear of gloom. She felt compelled to learn the identity of the lone dissenter.

"You're home early," Sara said when Ben followed her into the house less than an hour later.

"My secretary said you had called earlier today when I was in a meeting. By the time I called your office, Ruth said you'd left without mentioning your destination."

"I went to the children's center. The matron called and said the board had approved our adoption request. I met our children, Esther and Joseph."

"You met them? That's wonderful! You must be ecstatic." Ben reached out to hug her. "For some reason, you don't look as happy as I'd expected you to be. Is something wrong? Don't the children want us to be their parents?"

"No, no, that's not it. The children are beautiful, beyond anything we deserve. I can't wait until they are officially ours." Sara peered into his eyes. "In confidence, the matron shared a behind-the-scenes scenario. One of the board members objected to our adoption application."

"Who objected . . . and why?"

*Smoke in the Kitchen*

"The matron wouldn't say. I can understand her hesitation. She just wanted me to know the decision wasn't unanimous. Ben, I'm worried. I have this dreadful feeling that something is going to go wrong. You don't think my cousin Thomas has anything to do with it, do you? He probably knows we have applied for the adoption of children. It's just like him to try to throw a monkey wrench into the proceedings. What if he got to one of the board members, and, you know—"

"Bribed him or her into causing a ruckus? We really shouldn't make such an assumption on no evidence, Sara. It won't matter anyway. You say the board has approved of us, and the matron even allowed you to meet the children. Focus on that, my dear. Keep your eyes on the prize and not on the fly on the wall."

"I knew you'd have all the right things to say, my love. That's why I drove directly home. I'm so glad you're here. I feel the urge now more than ever before to be a mother."

"I don't have an ounce of doubt. I remember an old proverb my father used to quote on occasion, especially on days when my mother was especially supportive despite the antics of my brother and me when we were determined to upset the serenity of our home. He said that God couldn't be everywhere and that's why he created mothers. The good ones know exactly what to do on every occasion. I believe wholeheartedly that God created you to be the mother of Esther and Joseph. They will learn to love you as much as I do."

Sara felt the familiar fluttering in her heart and reveled in the love she shared with her husband. Whenever she was with him, it seemed that all time stopped. Nothing else mattered. They had each other. They understood each other's needs, and now, more than ever before, she was eager to cement their love for the sake of their children.

## Chapter 18

Sara had arranged an appointment to see the *headmen* and elders from villages in the Peninsula area regarding their participation in the Reforestation Association, but after the meeting with the matron, she had been too preoccupied with learning of the board's dissenter to drive there. Now that she had discussed her concerns and distress with Ben, she realized she could still keep the engagement. She rushed to her bedroom to change clothes. A few minutes later, she was dressed in a green tie-dyed *boubah* and *lappa,* red casual shoes, and a green head wrap.

Ben looked up from the newspaper as she entered his study. "Are you going somewhere?"

"I'm going to Funkia to meet with some people regarding the Reforestation Association."

"You mean Kelitia's hotel?"

"No, not the hotel; I'm going to the Funkia village."

"Why not cancel? You've already had a full day."

"You know the old adage; I don't want to put off until tomorrow what I can do today. If we're going to become the parents of two active children in the very near future, I want to have the association up and running. Besides, it would create a bad first impression if I were to reschedule. Older people, especially those in the villages, would consider it a sign of disrespect." Sara adjusted her head wrap. "I'm actually looking forward to meeting with them. I know they'll see the benefit of their participation, and once I've signed on representatives from the peninsular villages, others will follow suit."

"The driver's taking you . . . be careful! Sorry I can't go with you. I've got a mountain of work to take care of myself."

If the streets in Freetown were in disrepair, those in the villages were in a you-won't-believe-it-until-you-see-it condition. When they became utterly impassable, the youths in the area went out to perform a haphazard fix-it job by ramming stones and dirt in the potholes. In the process, they would put up roadblocks for drivers and strongly persuade them to pay their way. It was a makeshift means for collecting tolls to support them and their families from those drivers who used the road. Sara paid several such toll collectors on her drive to Funkia. When she finally arrived, only five people had already congregated.

"Oh, madam, *kabor* . . . *kabor*." The headman welcomed Sara with a broad smile. "You know *black-man time*, we are still waiting on the other elders. According to the clock, it is seven o'clock, but according to their clock, it is six. Be patient, madam. They will drag themselves here very soon."

Sara shook his hand. "Headman, please, do not concern yourself. I can wait. I have nothing to do after the meeting except drive back."

*Smoke in the Kitchen*

The meeting started at seven forty-five. Sara had expected her arguments to be so convincing she would be back in her car within the hour. But neither the headman nor the elders could be persuaded that the program would have a beneficial effect on their lives. After two hours of discussion and deliberation, each side decided to give the topic more thought. The headman promised to get in touch with Sara when a new date was set.

Disappointed, Sara struggled to maintain her composure. She had no right to assume immediate compliance with her newly formed league's goals. Some things took longer than others to digest. Change of such magnitude would take time, especially when it involved a change in thinking and attitude. Old habits die hard. Her father had drummed that into her head.

All the way home, she thought about the discussion and the concerns that the elders had voiced. She definitely had more homework to do. She needed more than a litany of facts. She needed pictures and definitive methods that could be easily understood and initiated—ones that made sense to ordinary workers who were illiterate and couldn't do the research for themselves. Above all, she needed to do some coaxing.

The next day, Sara arrived at her office fifteen minutes earlier than usual. Ruth had asked for the day off that Friday, and she would be on her own. No sooner had she sat at her desk than the phone started to ring. Callers needed a plethora of information about the new barter system she had introduced to help those with needs, but without cash to make purchases. She spent an inordinate amount of time explaining how it worked over and over again.

With each passing moment, it became increasingly hard for her to concentrate on other things. Finally, she gave up and went to search for another employee who could take over the phones in Ruth's absence.

Not five minutes later, she received a call from her lawyer, Othneil Baker, who had been communicating with her cousin Thomas's lawyer.

"Sara, I apologize for not getting back to you sooner. I know you've suffered a great deal of anguish over this case, but it has me completely baffled. I've gone over your papers several times, and I don't see how your cousin's case has any merit. The law is quite clear. There is nothing in your grandfather's original will that the property be handed down to a male grandchild as opposed to a female grandchild. He could possibly challenge your father's will if he could prove he were mentally incapable or senile at the time of its creation or that he was somehow coerced into turning the mart over to you, but I don't believe either of those things is true. Now, we may have missed something in interpreting the deed that made your father the owner of the mart instead of his brother, Thomas's father. I have assigned one of my assistants to look into that angle. You say you haven't spoken personally with your cousin about this matter?"

"I haven't spoken with Thomas for several years," Sara said. "As I told you before, he moved out of the country, and we lost touch."

"All I've been given is the lawyer's name and information, which is odd at the very least. Well, I don't know what to say, Sara. Something about this situation doesn't sit right with me. Thomas's lawyer stated in his last communication that he intended to explore all avenues, whatever that means. Whenever I place a call to him, he's out of his office. When I leave a message, I receive no reply. The man is keeping things close to his vest. I'll stay on this. Sorry it's taking so long. Unfortunately, property cases are seldom hurried affairs. They can go on for months or even years."

"I have a great deal on my plate right now," Sara said. "I'm in the process of adopting a couple children, and I'm organizing a national association to assist users of firewood in maintaining their lifestyle, but not depleting our forests. In the meantime, I must carry on with the business of increasing profits from the business. I won't allow the threat of my business being literally stolen from me to stop my plans for its expansion."

"I understand, Sara. I encourage you to continue as you are. Let me handle this sticky issue for you. I'll get back to you as soon as I have something new."

After the lawyer had hung up, Sara settled down to study the contract for a new warehouse. She was reading the last page when her phone rang again. This time, it was Wyatt North from the children's center, calling to confirm the time of the required home inspection for later that afternoon. Since it would only take an hour or so, she decided to go for an extended lunch break, providing ample time for the inspection and to answer any follow-up questions from their tour of her home.

The three inspectors from the center arrived in a Mazda 626 pickup truck at 1:00 p.m. sharp. Wyatt North, whose moustache had specks of salt and pepper, was the head of the team, which consisted of two women and himself. He was about six-foot-two and carried a stern, authoritative appearance. Sara introduced herself and invited them into the house.

"Is your husband at home?" North asked.

"I'm sorry; he couldn't be here, but I can supply whatever information you require."

"We really prefer to have both parents available for the home inspection, Mrs. Moses, but we shall proceed anyway. We'd like to take a look at the outside property first."

Sara let them into the backyard and pointed out the expansive grass areas. "There is plenty of room here for football or other outdoor games with the children's friends," she said. "You will notice that most of the yard is either fenced or surrounded with shrubbery for privacy."

North shaded his eyes from the sun and walked in a full circle around the yard. "With those dozens of fruit trees, how do you intend to keep the children from climbing them and potentially falling and injuring themselves?"

"To be frank, sir, I have never thought of fruit trees posing a danger to anyone."

Both of the women nodded in agreement.

Sara considered some of the questions nonsensical and wondered whether they were routine or tailor-made to suit her and her environment—or even personal. Each time she responded, North would scribble in his notepad. He even asked to see the generator house. She marched across the yard and pushed the door open, barely concealing her shock at the sight that greeted her. Although she had mentioned to Ben that the generator house could be included in the inspection, he had forgotten to ask the house assistant to clean it up. She saw oil spilled on the floor and the gallon container of diesel oil left just inside the entrance instead of on the shelf. A heap of sand decorated one corner of the shed, and a pair of boots and rubber gloves had been literally tossed inside. The three shelves were vacant.

"I apologize for the mess," she said with a nervous laugh. "It's usually quite orderly. I know very little about how the generator works, but it provides us with the power we need when NPA decides to take a break. Please be assured that this door will always be locked. Since we don't currently have children, that task has not been a necessity. Just as parents of new babies have to learn new routines, so will we."

She closed the door behind them and led them toward the house. "Why don't we go indoors now? There is a lot to see." She conducted a thorough tour, showing them the downstairs rooms first, including the kitchen area and the bathrooms. They asked a plethora of questions involving safety, and she answered them to the best of her ability. Clearly, their home was above and beyond the average home in the area. At times, she saw that the women were whispering about her decor and the various antiques visible in certain rooms. Sara was highly suspicious about the inspection and considered their visit wasted effort.

"Thank you very much, Mrs. Moses. I believe we have seen all we need to see," North said, shaking her hand.

"Thank you for coming," she said. "I hope you've seen that Ben and I are well equipped to raise two children in our home."

Immediately upon their leaving, she dragged herself into the living room and flung herself onto the sofa, her nerves twisting into knots. Unable to sustain one complete thought, she finally gave up and checked her watch. It would do no good to hang around the house and fret; she'd make better use of her time at the office.

She jumped when the phone rang, rushing to pick it up with a sense of trepidation; it was Ben.

"I called your office twice. Some stranger said you'd gone home. Then I remembered the inspection was this afternoon. How did it go?"

Sara's mind was like a ship bouncing through an ocean of waves. "As well as could be expected, I suppose," she said. "There were three of them. Mr. North asked endless questions about safety. I couldn't read his mind, but he never smiled. Not once. No compliments. No nods of approval. I'm at my wit's end, Ben. What if—?"

"Stop it, Sara! Enough of that negativity. We have a fine home, perfect for any number of children. We passed with flying colors. I am confident of that. Put any other concerns out of your mind and find something to do."

"I was just thinking I should return to the office. Ruth has the day off, and the phone has been ringing off the hook. How she can handle all those pesky calls is beyond me.

"Can we go shopping this afternoon, Ben? I'm eager to get the children's bedrooms set up. I'll pick you up at your office since the furniture store is closer to you."

"Sounds like a good idea. I'll wait for your call."

After spending the rest of the afternoon at the office, Sara left for Ben's office early in order to avoid the rush-hour traffic. Freetown depended heavily upon the presence of traffic police at strategic corners to control the flow of both pedestrians and vehicles. While waiting for the signal to proceed during several stops, she couldn't keep from looking at the schoolchildren as they walked home from school on the shoulders of the road. She thought of Esther and Joseph. They would attend the school near their home.

As she drove, she became aware of the overcast sky casting a gray gloom over the town and her mood. The gray patches of clouds appeared to join in increasing speed and seemed to be moving faster than her car. "I hope it doesn't rain," she mumbled to herself. "Knowing Ben, he'll want to postpone the shopping trip." She continued to drive with one eye on the sky. By the time she reached the roundabout in front of Ben's office, the clouds had miraculously dissipated and given way to clearer skies. "A good sign!" she declared.

Ben was already outside waiting for her. He motioned to her not to park, since she would be driving. She pulled up in front of him, and he jumped into the passenger seat. "Where are we going?" he asked after giving her a kiss.

"The furniture store is on Eastern Street." She maneuvered out into the traffic again.

"How was your day? Were you able to focus on anything other than Mr. North this afternoon?"

"The entire day was busy." Nonstop, she informed Ben about what happened in the office without Ruth and the callers that were relentless.

Sara stopped at a junction for oncoming traffic. "How was your day?"

"Uneventful. I'm glad I could leave early today, even though you know how much I dislike shopping trips."

Luckily, the traffic had eased off. As they drove along, Sara shared more about the home inspection. She became so carried away with their conversation, she found herself going on past the shop and had to turn around. Laughing at her discombobulation, she retraced the twenty yards they had already traveled and finally drove into the parking lot at the back of the furniture store.

"Here we go," she said. The popular fabric establishment didn't limit its offerings to only clothing and upholstery fabrics; it also offered bedding, draperies, and hard furnishings for every room. Sara had purchased all their furniture from the store.

As soon as they entered the store, the Lebanese proprietor and his wife rushed to greet them. "*Howa yoou,* Pa and Madam Moses? A long, long time. Happy to see you. What can we do for you?"

"Hello, Mr. and Mrs. Bram. Nice to see you too." Sara greeted them warmly as they exchanged handshakes.

"You've added an extension to the store. I didn't remember it being this big," Ben said. "It looks great."

"But, Madam Moses, *yoou cam here* before Christmas. *Yoou*'ve seen this store. Pa Moses don't come often. Looking for something special? Want like the last time?"

Before Sara took up residence in her marital home, she had shopped extensively for the entire house. Now Sara took stock of the fabrics lower down on the shelves and those on the counter. Mrs. Bram asked her shop assistant to bring in some more samples.

"Oh, no, no, Mrs. Bram. We don't want as much. We only need a few items for our children's bedrooms."

"Children, *yoou* say? My, my, we *don't* know about them. Look, these, nice. Special for children. These are *butifel* for the windows, for the chairs, and for the beds."

Sara and Ben were spoiled with choices as Mr. and Mrs. Bram were determined to make a sale. After she had finished reviewing the many fabric options, Mr. Bram escorted her and Ben to the annex of the store, where the hard furnishings were displayed. They selected beds, dressers, desks, and chairs. Ben then made a check out to the couple and requested that Mr. Bram arrange delivery for the next day.

\* \* \*

Tuesday evening, they had just entered the dining room for a late dinner when the doorbell rang.

"Someone's at the door, Ben," Sara said, feeling her heart leap into her throat. "Do you suppose it's a neighbor? Maybe it's Martha. I haven't heard from her in days."

Ben went to the door. A young man in his early twenties, dressed in military khaki pants and a white shirt and holding a helmet under his arm, introduced himself as the dispatcher from the center. His motor scooter was parked at the entrance of the house.

"Good evening," he said politely. "I have a letter for Mr. and Mrs. Benjamin Moses."

"I'm Benjamin Moses."

"Sign here, sir." The young man handed Ben his pen and waited while he scribbled his name in the designated space.

By this time, Sara was right behind him, tiptoeing to peer over his shoulders. "Is that the letter from the children's center?" she asked, barely able to suppress her excitement.

"Sure looks like it."

The large brown envelope contained not only a letter addressed to them, but several other enclosures. Ben handed it to Sara. "You do the honors," he said.

She pulled out the letter and read it aloud. The opening paragraph expressed delight over the approval of their application for adoption of two siblings, Esther, eight, and Joseph, six. Their photographs were attached. The other enclosures included the affidavit to determine their ages, their medical records, school records, school transfer certificates, and a copy of the letter, which would be signed at the center on the day they collected the children. There was also a notice that a home-care worker would visit the children once a quarter for two years, to ensure that the children were doing well in their new environment.

As Sara read the letter, she finally reached the paragraph she was the most eager to read. "The children will be free to join your family on Saturday, April 30, 1983. All other legal documents will be signed in the presence of our retainer." The final paragraph congratulated them. She flung her arms around Ben and sobbed aloud against his chest. "It's been such a . . . a long, l-long road," she stuttered. "I am so . . . so happy, Ben."

Ben cradled her in his arms. "I am too, my dear. I am too."

Sara kissed the photographs, rubbed them on her chest, and danced around the room. "Oh, my precious children, I love you, love you, love you."

It was another new beginning, the birth of a family. Sara had never been so happy.

# Chapter 19

Still reeling from the exciting news, Sara and Ben arranged the new furniture they had purchased for the children's rooms. Once everything was in place to her satisfaction, they made up the beds with the new sheets and hung curtains. Ben installed bookshelves in Joseph's room, and Sara put together a doll section in Esther's bedroom. Soon the little girl's pink cotton-candy bedroom was outfitted with a wall clock, combs and brushes, and a manicure set on the dresser, and a small Bible on the bedside table.

Joseph's bedroom was painted sea blue and featured pictures of a football team. Then Ben propped a new football in one corner of the bedroom.

Sara placed a Bible on the bedside table and smiled. "And while he learns to play football, he'll also learn how to be a role model for his fellow players. I want him to be someone who treats others as he'd like them to treat him."

Sara called Kelitia to share the good news, and they laughed and talked on the phone for a good half hour. "I am beyond happy," she said. "I feel as though my heart will burst at any moment. Nothing . . . absolutely nothing can bring me down from cloud nine. Everything is finally moving in the right direction. Ben and I are to become parents, Ben is happy about my involvement in the reforestation efforts, and I'm even more positive about the outcome of the issue with Thomas."

The next couple days passed quickly. Sara informed everyone at her place of work of how her life would change. "I intend to stay at home for at least a week," she said. "I will leave everything in your very capable hands. All of you know the routine as well as I do. You may call me concerning any urgent matters, of course, but I want to focus on the children. They're bound to feel uncomfortable at first. It's important for them to learn to trust us and know that they will always be our children, even when they misbehave or don't live up to what they think our expectations for them are. And I have to enroll them in school, purchase their books and other supplies. All of you know that routine too." She laughed good-naturedly, and they joined with her in celebrating the joyous occasion.

When Friday morning arrived, Sara was counting the hours until she could hear her children's footsteps in the house. She climbed the stairs several times to check and recheck their rooms. Finally, convinced that everything was in place, she waited for Ben to return from his office. He had promised to be home by noon.

In the evening Sara started to remove food items from the freezer. According to Ruth, whose advice she had sought, okra and rice were enjoyed by children; she remembered that she had also enjoyed them when she was young. She would use those ingredients to cook something special that would bring smiles to the children's faces. Soon, she had packages of meat, chicken, fish, okra, bitter leaves, and *foo-foo* on the preparation table. Just as she was about to start the precooking routine, the doorbell rang.

*Smoke in the Kitchen*

"Who's there?" she wondered. She wiped her hands on her apron and hurried through the living room. As soon as she had pulled open the door, she recognized the dispatcher from the children's center. "Good evening, young man," she said as she smiled excitedly.

"A letter for Mr. and Mrs. Benjamin Moses," he said formally. As before, he removed a pen from his pocket and handed it to her.

Sara signed the receipt, accepted the envelope, and shut the door after him. "Another letter from the center?" she mumbled aloud. Had there been a time change? If so, why hadn't they simply called her? Panic surged through her like a tidal wave. She slit the envelope, removed the letter, and read it. "Oh, no! *No, no, no.* This can't be. Oh, no, it can't be! Ben! *Ben! Come quickly!"*

Ben hurried toward her, fear darkening his eyes. "What happened? Why are you standing there with your mouth hanging open? Is it Kelitia? Martha?" He reached her just as she was about to crumble to the floor. "Sara, speak to me."

Numb with shock, Sara could not find her voice. She clung to his shirt with one hand and waved the envelope in the other.

"What is it? A new letter? Did it just come?"

Sara nodded. Her lips quivered, and two giant tears clouded her eyes. She pointed at the door.

Ben looked, but saw no one. "Come into the living room and sit, before you collapse. Let me get to the bottom of this." With an arm wrapped around her waist, he moved her toward the sofa. Once she was seated, he took possession of the envelope still clutched in her hand and pulled a chair closer to hers. "It's from the Freetown Children's Center. Why would they send a letter to us so late on a Friday afternoon?" Ben read the letter and then read it again. This time he read it aloud.

"'Due to a grave administrative problem, we ask that you disregard the former letter regarding the adoption of Esther and Joseph. The approval has been rescinded. We shall contact you in the near future if the situation changes.'" Ben peered glassy-eyed at Sara. "This can't be right! A one-paragraph notification with no explanation?" He leaped from his chair and paced the room. "Are they out of their minds? They can't do this to us. *To the children.* This makes no sense. No sense at all. And they waited until the very end of the workweek to inform us, with no opportunity to answer back." He was angry and shaking with rage.

Sara cried openly, burying her face in her apron. "My children . . . my d-darling children. Do you think they k-knew? Do you . . . ?" She couldn't speak anymore. She was choking on her sobs.

Ben rushed to her side. "Please don't cry, Sara. We must talk about this. We must decide what action to take." He pulled a clean handkerchief from his back pocket and handed it to her.

Sara blew her nose and wiped her eyes, staring bleakly at her husband's dejected face. That's when she knew he had already come to love the children too. Her mind flashed to the conversation she'd had with the matron. "Do . . . do you think this was because of that one board member who didn't want us to have t-two children?" she asked.

"I can't imagine that one person could wield so much power over the other members, but I suppose it's possible. I intend to use my own power through the government and investigate the situation. Esther and Joseph are our children, and they *will* become members of the Moses family! Come Monday morning, I'll get in touch with the chairman." Ben spoke emphatically as he folded the letter and placed it on the table. "Sara, I've always admired you for your strength and courage. Now I want you to show some of it. Don't allow this setback to defeat your optimistic spirit. You need it now more than ever before."

An hour later, Ben phoned Kelitia. He assured her Sara was fine. She apologized for not being able to come over. She was leaving town for a few days—a hotel commitment. "I understand. We'll talk again when you return. Hopefully, we'll have better news."

Sara moved listlessly from the living room back to the kitchen to replace the items she'd removed from the freezer. Back in the living room, she leaned her head against the back of the sofa and shut her eyes. A surge of anger made her sit up and take a swift swipe at her still-damp eyes. The matron had some explaining to do! What was she thinking? In the day of telephones, why had she and the board resorted to sending an impersonal three-sentence note? It was cruel, to say the least. With her mind in continual torment, she thought of the time she'd spent preparing for the children. It had been time given willingly and with heartfelt love. She had informed so many people that the children were expected on Saturday. Tomorrow! What could she say to them?

Ben moved about the room like a caged lion, suffering as much as she was. He had to provide enough strength for both of them. Sara rose from the sofa and sorted through their record collection to find several soothing pieces that would promote peace of mind. It would do neither of them any good to nurse their anger. Anger rarely solved problems.

With the music playing, she went to the kitchen and boiled a kettle of water to make hot chocolate. Saying little to each other while they listened to the music and sipped their chocolate, she prayed for understanding. Why would God put them through such an ordeal when their hearts had been opened to accepting the children into their home? There must be a reason. Was it God's will that the process be delayed?

Hours later, they both lay next to each other in bed, still not voicing the depth of their pain. Both had purposely avoided even looking at the two bedrooms they had prepared with such love all week. Sara lay stiffly under the covers and wondered what the next day could possibly bring other than the misery she fully expected. The music had done little to soothe her deeply troubled soul. She finally shut her eyes and allowed the questions to parade through her consciousness. She had so many questions. So very many questions . . . and no answers. Not a single one.

On Saturday morning, Sara woke up early. It didn't surprise her that Ben was already awake. "Did you get any sleep at all?" she asked.

"Not much," he said, rolling off his side of the bed and heading for the bathroom. "I'm going to take a long shower."

Sara didn't offer a protest. She shuffled over to her desk and lifted her to-do list. She had completed every task.

"Sara," Ben shouted from the bathroom, "I want us to get out of here today."

"Leave the house? Why?"

"It won't do either of us a bit of good to hang around and mope."

"I don't know, Ben. Do you think we should?"

"I know we should." Ben reappeared in the bedroom. "Dress in something casual—a pants outfit. Have confidence in me. I know what I'm doing."

"Where are you taking me?"

"You'll know when we get there. Trust me. You won't be sorry," Ben told her. "No matter what, my darling girl, we have each other. Neither Esther nor Joseph would want their future parents to become sourpusses. We're going to keep our hopes high and go on with our lives. 'Today is the first day of the rest of my life.' Isn't that one of those adages you're always quoting to me? I want you to learn how to keep from brooding over things you can't control."

"Well, I don't know. I'd hate to be—" Sara's brow arched. She struggled to keep from smiling too broadly. Ben had a way about him. He could be mighty persuasive. "All right," she said, finally giving in.

Thirty minutes later, they were in Ben's car heading toward the beach. In the early morning hours, the air was crisp. As they drove along the coastline with the car windows open, she took in deep breaths, enjoying the freshness and the smell of the sea. She was comforted by it, and a load was lifted from her heavy heart.

Ben parked the car near where fishermen were pulling their nets ashore. They got out and tottered across the sand to watch them. About twenty fishermen, each grasping hold of the heavy net and pulling with all the energy he could muster, finally succeeded in dragging the net ashore. Hundreds of fish flopped in the net and on the sand, looking like gilded silver nuggets, luminescent in the early sunshine. The fishermen joked and laughed as they worked, pleased with their catch. Some sang familiar tunes that Sara recognized from her youth. While they watched, scores of fishmongers arrived with baskets to hold their purchases after bargaining with the fishermen.

"It's been a long time since I've been down here this time of the day," Ben said. "I wanted you to experience something different today. Let's go have breakfast. What do you say? Want to?"

They removed their shoes and walked along the beach, passing several groups of joggers and other early-morning walkers. They met one couple they knew from church and stopped to talk, not mentioning why they were on the beach so early on a Saturday morning.

On their way again, Sara peered up at her husband. "This is amazing, Ben. It's more relaxing than I imagined it would be. We've never done anything like this before. I like it. We must plan to do this more often." She didn't add, with our children.

"We will. And we'll try many other new things too. I want you to be happy, dear. I don't want to see a repeat of what I saw happening to you last night. That frightened me. You say God has a plan for each of us. You must learn to believe what you say. Sometimes things happen to teach us patience. Everything in its own good time."

"Thank you for that reminder, Ben."

"Are you hungry?"

"Yes, I'm ravenous." She looked at her watch. "It's almost nine o'clock."

"I love you with all my heart, darling. Thank God the center wasn't involved in our courtship, or else I would likely be without a wife today. With their track record, I would still be negotiating for your hand in marriage!"

Sara laughed and punched him playfully in the side. "You're too witty, Ben Moses."

"That's my lady. I like you best when you're smiling and upbeat. Nothing can deter you when your mind is set on something."

"You're absolutely right. The center has experienced what they call a 'grave administrative problem,' and I will find out what it is and solve it."

He held her hand, and they strolled toward one of the beach hotel breakfast bars. They ordered from the menu, and while they waited for their order to arrive, she said, "I feel sorry for the matron. I can't imagine that she's not embarrassed over this glitch. She was honest in letting me know that she wanted us to have Esther and Joseph." She stared across the waves lapping the shoreline and abruptly changed the subject. "After we eat, let's pull a couple of those deck chairs closer to the water and just relax. I'm not ready to go home yet."

"That's a good idea. We can watch the waves roll ashore until we fall asleep."

Surprised by her appetite, Sara found herself cleaning her plate of all the breakfast items. She had three steaming cups of coffee and was finally ready to join Ben in the deck chairs. They watched seagulls swoop into the water for fish and carry them off for a feast. They watched other joggers and beach lovers as they enjoyed a morning swim. Silent most of the time, Sara finally plied Ben with a few questions about what the week would hold for them.

When she received no response, she turned and noticed he was fast asleep. Shortly thereafter, she finally gave in to the urge and fell asleep herself. Soon she was dreaming of running through the sand while holding onto the hands of her children, one on each side of her. They were laughing and lifting their faces to the sun.

## Chapter 20

Sunday morning, the chatter of birdsong awakened Sara as though it were the dawning of a day worth celebrating. Her first thought was of how she had expected to waken her children and prepare their first breakfast in their new home before attending church services. She turned her head to see if Ben were still sleeping and found his side of the bed empty. Rising despite her heavy lethargy, she mechanically performed the morning ritual and found her way down the stairs.

"Good morning," Ben said from his position by the stove. "I have coffee prepared." He filled her usual ceramic mug and placed it on the table, pulling out her chair.

She saw his grim demeanor as she slid onto it and knew his thoughts were in the same place as hers. She could only focus on her own sorrow, though. She didn't have the energy to be sensitive to his feelings, and she didn't want to discuss the issue. "What time were you up this morning?" she asked.

"A couple hours ago." He brought his cup to the table and sat across from her.

"I feel it in my bones . . . it's going to be a nice day," said Sara.

"Is it?" He peered more closely at her.

*Smoke in the Kitchen*

He glanced at her pantsuit. "I'm assuming you've decided to skip church this morning. I don't know about you, but I'm not ready to hash over our situation a dozen or more times with those who will be expecting us to show up with . . ." He coughed into his hand and drank the rest of his coffee. "I didn't mention this before, because I expected us to be otherwise occupied today, but the Swiss Consulate General is having a gathering at the Number Two Beach this afternoon—sort of a casual picnic and kite-flying competition. A few other diplomats will be there. I've been thinking we should attend."

"I don't know. I'm not really up to it." She peered about the kitchen as though to find something that needed her attention, but there was nothing. Everything was ready for company.

"Of course you are. It will do you good to meet some new people. You may be able to drum up some support for your Reforestation Association. Have you heard from Martha yet? Does she have a telephone? We could invite her to go with us. Kelitia isn't available for a few days."

Sara sipped her hot coffee and lifted her eyes to the window. The relentless sun was already beating down on every inch of the house and yard. It would be hot and muggy. "I have no way of reaching Martha yet."

"Then we'll go by ourselves. It's an opportunity for me to make myself known. We need all the contacts we can make these days. Sierra Leone depends upon the good graces of foreign monetary assistance and—"

"All right. I'll go with you. I know you enjoy kite flying. It will be fun to participate in something that gives you so much pleasure. It's the least I can do for you; you've been such a—"

"If you tell me I've been a good husband one more time, I'll go crazy, Sara! I love you. We're going through a trial right now. We support each other. That's what loving spouses do. We're not whiners. We're not people who wring our hands and give in to useless emotions."

Sara thought of the ten years she'd spent grieving over something that couldn't be changed. Ben was right. This was a time to concentrate on only positive thoughts and to live each moment with the strength God provided. To do anything else would show her lack of faith. Compared to what Job endured, she had little to complain about. Patience and understanding, that's what she needed to exhibit. That, and hope.

"Once again, my darling, you know exactly what to say to lift me from my doldrums. What time should we leave here?"

"By noon. I'm going to do my best to win the kite-flying competition! I'll need you for support."

She watched him leave the kitchen. Somehow she'd gather the strength to get through the day. She owed him that.

Shortly after noon, they parked near the beach and strolled across the sand toward the group that had gathered under huge white canopies, erected to offer relief from the sun. Tables were laden with several types of cold beverages and trays filled with fresh fruit. There were also chafing dishes holding both local fare and several typical Swiss delicacies, which were being offered by servers dressed in pristine white pants and shirts.

While Ben went off to sign up for the kite-flying competition, Sara filled a plate and wandered about the area, trying to look as though she were enjoying herself.

"Excuse me," a pleasant-looking man said, bumping into her. "I wasn't paying attention to where I was going. Those kites caught my interest. Reminded me of my youth back in my home state. We knew the long winters of snow had finally melted and spring had arrived when kites appeared in the stores."

She forced a laugh. "No need to apologize. We're all rather enthusiastic about the kite-flying contest. My husband is participating. I was hoping to catch a glimpse of him and wasn't watching where I was going either. I'm Sara Moses, by the way. My husband, Benjamin, is an economic adviser for the government."

The man reached into his shirt pocket and pulled out a business card to hand to her. "Mark Harris," he said. "I have just recently arrived for my term of duty as a foreign service officer representing the United States."

Sara read the card, and her eyes widened. "My goodness," she exclaimed. "I am so honored to make your acquaintance. It says you're the Ambassador Extraordinary and Plenipotentiary. I must confess to not knowing the meaning of that last word, but it sounds most impressive."

Harris laughed. "Few people do. It simply means that I am the highest-ranking diplomat representing my country in Sierra Leone. Big titles make us feel important."

"But you're the ambassador of the most powerful country in the world. Again, I will say that I am deeply honored to be speaking with you." Sara reached for her sunglasses, because the sun was glaring into her eyes and she wanted to be able to converse without squinting. "Is your family here with you?" she asked.

"Not yet. I'm expecting them in about three weeks."

Sara hoped he wouldn't ask about her family and was happy when he changed the subject.

"We have quite a few programs at the embassy that might interest you," Harris said. "One group is called Women in Development. There are quite a few others. Women and Children in Conflict is new. You would fit very well into an organization like that. We need new members to form an activist group."

"I'm afraid I can't obligate myself to another organization right now," Sara said. "I'm in the embryonic stage of developing an organization that will affect the lives of our citizens for decades to come. It concerns a subject dear to my husband's heart. I want to do this for him, as well as for our citizens." Sara really wanted to run out to the kite area to search for Ben, but was too polite to leave the diplomat alone. She sipped at her watered-down lemonade and gazed across the beach, looking for his familiar face.

"Is it a political group?"

"Far from it, Ambassador. The politics of this country is always in flux. I'm not sure where I stand from one moment to the next. I'm not ready to discuss the project yet." She smiled at him. "I'm sure you understand."

"Fully." He looked up at the colorful kites bobbing over the sea. "Quite a spectacle, isn't it? I admire your dedication to seeing that your country advances. I've never seen so much poverty as I have in the short time I've been here. To tell you the truth, it is heartbreaking."

"The older I get, the more concerned I've become about the many thousands who go without food or education," Sara said, warming to the subject. "I was one of the lucky ones. My family could afford to send me to college. Too many countries in our continent continue to be ravaged by civil wars. Our women and children suffer the consequences. Families are torn apart, and optimism completely disappears. Without hope, despair takes over; and pretty soon, our people simply exist, with no incentive to improve their living conditions."

Harris took her empty plate and tossed it into a trash container. "Unfortunately, starvation is an international issue and not easy to eradicate. We need more people like you to work alongside agencies to raise the awareness of social injustices. I've been reading about the history of Sierra Leone. It is a travesty that just when progress seems to be made, there is unrest and people become dissatisfied. This is the situation in most African countries." He watched the kites with her for a couple minutes without talking. "Do you work outside the home, Mrs. Moses? Are you a teacher perhaps? You mentioned your family."

"I own and operate the Family Auctioneer Mart." Sara smiled again. "It takes up a great deal of my time. It's at Kingtom, west of the city center. A number of people in the community have used it at one time or the other. Our auction sales cater to those from all walks of life. Since I took over, our capital expenditure has increased significantly. I just initiated a barter system that allows customers to exchange something they have for another item of the same value, while paying us only a token commission for handling the swap. Many of our citizens have little or no money. Often, they come to offer their labor for an item they need. If the owner of the goods is agreeable, he or she accepts assistance with yard work, carpentry, roofing in lieu of money . . . whatever skill the individual has."

The ambassador looked at her more intently. "You thought of that on your own? I'm even more impressed, Mrs. Moses. Your staff must think highly of you."

"We share a mutual respect. I hold regular staff meetings each week, and we formulate policies on our joint consensus of what would best serve our customers, while bringing in enough profit to pay our expenses and salaries."

*Smoke in the Kitchen*

"How did you get involved in auctioneering?"

Sara was pleased with his interest. "I inherited the business from my father, and he from his father. I was an only child and enjoyed working with him in the mart, so it made sense for me to carry on with it. I graduated from our local college with a degree in business administration. We hold big sales every six weeks—on Saturdays between nine and five. We hold mini-sales between the big ones. You must plan to attend sometime . . . when you're free. Perhaps your wife would enjoy it. We offer some wonderful items."

"I wouldn't miss the opportunity to experience such a fine local event. What sort of things do you auction?"

"Everything from real estate to furniture to used clothing and books. Because my line of business involves buying *and* selling, I am particularly careful about the authenticity of the goods we purchase." She stopped briefly to wait for the passing noise from an overhead helicopter to diminish. "I impress on my staff that all transactions must be supported with a completed verification form. This includes a section to indicate the reason for the sale. After completing the form, it has to be signed by the owner and countersigned by a witness. If a receipt cannot be produced, a lawyer countersigns and stamps it. Some people think they can easily dispose of stolen goods by selling them to auctioneers, but that doesn't happen in my mart. In fact, our verification policy has provided leads for those in law enforcement agencies to locate and break up gangs of thieves. Wherever you have poverty, you have those willing to exploit it."

"I've been told that auctions occur at the embassies too, especially when ambassadors and their staff members leave to make room for new appointees. Some of their used goods are put up for auction. If you're interested, I may be able to put in a good word for you."

They spoke about a few other subjects, and then Harris turned to shake her hand. "I'm sure you're eager to find out how your husband is doing, Mrs. Moses. Thank you for allowing me to chat with you."

"I enjoyed it, Ambassador. When I'm ready with my organization, I may call on you for your support. Would that be all right?"

"Of course. That's why I'm here. Feel free to call on me at any time. I am unlikely to forget you."

Sara shook his hand and immediately made a mental note to ask him to speak at the launching of her Reforestation Association. She was well aware of the sales at the embassies and the high commissions. She had purchased a few items from some of them in the past. When she took over the business, this was one area she had intended to explore in more detail. The furniture items were always in good condition. The procedure involved a sealed bid after the inspection process.

As she walked toward the area where the competition was being conducted, her thoughts returned to Esther and Joseph. They would have enjoyed this day at the beach and watching their new father fly his kite. Hopefully everything would be straightened out by Monday afternoon, once she had learned more details about the so-called grave administrative problem. A hint of depression slipped through her carefully constructed pretense of contentment, but she quickly replaced it with interest in the competition.

She stood next to a woman who explained that each participant was given the same quantity of string and the same type of kite, but in different colors. The person whose kite went the farthest and used the most string was declared the winner.

Sara found an empty deck chair and carried it to a section of the beach where she could watch all the activities, including the kite flying. In order to keep her mind from wandering, she snapped mental pictures of the wide stretch of white sand and contrasting aqua sea. She watched the unending gentle waves roll toward her, only to crash against the hidden sandbars and erupt into high-flying white froth. She took a long deep breath and lifted her face to enjoy the sea breeze.

"My goodness, Sara Moses, is that you?"

Sara startled at the familiar voice and sat up to sweep the shoreline while cupping her hand over the top of her sunglasses to cut the glare. "Martha! I have not stopped thinking of you! Where have you been? Why are you here?"

Martha strolled across the sand and plopped down beside Sara's chair. "I'm taking a couple hours to relax. I apologize for not getting in touch with you. I'm still without a phone. I've been busy since moving back here from London. I've been attending interviews for a job as a matron in the Eastern Province, Yengema to be precise. I just got word yesterday that I got the job, so I'm relocating there in the next two weeks, much to my brother's chagrin. He just finished remodeling my upstairs apartment. Between going for an interview and the job, I was out more than I was in. I wanted to see you before I left town, though. I didn't dream I'd meet you here. How's Ben?" She brushed sand off her arms.

"I am happy for you . . . So, you will be in the diamond area. How nice."

"As if I'll see any of the stones!" Martha smiled at Sara.

"Ben's fine. He's in the kite-flying competition." Sara pointed in that direction. "You look more relaxed and happy than you were the last time we were together."

"Well, there's happy, and then there's happy." She shrugged. "I'm as happy as can be expected, I guess. Listen, Sara, there's something I need to tell you."

"Same here. You go first."

"My brother shared some information you may find interesting." Martha peered over her shoulder to ensure no one was listening. "He said your cousin's lawyer has been searching the records in the registrar's office to find the original documents for the mart—the ones that your great-great-grandfather registered.

My brother's friend, who works with the registrar, told him that he's been going to that office regularly for the past few months."

Sara nodded. "My lawyer, Othneil Baker, told me about that just a few days ago. The man doesn't seem to know exactly what he's looking for. I have the original documents in my possession, and I've given copies to Othneil. Neither of us knows what to make of it. It seems like an exercise in futility."

"You don't suppose they're still of the mind that only males can inherit property in Sierra Leone, do you? Far too many in this city believe women are unfit to operate a business."

"Well, times have changed. All I know is that the Family Auctioneer Mart is my property and I'll put up a good fight to keep it. Everybody knows that when Papa took over the business, it was at the point of bankruptcy. He worked all his life to restore it to its original state and solvency."

"Thomas must have a great deal of money to support such a long search. It takes time to go through records going back to the 1920s."

"It's money misspent," Sara said. "Nothing will come of it. I could certainly put the money it's costing me to keep Othneil on my payroll to better use."

"What was the news you had to tell me?" Martha stretched out her legs and leaned back on her elbows in the sand. "Is it about Ben?"

"No. It's about the children we had hoped to adopt." Sara felt herself stiffen. It was still difficult for her to talk about the subject.

Martha bolted upright. "What do you mean by 'hoped to'? Has something happened to stall the process?"

Sara nodded and swallowed the lump that had magically appeared in her throat. "We expected them to join our family two days ago, Martha. I had everything all ready. Then we received a special delivery letter late that Friday evening. They changed their mind. Some sort of administrative glitch, it seems."

"That can't be true!" Martha sat upright, pulling up her knees and turning to face Sara, placing her hand on her friend's hands where they lay in her lap.

"The letter said the center was withdrawing its letter of approval. That's all we know."

"Can they do that? It's inhuman!"

Sara sat with pinched lips and just nodded.

"What does Ben say about this? Is he as irate as I'd be? Is he going to demand an explanation?"

"Ben has been wonderful. He's determined to get to the bottom of this. He's more than supportive. He's my rock. Neither of us will rest until the children come home with us."

"That guy loves you so much, considering how much you bully him."

Both of them laughed, but there was no jollity in the sound.

"It isn't about money or the condition of our home," Sara said. "I'm convinced their so-called 'grave administrative problem' didn't occur overnight either. Something doesn't make sense. Someone is behind this. I know it isn't fair or even logical, but I can't help thinking Thomas has something to do with the abrupt change in decision. Do you know I haven't even seen the man for years, let alone spoken with him? My lawyer can't find him anywhere, and his lawyer won't share any information about how we can contact him."

Martha pursed her lips. "Hmm," she said. "That's more than strange."

The two of them sat silently for several minutes, watching the kites and the lapping waves of the sea against the shoreline and thinking about their childless lives. Finally, Martha jumped to her feet. "I've got to leave now. My dear Sara, I wish you bushels of luck with both the adoption and mart matters. You've got more on your plate than you deserve. If there is anything I can do to help, please don't hesitate to let me know. I'll call tomorrow with phone details. I'll get in touch with you. And don't worry. With your determination, I'm certain everything will work out just fine."

Sara got out of the deck chair to hug her. "Thank you, Martha. You are such a dear friend and the exact medicine I needed today."

Once Martha was on her way, Sara strolled with the burgeoning crowd heading toward the kite-flying area. The contest was about to end, and the winner would be announced. She waved when she caught sight of Ben. "Over here!" she shouted.

"It's been quite an exciting activity," he said, smiling. "I think I'm a front-runner. Let's go closer to the judges' stand. There! Look at the judge on the far right. He's holding the string of my kite."

When Ben's name was announced, they both jumped about like children. "Well," Sara said, "never in my wildest imagination did I believe I would be married to the finest kite flier in the land. I don't believe congratulations are enough. I'll serve you a glass of wine when we get home."

"The first prize is a ticket for a weekend-for-two at a seaside resort," Ben said. "We can take that second honeymoon we've been wanting for so long—to celebrate our first anniversary."

As they left the picnic area, he looked at all the cars already leaving. "Traffic's going to be chaotic," he said. "Let's try to get out of here as soon as possible. Keep your head down. Maybe if we don't meet anyone's eyes, we won't have to stop to talk!"

Once they were in the car, he glanced at her. "Did you have a good time? I'm sorry about having to leave you alone while I was flying that kite."

"Actually, I'm glad you were off on your own. I met a very interesting man." She told him about the long and interesting conversation she'd had with the American ambassador. "Can you believe my luck? Of all the people there today, I spent at least an hour talking with the most important one. I believe he likes me. When the time is right, I'm going to ask him to speak at the launch party for the Reforestation Association."

Ben grinned at her. "You're going places, Sara Moses. I met Ambassador Harris's predecessor at an economic conference last year. He was on his way out."

Even though they had left earlier than most, traffic remained a problem. They were stalled several times on their way back, but eventually got home. As they pulled into the garage, Sara felt her spirits fall. She wasn't interested in becoming well-known in political circles of power. All she wanted was to become a much-loved and respected mother, one whose children would accomplish great things because she encouraged them to reach for the stars. Even in Sierra Leone, that was possible. She believed that with all her heart.

## Chapter 21

Although she had not informed her office of the change in plans regarding the adoption because she intended to take the day off anyway, Sara was still wide-awake at six o'clock on Monday morning and decided to get up. Throughout the night, she had structured a fact sheet in her mind with the chain of events that had taken place from the moment of her first contact with the Freetown Children's Center. She tiptoed around the bedroom to let Ben sleep another hour and finally picked up the file on her dresser and headed downstairs.

Soon after their marriage, she had reorganized the house to be more functional and turned what had been intended to be Ben Jr.'s playroom into a study. It was equipped with a desk, a library table, a typewriter, and a filing cabinet. The file she had been keeping on the adoption process included notes she had made to herself, copies of the application forms, the letter requesting an interview with the board members, notes after speaking with the matron and the board, and the acceptance letter and the one that followed, rescinding the adoption. As she flipped through the documents, she saw that she had also kept records of the phone message informing her about the home inspection, details about the inspection, and even a note written after having her first conversation with Jeremiah, who had informed her about Esther and Joseph and how they had come to be wards of the center's founder.

While reading the material, she spoke aloud, rehearsing what she intended to say to the matron later in the day. "From the very first day, you led me to believe that you had already decided Esther and Joseph were to become members of our family. Your nephew Jeremiah had informed me even before that first meeting that you had—"

"No, no, Sara, you can't mention that." Ben's voice interrupted her speech as he entered the room.

She jumped up as she glanced at him over her shoulder. "Did I wake you up? I tried to be extra quiet. Why can't I mention how we were encouraged from the very beginning?"

"Because both Jeremiah and Mrs. Brown spoke in confidence."

"I just want to remind the matron of the enthusiasm she exhibited over our eagerness to adopt the children. Most applicants want babies. With so many children without homes in our country, it is baffling to me why they would find us, of all people, not suitable to adopt Esther and Joseph."

"We need to keep the matron on our side. You don't want to antagonize her or get her in trouble with the board members, in case she was speaking out of turn. That boy . . . Jeremiah, perhaps you can speak with him again this morning. You know, to sound him out, just in case he's learned something about the halt in the process that can make us understand what happened."

"Jeremiah isn't available, Ben. He's in college at Njala, a long way out. He won't know anything about this. And you know how unreliable the phone system is. I doubt I could reach him even if I tried."

"So, we must strike him off our list. Let me read through the material you've collected. You have a better idea of what has transpired, but I'm still in the dark. I know this setback seems insurmountable, but each time we confront a problem headlong, it makes us stronger, my dear. We learn important things in the process. I've gone through so many trials in my lifetime, I've come to expect them. Not all of them were resolved to my satisfaction, but enough of them contributed to my future in ways that have kept intact my trust in fairness and justice. We set out to go by the book in this adoption. We wanted the children to be legally ours. If it doesn't work out, we'll find another way to become parents. I want you to remember that. We'll take one day at a time and work toward keeping everything in balance. We both have jobs and people who depend on us. We can't let them down."

Sara bit her lip. She knew her husband was thinking of his birth son, who was so many miles away from him. "You're right," she said. "I have endured many challenges too, and now I have a fine husband to share my life with me. I thank God every day for you. You never stop reminding me of God's grace. We were blessed with the intelligence and means to know what to do. That, in itself, is something to keep me going."

All the while they talked, she remembered Ben's family history. He had built the very home she was expecting to share with their adopted children for his first wife and son. His plans had been to provide for his flesh-and-blood son in a way his own father had not been able to provide for him. Not only a physical home, but the warmth and companionship that enabled a son to grow and thrive. His own father died when he was nine. He'd been determined to be the father he'd never had, and now he was deprived of that experience.

"I wish I could stay with you all day, but I have a meeting with a delegation from India and I have to attend," he said. "Call me as soon as you've spoken with the matron. If she agrees to a meeting today, I'll try to make it. Otherwise, do you think you can handle it on your own?"

"Of course! You go to your meeting and don't worry about me. I'll be fine."

At nine thirty, Sara called her office to ask Ruth if the matron had left her a message. She didn't mention the children or the problem. When Ruth said there were no messages, she thought it strange that Mrs. Brown hadn't called her first thing upon reaching her office. For the next three hours, she attempted to reach her at least ten times. No one answered the phone. Not even the usual receptionist.

With her hand still on the phone, it rang. "How are things going?" Ben asked. "I have a little free time in my schedule. When will you be visiting the center today? Did you get an appointment?"

"I haven't been able to reach anyone. No one answers the telephone. I dialed several times over the past three hours. I'm worried. Why would they avoid answering the phone? I think I need to get there."

"I'm free right now. I can meet you there."

"That isn't necessary, Ben. I'll go alone and call you later."

"Is there something else I can do to help out? I could make a few waves and use my influence, but I'm reluctant to do that until we know more about why we received that last letter."

"I think you should wait, Ben. Why don't you keep trying to reach the matron or even the chairman of the board? I'll drive out there. Hopefully, one of us will be successful." She gave him the phone number and then called Ruth for a second time. Again, no messages.

With a heavy heart, Sara went over what she intended to say once she was in the presence of the matron. She had so many questions, and she would demand answers. Logical answers. Ones that proved the center had made its decision based upon what was best for the welfare of the children. First, she wanted to know why the matron hadn't immediately gotten in touch with her when she learned about the rescinding of the adoption. She was only a phone call away. She had several phone numbers at her disposal: Ben's office, her office, and their home phone.

With each roadblock, her agitation grew. Why couldn't one thing go right? The trip to the center was taking far too long. Finally, her car pulled into the driveway of the compound. She saw no other cars in the parking spaces. That was strange. When she entered the building, an eerie feeling passed over her. No one was manning the reception desk. The lights were off. As she walked along the corridor to the matron's office, she could hear the heels of her shoes clicking on the wood floor. She knocked on the matron's door and heard the familiar sound of her secretary's voice.

"Hello," Sara said, approaching her with an outstretched hand. She had always shaken hands with her and didn't want to alter her greeting. "I'm so happy to find you here, Emily. I've called several times today, and no one has answered the phones. Are they down today?" She smiled and hoped her voice reflected a warmth she didn't feel.

"As far as I know, the phones are fine, Mrs. Moses. I've been out all morning. I just got here a few minutes ago. How can I help you?"

"Is the matron in? Or Chairman Emmitt? I'll speak to whichever one can see me first."

"Dr. Emmitt is never in on Mondays."

"Will he be here tomorrow then, and what time?"

"Unfortunately, Dr. Emmitt had emergency surgery last Thursday. He's still in the hospital and will probably not be able to resume his duties here for a couple months."

"Oh, my goodness! Surgery? What happened! I hope it wasn't anything too serious. If you speak with him, please let him know Mr. and Mrs. Moses wish him a speedy recovery."

"Yes, Mrs. Moses."

"I'll speak with the matron then."

"I'm afraid that will be impossible, Mrs. Moses. The matron is out of the country." The secretary didn't make eye contact with Sara as she delivered the unexpected words.

Dazed by the revelation, Sara gasped aloud and felt the blood rush from her face. "Out of the country?" she exclaimed, barely keeping control of her shock. "For how long?"

"She is on vacation."

A feeling of dread passed through Sara, and she hated where her thoughts were taking her.

The secretary sat mute and offered no explanations.

"I received a letter from the center on Friday evening withdrawing its letter of approval for the adoption of Esther and Joseph into our family. Do you know anything about it?"

*Smoke in the Kitchen*

"No, I'm sorry I don't."

"You didn't type the letter?"

The secretary shook her head.

"Someone did. I want answers today, Emily. Who is here to speak with me about this matter?"

"Unfortunately, I'm the only one here."

Feeling decidedly woozy from the pounding in her head, Sara heaved an audible sigh and clenched her jaw. "This, of course, is entirely unacceptable. This institution receives support as well as sizable donations from individuals. We have already paid over half of the stated fee for the legal adoption of Esther and Joseph and consider them our children. I would like to see them."

"I'm sorry, Mrs. Moses, but it is against the policy for the children to have any contact with a member of the public without prior approval. I'm not authorized to give that approval."

Sara stared at the woman. Her explanation seemed scripted. She raised a brow and pursed her lips. What should she do? For a moment, she went completely blank. It would never do to be too aggressive with someone who was not in a position to make decisions. "Surely you don't regard me as only a member of the public, do you? You have spoken with me several times. You have seen how delighted Mrs. Brown was to have me apply for the adoption of these children. They should be in my house right now.

I am not a mere member of the public. I am, for all intents and purposes, the children's new mother."

"I-I'm so sorry. I've been told that until all the legal documents have been signed, they are not your children."

On the verge of tears, Sara worked at controlling her frustration. Something wicked was going on in the Freetown Children's Center. She would state that categorically to anyone who had an ear to listen. She felt like stamping her feet and shouting at the top of her lungs. She was too much a lady for such behavior, however, and if Ben ever got wind of it, he would certainly lecture her on the proper decorum for someone of her status. "Exactly what do you know, Emily? What have you been told? Has no one been appointed to take Mrs. Brown's place until she returns?"

Emily shrugged. "All I know, Mrs. Moses, this is a temporary situation. Things have happened very fast. Mrs. Brown is on vacation, and no one knew the chairman would fall ill."

"How long will this last?"

"I honestly don't know. Mrs. Brown has been due to go on vacation since last month. I don't know how long she is away for. I really don't know."

Sara shifted her weight to her other foot and leaned over the counter, staring directly into Emily's eyes. "Who is causing the ruckus here? Something is dreadfully wrong. Someone pulled the rug out from under us, and we deserve an explanation." When she received nothing but a blank look, she took another approach. "Will somebody of authority be in tomorrow?"

"Yes, the person who is standing in for the chairman—a Mrs. Leona Murray."

"I would like to meet with her. Please set me up for an appointment. I'll come in anytime.

"Let me check her calendar."

"I'll wait while you check."

"I, uh, I don't have an appointment book for her yet. May I call you later, once I have had an opportunity to speak with Mrs. Murray? It may be tomorrow before I can call you."

Brooding all the way home, Sara blinked several times to water down her smarting eyes. *Something is not right*, she kept muttering to herself. The grave administrative problem appeared to be even worse than she had imagined. Was the chairman really in the hospital after emergency surgery, or was this a cover-up? She'd have Ben check. And why didn't the matron mention she was going out of the country? Maybe she thought she would do a good deed before she left.

*Leona Murray.* That name rang a bell, but she didn't know why.

Ben was just climbing out of his car when she cruised into the yard. "Any luck?" he called, striding toward her to open the car door. "What did you learn?"

"A great deal of nothing and lots of unanswered questions," she said.

Five minutes later, she had filled him in on everything she knew. "I wasn't allowed to see the children, and Emily, the matron's secretary, actually told me they weren't considered ours until *all* the papers had been signed. She said members of the public were not allowed to see the children without prior permission."

"Members of the public?"

"That's right. I am only a member of the public. A stranger. All sorts of questions have come to mind during the drive home, Ben. I think we need to initiate a full investigation into what is going on. Something's not right. Someone there is wielding a strong fist, and we are on the receiving end of the blow."

"I'll check which hospital the chairman is in and see if we can get some information on whether or not he is well enough to receive visitors."

While Ben went to the phone, Sara went to the kitchen. Suddenly she dashed to her study and pulled two papers out of the folder on the desk. "Ben," she called. "When you're ready, I've got something to show you."

Once he had seated himself at the table, she shoved two sheets of paper toward him. "Read these," she said. "What do you see?"

"The approval letter and the rejection letter."

"I know, but take a look at who signed them."

"Dr. Emmitt signed the first one, and an illegible signature, probably Leona Murray, appended on the second one 'for chairman.'" A frown furrowed his brow. "Who is this Murray woman?"

"According to Emily, Leona Murray is taking over for Chairman Emmitt in his absence. Which of them has the authority to make binding decisions, Ben? The board in its entirety approved of our becoming the parents of Esther and Joseph. Then, the day after Dr. Emmitt ends up in the hospital, everything changes? Doesn't that smell a little fishy to you? I'm sure the letter withdrawing the approval was written *after* he was absent from work." Sara took a second look at the letters.

"Well, well . . . we have a problem here. I can bet my last cent that someone was busy last Friday." Ben folded his arms over his chest and rocked back in his chair. "The chairman fell ill and phoned the matron and his deputy to contact all the parties concerned. Someone decided this was the perfect opportunity to cause trouble for the Moses family. I wonder whether the matron really is out of the country on vacation. Was it a coincidence? Of course, the secretary was advised to take messages, but not to give out any information."

"Your scenario makes some sense. I just don't know who the instigator of this entire trauma is or why anyone would want to keep two innocent children from finding a home. Someone is being more than a little callous."

"We'll wait and see what happens."

"Wait? How long? Can't we get someone to investigate this? Can't we get Othneil to look into the matter for us?"

"Sure. We'll call him in the morning. Nothing is likely to happen this week, Sara. Get your appointment with this Leona Murray and sound her out. See what she has to say. For all we know, everything is on the up-and-up. On the other hand, you know how things go in this country. Corruption is rampant. Red tape is involved in every situation. Sooner or later, we'll end up with two wonderful children. We'll just have to take a circuitous route."

"I know. Keep busy. Wasn't it Albert Einstein who said we should learn from yesterday, live for today, and hope for tomorrow and that the important thing is not to stop questioning?"

Ben laughed and poured himself another glass of wine. "You have all the answers, my dear, and then you let yourself fret over matters you can't control anyway."

"Not tonight. I'm going to plot my discussion with the mysterious Leona Murray."

## Chapter 22

Two weeks later, Sara still had no indication as to how soon the grave administrative problem would be resolved. She had received no appointment with Mrs. Leona Murray, despite several phone calls. Two of the influential board members were out of the country on business. Since the auctioneer mart was running well without her hands-on input, she had time on her hands for other things. She sought refuge in the public and university libraries in order to save herself from the embarrassment and distraction of endless explanations to well-meaning friends and acquaintances.

Fortunately, in this self-imposed seclusion, she did some more research on reforestation that she found both fulfilling and rewarding. At home, she was able to distract herself on the sofa with the reading of her notes and endless jotting down of notes regarding the formal organization required for a national association involving so many people.

On Thursday evening, she was half asleep and not at all ready to begin preparing dinner when Ben returned from work a little earlier than usual. "Did you see the article in the *Daily Mail* today?" he asked. He opened his briefcase, but couldn't find the newspaper. He went to check in his car and came back five minutes later without it. "I must have left it at the office," he said.

"What was the article about?" Sara rose from the sofa and piled her notepads on the table next to it. "You didn't see the newspaper? Where did you leave it?"

"Maybe it's on my desk. Never mind. I'll tell you about it. There was a long article rehearsing the complaints of the woodcutters and timber producers."

"Oh? What's so upsetting about that? It's old news, isn't it?"

"The woodcutters are blaming the timber people for depriving them of a livelihood, and with rather harsh words too. Trouble is brewing, Sara. I understand the newspaper sold out like hot cakes."

"Several months ago, Cano hinted to me that this would come about if the timber bosses didn't let up on their pressure and demands for increasingly higher bribes. So, it's to be a war between the timber giants and the flies." She perched on the edge of a chair. "Oddly, I was stuck indoors the whole day and didn't see a copy of the paper or hear anyone talking about it."

Ben removed his suit jacket and flung it over the back of the sofa. "The woodcutters claim they've been discriminated against for far too long, and they are determined to be heard this time. They say the forest rangers favor the timber producers with better forest areas and longer work hours to extract their wood requirements. On the other hand, they apply undue pressure on the woodcutters to stay away and charge exorbitant fees they can't afford in an effort to dissuade them from operating in certain areas. The charcoal producers joined the woodcutters in their complaints,

*Smoke in the Kitchen*

while the pole producers joined the timber people. A spokesman from the timber producers claims the allegations are false. As far as they are concerned, no discrimination exists."

"It exists all right." Sara crossed her arms over her chest. "You can't fault the woodcutters for playing the blame game. It's time for everyone to know that it's mostly the timber and mining cartels that are depleting *all* our natural resources. Don't forget, the mining companies are responsible for an enormous degradation of our forest areas and vegetative cover. My research has shown that indiscriminate artisanal mining has resulted in a great deal of deforestation. Their activities cause no end of other problems too—soil erosion and contamination of our water sources. That's one of the reasons why malaria and cholera are still so rampant in our villages. The standing water breeds mosquitoes and no end of other hazardous conditions."

Ben grinned and shook his head. "By the tone of your voice, this subject has taken on considerable importance to you."

"That's right, Ben. You wanted me to get involved, and I don't do anything halfway. I'm on the side of the villagers and the woodcutters in this issue. I'm just trying to find a way for them to provide a living for their families, while at the same time, contributing to the rebuilding of our forests so that we always have them. It's being done in other countries. I'm convinced it can be done here too. We're just behind the times, because no one has taken the issue to the people. The timber producers clear large areas of forest at a time, but you don't read about that in the newspaper reports. The woodcutters come in and make use of some of what's left after they leave. The woodcutters and users of firewood, like me, are victims of bad press. And where does the fodder for their articles come from? The timber producers, who use finger-pointing to distract attention from what they're doing. Think of it, Ben. Outside Freetown, most of the villagers throughout the country rely on coal and wood as their only fuel for cooking. It's cheap or free if they can gather it up themselves."

"I understand, Sara. I'm not your enemy. But I am employed by our government. I have to deal with corporations and importers and exporters. By the way, the article hinted that an unnamed entrepreneur is in the process of launching a program to put a stop to the indiscriminate leveling of forest areas. Evidently, this news has stirred up more controversy. It has infuriated the woodcutters too, who have requested a meeting with this so-called capitalist. And who do you suppose called for the meeting? Your old pal, Cano. And who do you suppose this unnamed entrepreneur might be?"

Sara shrugged. "Your esteemed wife, I assume. I'm sure the newspapers got some of their information from someone at the Department of Agriculture. When I presented my letter of intent regarding the formation of the Reforestation Association, I requested that the information be kept confidential."

"It doesn't seem to have stayed that way."

"I'm not surprised." Sara headed for the kitchen. "So I guess there are those from several sides out to get me without even knowing what I'm about to present. I'm not an entrepreneur. I'm a volunteer citizen forming a community member organization. I'm not ready to go public yet, though. I could use any advice you could give me on my next step."

"I wish I had some. The situation is complex and comes at a time of great uncertainty in our country. Try to tell people who can't find a way to put food on the table for their families to stop cutting, selling, and using firewood. We'll have even more riots in the streets. You've got your work cut out for you."

Ben unknotted his tie and pulled it off, flinging it over his suit jacket. "You know my feelings about the forest depletion, Sara. But we can't forget that the companies cutting trees have permission to do so. They pay for the right to cut and sell and export this commodity and to make a profit. Some or all of them may corrupt the system, but in the process, they employ hundreds of local citizens. Your plan must include suggestions on how the forests can be preserved, without endangering the stability of the industry or the lives of the local men and their families."

"It's because I care about the small man that I'm forming this association. That's why I'm getting village headmen, chiefs and elders, the woodcutters, and even the timber people involved. Everyone's voice deserves to be heard and respected. Even mine. I'm not denying I'm a little prejudiced about the subject. I buy wood from Cano and cook with it. I'm fully aware that I can't call for nationwide meetings and then watch them erupt into free-for-alls, with people shouting at each other and slinging around accusations. Someone has to put in the time required to come up with solutions."

"According to the newspaper article, people consider the woodcutters were right to cry foul, but if they go on strike—which they are threatening to do—poor people would suffer the most." Ben pushed past her and headed for the refrigerator for a bottle of cold beer and then drank thirstily from the bottle. "You should know that the government has asked me to become involved . . . to urge a truce of sorts, however tenuous.

"The Department of Agriculture is organizing a meeting concerning this issue, Sara. If you're asked to participate, I'm caught in the middle. My wife is working on a project to save the forest and has to maintain her confidentiality. At the same time, I'm a senior official of government, and I'm expected to make recommendations to prevent a bad situation from getting worse."

Sara watched him pace the floor and remained silent. The woodcutters were experts at what they did. That was one of the reasons Cano and the others who worked with him were so disheartened when they were moved from the areas in which they were accustomed to working. Their customers required a certain type of wood—a kind that retained the proper heat while cooking. If they couldn't provide it for them, they could lose the business of those customers. The area they had been ordered to use in recent weeks produced wood that burned too fast, didn't retain heat, and produced loads of ashes. Users called it *pow-pow*.

She remembered asking Cano about that the last time she had bought firewood from him. "Exactly what is *pow-pow*?" she had asked.

*Smoke in the Kitchen*

"The sound the wood makes," he said, laughing. "Pow! Pow! Pow! We have to go undercover to find the good wood for our customers now."

Early the next morning, Sara sent a message for Cano to see her. By two thirty that afternoon, his rickety truck stopped in front of her house. She invited him into her kitchen. "Cano," she said, "I want to be the first to tell you that I am the one the news article is speaking about. But I am not an entrepreneur. I'm a volunteer determined to become a national spokesperson on your behalf. I have alternative means to cook, but many other people depend on firewood. But the government is concerned about the depletion of our forests. If we don't do something soon, we won't have any wood left for anyone. I'm working on solutions and need your input and support."

Cano listened, his eyes widening with her confession. He sucked in air through the wide spaces in his front teeth before finally speaking. "Maybe you don't know what those crooks are doing, Aunty," he said. "You know this Matthew Wiseman? The new supervisor? He has a makeshift prefab office right there at the entrance of the forest. I don't like the man. He speaks lies."

"What has he done that makes you say that, Cano? Surely he'll make sure everybody is fairly treated."

Cano violently shook his head. "No, Aunty. I listen in on every detail of the meeting he had with the forest rangers . . . the ones that stated the new policies. Aunty, that man is tough. He told those rangers that in order for them to guarantee proper monitoring of the forests, the new guidelines will be enforced. He waved those papers in the air." Cano demonstrated by picking a napkin from the table and waving over his head. "He said every ranger better follow the new rules to the letter. He said they must be watchdogs and should walk every acre of forestland to see that no tree in the restricted areas is felled." Cano asked for water and gulped it down fast.

"As soon as he finished the meeting, he called for the timber producers and woodcutters like me." Cano stopped to eat some of the *akara* Sara served him. "The number of days we can work in the forest has been cut short. If any of us violate one of these new rules, we pay serious consequences. Aunty, everything is stiff now."

"Exactly what are these stiff new rules, Cano? As long as they apply to everyone—"

"Those penalties are too strict, Aunty. The first time we get a warning, the second time a warning and a fine, and the third time a *three-month suspension*. Woodcutters are not happy with those rules. They work one way all their lives . . . the only way they know."

"Any change to the way in which we have always lived is difficult. But this time, Cano, the change will benefit everyone, and especially our nation's children. We want to leave them a better world, don't we? We want them to have wood available twenty years from now?"

*Smoke in the Kitchen*

Cano pushed back his empty glass and headed for the door. He didn't want to listen. Just as he was about to push his way into the yard, he turned and pulled a torn paper from his back pocket. "Listen to these rules, Aunty." He came back.

Sara reached for the paper and read it over. "'Workers must abide by the forest hours, which are from eight in the morning to four in the afternoon.'"

"In past days, our hours were from six to six," Cano said. "The government says the reduction of time will reduce the number of trees cut down. But we don't cut many trees. At times, we cut up firewood from the trees already felled before we start to cut new ones." Cano struck the palm of his left hand with the wedge of his right hand, and his eyes flashed sparks.

"'Workers must produce a license and an ID if requested to do so. Violators will be fined and disciplined.'"

"IDs cost money, and my workers don't have the fees. Most can't read, so they don't know what they must sign."

"'Workers may cut down trees only within the designated areas. Workers must clean up each area at the end of the day. Trucks are not allowed to park in the forest area, unless loading timber. Cutting of trees will be allowed only six days each week.'" Sara handed the handwritten rules back to Cano. "Those rules make sense, Cano. You know that. I understand your fear. You think the government wants to stop you from earning a living the only way you know how, but that's not true. The government simply wants some monitoring and control over wasteful and destructive cutting. They are aware that woodcutting is your livelihood and that firewood is the only source for fuel energy for some of the people."

"No, Aunty, you are wrong," Cano refuted. "You want to believe, but your man, Mr. Ben, he is part of the government. They want the good areas for themselves . . . to sell rights to foreign timber cartels and take rights away from us. They want money. Always money. The government will raise our fees. They will make more rules. They care only about the people in Freetown, not the villages."

"I will work to see that such a thing doesn't happen, Cano. I'm not the only one in Freetown who cooks with wood. Your task is a hard one—extremely tedious and labor intensive. Everyone knows this. I understand why you think this new policy won't work. The government wants everyone to benefit from the new policy, not only those in positions of power. But, Cano . . . it doesn't do any good to threaten strikes or cause riots. It works best to find solutions that everyone can accept. That's my goal, and I need your help. To find solutions." She rose from her chair and motioned for him to sit down again. "I'll be back. I want to get something."

Sara gathered her reforestation files and brought them to the kitchen. She searched for relevant documents to support her case. "You're an intelligent man, Cano. I know you will try hard to view things objectively. Let me show you a few things I've researched on this subject."

She showed him photographs of forest areas that had been replanted with trees. "See, Cano, other countries share our concerns over forest depletion. They are replanting as they cut down. In time, the forests are rebuilt to their original state."

Cano took his time looking over the pictures. He picked up several and held them close to his eyes, studying the details.

"My goal is to encourage both the government and the timber and mining cartels to develop a plan for reforestation," Sara said. "They will hire village people to do the work. It will be another job opportunity for woodcutters. Education can change the thinking of everyone, even the elders and headmen of the villages and tribes. Once they understand how important this system is and how it will ensure a future for their children and grandchildren, there will be less suspicion and anger."

She waited for Cano to say something. He was silent for such a long time, she grew uncomfortable. "There's a fancy copy machine at Ben's government office," she said. "I'll ask him to make copies of those pictures for me so that you can have a set of your own. You can show them to your fellow woodcutters. Talk to each other and see if you can come up with a plan. I'll listen, and then I'll go to the authorities to see that a program is started." She paused to gauge how well her presentation was being received. "I'm forming what I call the Reforestation Association, Cano. I want its members to include woodcutters, village elders, mining and timber representatives, and government people concerned about preserving the natural resources of Sierra Leone—especially our forests."

Cano nodded. "I will come back in a few days."

"Thank you for listening, Cano," Sara said. "I want you to know that I understand your issues. I will see that you have an equal position in the association . . . one of respect. Your voice *will* be heard. Between the two of us, we have an opportunity to work toward creating a new and better Sierra Leone. Sharing ideas, sharing the work, and sharing the goals will bring about satisfaction for everyone."

Two hours later, Sara fired up the wood in her outdoor kitchen and worked at preparing meals. All the while, she sang her favorite hymns, thanking God for giving her the ability to reason. "I understand that nothing has been accomplished yet, Lord," she prayed. "I have only planted a seed. But if you provide all the other elements that will make that seed germinate in the minds of my fellow countrymen and grow to fruition, I know we can restore one of your creations to its original glory."

## Chapter 23

After canceling three scheduled appointments, Leona Murray finally decided to see Sara. Ben wanted to accompany her, but she insisted upon meeting with the acting chairman alone. "I'll call you if she releases the children into my custody today." She straightened her spine and stood tall, determined not to let Ben see the extent of her doubts. He had enough on his mind without having to worry about her. She flashed him a quick smile. "We'll leave it in God's hands."

He hugged her one more time. "I haven't forgotten that we put off celebrating our first wedding anniversary, Mrs. Moses. Remember that we still have the kite-flying prize and can enjoy ourselves at that fancy resort as soon as we can find a weekend when we're both free to relax."

"Don't worry about it, dear," she said. "Every day you come home to me is a celebration. Love like ours doesn't go by the calendar."

Although the meeting was set for nine o'clock, Sara arrived ten minutes earlier. When she was finally ushered into Leona Murray's office, she looked closely at her to try to interpret what was going on behind her carefully camouflaged exterior. The woman was in her late forties, slightly overweight and well dressed in a finely tailored black short-sleeved suit and coral blouse, but her stern face was totally devoid of any hint of friendliness. As they shook hands,

Sara felt her piercing eyes boring through hers with a degree of indifference. Determined to keep her composure and not be intimidated, she lavished Mrs. Murray with a broad smile.

"Thank you so much for meeting with me today, Mrs. Murray. I know you must be very busy in the absence of the chairman and Mrs. Brown. I hope the chairman is getting better."

"What can I do for you, Mrs. Moses?" The interim matron gestured toward a chair and then seated herself behind the desk, opening a file folder lying in front of her and giving it a cursory glance.

Sara smothered a gasp. The woman knew exactly why she was there! "I'm here to take my children home, Mrs. Murray. I've phoned many times and had three appointments with you, which were canceled at the last minute, over the past few weeks. I came here in person last May 2 and no one was here to receive me. My husband, Benjamin Moses, and I received a letter with documents that gave us the right to adopt two children from the center—the siblings Esther and Joseph. The letter was dated April 26, 1983, and was signed by the chairman of the board, Dr. Emmitt, and the matron, Madeline Brown. The following week, this permission was rescinded in a letter signed by you. We are deeply troubled by this sudden change, especially since we had signed documents and paid half the required fee for the privilege of parenting Esther and Joseph. My husband and I would like an explanation."

Mrs. Murray closed the folder on the desk with a quick flip and covered it with her folded hands. "As you have probably already been told, Mrs. Moses, unexpected events occurred about that time that required us to put everything on hold. Dr. Emmitt was hospitalized, and he had to be flown out of the country. Mrs. Brown traveled out of the country on vacation. In the meantime, we are doing our best to carry on here. You will *not* receive—and should not expect—special treatment, regardless of your position in the community. *All* adoptions are being put on hold."

Sara was shocked into momentary silence. *"On hold?"* she finally gasped. "Until when?"

"Until we are ready to proceed with the paperwork. I can't give you a date."

"You mean our children will have to remain here . . . *indefinitely?*"

"In simple English, Mrs. Moses . . . yes."

Aghast at the way in which she was being treated, Sara peered more sternly at the bordering-on-insolent woman. "Mrs. Murray, do you realize your inaction has had a profound effect on my family? I'm sure it has affected the children, as well. I'm talking about all children who will be detained in this institution because of such a delay in paperwork. They need to be in a home with parents who will love them and provide for their futures. Esther and Joseph need me. There is more to nurturing than merely feeding children and providing them with a bed."

"My goodness, you do have an elevated opinion about yourself! May I remind you, Mrs. Moses, that many of these children have been in our care for several years? They are thriving and are well looked after . . . certainly when compared to the destitute life they had before being rescued by the center. Some were even abandoned and lived on the streets." Her smile was patronizing. "The Freetown Children's Center has rules and regulations, and we strictly follow them . . . just as, I'm sure, you do at your Family Auctioneer Mart."

"I beg your pardon!" Sara said, rising to her feet. She loomed over the desk. "I don't understand why you are bringing my business into this discussion, but I will certainly agree that we have strict guidelines that are fairly dispensed for every transaction, but *we* treat our customers with respect and dignity. My sole concern today is for Esther and Joseph, whom I already consider part of my family."

Leona Murray also rose and stood behind her desk. "Our rules and regulations are written to protect both our children *and us*. And may I remind you again, Mrs. Moses, just as your company rules protect you, your staff, and your products, our rules protect our institution from undue outside pressures and the personal opinions of certain candidates."

A knock on the office door interrupted Sara's retort. Emily entered and motioned to Mrs. Murray to come closer for a whispered conversation. They huddled near the door for a couple minutes. Then, in a quieter tone, Leona Murray said, "I'm sorry,

Mrs. Moses, I will have to end our meeting. An urgent matter requires my attention." Without further ado, she left the room.

Sara stood in place while prickles of hot anger rendered her momentarily helpless. Never before had she been treated so disparagingly and with such rudeness. The woman seemed to be harboring a personal resentment toward her, and it made no sense. No sense at all. Standing alone in the office, she gazed sightlessly about her and finally took up her handbag and headed back to her car. She didn't even glance at the secretary, Emily, as she passed her desk. What could she do anyway? If she wanted to keep her job, she must keep her mouth closed. The situation called for outside action. Ben would have to use his influence to learn what was going on.

Back in her car, Sara headed directly for home. She had no desire to feel the eyes of her employees on her, and she certainly didn't want to field their questions. If only she knew where Madeline Brown could be contacted, she would try to reach her for an explanation. If only Jeremiah were still working for her, she could go to him for advice. He would know what was happening. She would make all efforts to get a letter to him. Young people had their own ways of finding out secrets.

As soon as she was ensconced in her home office, she dialed Ben and told him about her ordeal. "We need to get the lawyer or someone else to investigate," she said, on the verge of tears. "I am convinced this Leona Murray has a personal grudge against us. For the life of me, I can't imagine what it is, but once we find out, we'll know how to proceed."

Ben listened quietly and then soothed her with his measured voice. "I'll get on it right away, dear. Don't fret. We have many people in positions of authority who can speak on our behalf. If something is amiss, we'll find out what it is. When I get home, we'll talk about it some more."

Sara met Ben at the door after hearing his car cruise into the driveway. Searching his face with eyes wide with anxiety, she bit her bottom lip to keep from crying yet again. "Did you find out anything? Will Othneil work on the matter?"

"He's already been at work and found out several interesting things that may have influenced the outcome of our adoption proceedings. Give me a chance to change clothes."

While Ben was upstairs, Sara dashed to the kitchen and pulled out a tray. She loaded it with two bottles of Star beer and a few nibbles. She had the tray in the living room by the time he entered. "Don't keep me waiting, Ben. Please be quick."

He seated himself on the sofa and patted the cushion next to his. "Come and sit so I don't have to watch you pacing, Sara. When I see you so upset, it keeps me on tenterhooks."

When she had seated herself and he had drunk half his bottle of beer, he finally began. "I spoke with Othneil, and he went right to work. He called back only minutes before I left the office. It seems that your Leona Murray recently got married to the lawyer James Murray."

"James Murray. That name seems familiar." Sara frowned and rubbed her forehead with agitated fingers. "I remember now. That's the name of the lawyer who signed documents in the absence of the spouse of a customer of the mart—a Mrs. White. Mrs. Salma White. She was very angry when we wouldn't accept the sale of her furniture and antiques without her husband's signature. She claimed the mart had discriminated against her. Our rules are quite cut-and-dried, Ben. We have to protect ourselves against buying and selling stolen goods. We require that both spouses sign the verification form. She was trying to put one over on us and had her brother—this very same James Murray—sign the documents instead."

Sara clamped her hand over her gaping mouth. "So it *is* a vendetta!" she exclaimed. She leaped up from the sofa, almost overturning the tray of drinks and snacks. "Mrs. White was irate over having her plans upset to pull a fast one on her absent husband. She complained to her lawyer brother, and he told his wife about it. Together, they wielded their influence to stop the adoption proceedings to get even with me! Can they do that? Is it right? Do we have some recourse, Ben?"

Ben pulled her back to the sofa. "Stay calm. Hear me out. That's not the only connection." He waited until she had resettled herself next to him. "It seems this James Murray has another client with a reason to cause problems for the Moses family."

"Another customer of the mart? Who, Ben?"

Ben gulped some more beer. "None other than your cousin Thomas."

"Thomas!" With nostrils flaring, Sara jerked to her feet again. *"Thomas!"* she repeated, hating the very sound of the name. "Why is he so determined to ruin my life? And he's not even man enough to face me in a rational discussion. He has to hide away and let someone else do his dirty work. He must have had this Murray digging around in the registrar's office for months now. Since before we were married, Ben. What has he found? Does he know something I don't know? Is it something that will prevent me from getting my heart's desire?"

Ben rose to gather her into his arms. "You'll have your heart's desire. I promise you. No one is going to deprive you of getting what you deserve. I'll see to it."

\* \* \*

Sara had been busying herself with work at the mart and making more detailed plans for the formation of the Reforestation Association, and she continued with this scheduling. Several times with her chauffeur, she drove to villages within and out of Freetown to meet with the headmen, elders, and other select villagers. For the most part, her efforts were successful. That's not to say her mission was an easy sell. On several occasions, she took lecturer Dan Samuel, one of her key advocates for the formation of the association, with her. On these occasions, she asked the headman of the largest village to invite those from surrounding villages to hear him speak. Every day was long and stressful.

Most villagers were not accustomed to having a woman discuss such a topic of concern with them. It was still a man's world. But she seemed to have influence with the government and with the timber people, and for that reason alone, they treated her courteously. At first, few understood the rationale for replanting trees. They considered it a waste of time and money. One elder exclaimed that no one had planted the original trees making up the forest. They grew by themselves, and new ones replaced them from fallen seeds. If it happened once, it would happen again.

Dan explained that this was no longer a guarantee. Now, vast amounts of the tree wood were being used for building purposes and for furniture, as well as for cooking and for other products. "Take a walk to some of the surrounding forest areas," he said. "It's frightening to see all those barren fields. We have to do something about it for the sake of our children. There is a simple solution. We just have to decide the effort is worth it. We *can* replant the forest."

Cano came with her on occasions too. He was finally convinced the purpose of the Reforestation Association was worthy of his cooperation. He promised to do whatever he could to advise his woodcutter colleagues about their role in ensuring there would be a future for them. Most woodcutters respected him, because he was their leader and he looked after their welfare. He had spoken about Aunty Sara Moses's kindness many a time, and they knew of his close relationship with her. Now they listened as he explained that her association was meant to help, not to hurt, them in their work.

"*Me baba dem*," Cano said, using his pet name for them, "listen to me! I speak the truth. The forest is like our body. We have to look after it. God made us and gave to us a head with eyes, ears, mouth, and nose. He also endowed us with strong arms, hands and fingers, and legs to carry us where we need to go. We thank God for that. Life is more difficult for any of us who lack any part of our body."

"You preaching, man? Get to the point," someone from the crowd yelled.

Cano cleared his throat as if to speak, but then said nothing. He waited for everyone to be quiet. When he had their full attention, he continued, "We come to the forest every day to cut the live and fallen trees into firewood. There will come a time when there will be no more trees. What will we do then?"

"More will grow," a voice from the crowd bellowed.

"How can more trees grow when nobody plants anything to grow and there are no trees to produce fallen seeds? *We* have to plant."

"Plant *what*?"

Cano paused again. When he saw that all eyes were on him, he said, "Trees. We will plant and grow one tree for every tree the loggers cut down."

"*Shupid, shupid,*" one of the older men said. Then loud and angry talk erupted.

Cano held up his hand and shouted. "Wait, wait, wait! Listen to me!" The noise died down. "I am standing here to tell you how we can do this. The system is called reforestation. You see over there?"

Everyone turned toward the area he was pointing out . . . a mountainous area, with a huge section completely bare next to another dense with trees. "You see that treeless section? If we're not careful, the entire mountain will soon look like that. Maybe not in our lifetime, but in the lifetime of our children. If we don't do something now, Sierra Leone will have no forests. Aunty Sara has a plan. She knows how to help us save our forests."

"Is *she* that person . . . that one they write about in the newspapers . . . the one who wants to stop us cutting trees?" The man pointed at Sara.

"Aunty Sara does not want to stop you cutting for firewood," Cano said. "She has no power to do that. She no be the *gowanment*! She can't stop me or you."

"Her husband is the big man in *gowanment,* so she can tell *him* to stop *we!*" a voice from the crowd shouted.

"Listen to me! You miss the point. That can't happen. Look at these pictures. See how happy the people are? They are planting trees to save the forest!" Cano passed the enlarged pictures Sara had given him that morning. Some showed tree planting in other West and East African countries and different stages of tree growth. Other pictures showed reforestation efforts in the United States and Canada. Everyone crowded around to see them. Some in the crowd were far from being convinced. When the discussion resumed, everyone tried to talk at the same time.

"Wave your hand if you want to say something," Cano shouted. "Wave it, and I shall call you up."

"This is no school, Cano! You are no teacher!" Abel yelled back. "I need to talk when I have something to say!" He hopped up onto the temporary stage and stood next to Cano. "The people who cut down those big trees—the loggers and timber bosses—*they* should do all the planting."

The response was boisterous. "Good talk, man. Good talk. Good talk. Man, you talk good."

Sara touched Cano's arm. "Do you want me to take over?" she whispered to him.

He shook his head. "I can do it. I don't want to be too pushy today. Just introduce the subject to them." He waved at the men again. "It's getting late, and I think we should end this first meeting. We'll meet again next week and talk some more. *Tenki, tenki.*"

As he stood with Sara and watched the men return to their trucks, he voiced another concern. "We should have started the meeting earlier, Aunty. It is now peak hour for traffic. Wood trucks are not allowed to be on the road this time of the day. If they cause a traffic holdup, the traffic police will come. I'm worried."

Sure enough, Sara was on her way home when the police arrived and impounded all the wood trucks, ordering them to the sides of the road. They would be kept there until much later in the evening, when the road was clear. Cano and his friends had plenty of time to think about the subject of their meeting.

A couple days later, she took Dan Samuel with her again. This time they had a more diverse audience, which included representatives from several tribes. Sara had arranged for translators so that everyone could understand the purpose of the association. Several herbalists voiced their concerns. They had been having a more difficult time finding the bark and leaves for their potions because of the depleted forest areas and wanted to know how the reforestation efforts would affect their livelihoods.

"Where do we replant these trees?" a female voice from the crowd asked.

"You can plant where you are," Dan Samuel said. "Any of you can create a makeshift nursery, plant the seeds, nurse them to life, and when the little trees have grown several inches, we will purchase them from you."

Now the tribe representatives were interested. With very little effort on their part, they would have another way to support their families. "Good business, this is good business," they said, and their acceptance spread like wildfire.

Within the next two weeks, Sara's list had grown significantly. Each tribe turned in the names of two representatives to be members of the Reforestation Association, and soon the membership had grown to include those in the western and surrounding villages.

Sara had started the campaign with her own money. She was confident that once she had established the association, she would get sponsorships from government and local and international organizations for the project. Soon she had sent out hundreds of fliers and letters introducing her project to members of the community, schools, and colleges. She elicited assistance from teenagers to affix the green flyers to the electric and telephone poles. She had to smile when she saw them in the marketplaces and on taxicabs and buses.

During her research, she had acknowledged that education should be the key to open the door to the Reforestation Association's goals. On occasion, she wondered if it weren't a blessing that the children's arrival into their home had been delayed. After work every day, there was yet another meeting to attend. She made hundreds of phone calls, enlisted the assistance of a long list of volunteers with clout in the community, and finally felt she was ready for the formal launching of the association.

"Still at work?" Ben asked one evening. "How is it going, dear? You seem more tired than usual these days. I think you're doing too much." He stood at the entrance of her study at eleven one night. "Your launch is in two weeks, isn't it?"

She peered at him and sighed heavily. "There is still much to do. I want everything to be as perfect as possible. You know . . .

## Smoke in the Kitchen

so there won't be any unexpected last-minute glitches. We need positive press, Ben. If anything goes wrong and we get poor publicity for our efforts and intentions, it may set us back years."

"You've done most of this without my help, but I'm here to assist in any way you deem important, Sara. Just say the word."

"Believe me, I will, my dear. Many of the people on board the project are concerned about the social and economic aspects. Let me use you for a sounding board. The physical evidence of woodcutting and charcoal production is the topic most talked about, because that is what people see with their eyes on a daily basis. They see these products go up in flames, so to speak; they see smoke in the kitchen. Little mention is made of the vast amounts of timber being exported to other countries and bought up for the creation of furniture, building supplies, paper products, and other industrial uses. Few talk about the other reasons for the depletion of our forests. We have the mining industry cutting down trees by the thousands to make way for their activities. Then we've got farming and road construction to add to the list. It goes without saying that some of these activities in the forest are necessary and important to our economy."

Sara removed her reading spectacles and rubbed her eyes. "The Reforestation Association is not going to be limited to only telling the woodcutters to plant a tree every time they cut one down. The timber and mining industries must get on board and do the bulk of the replanting. That's the way it's done in other countries. It has got to be a national effort, with everyone taking the subject seriously. You can do a great deal to pressure the government into passing a law that makes this a mandatory service, Ben. Without muscle behind the effort, it will be doomed to failure. This is a big task. I know it, but I am prepared to give it my all."

"You know what?" Ben pulled her to her feet. "I'm so proud of you, I could explode! But I want to caution you. I agree with everything you've said, but you have to use as much diplomacy as you can with those in positions of power. And by power, I mean those holding the biggest purse strings. There will be some out there who oppose your efforts, because it will affect their financial operations. Profit is the name of the game in big industry, and those involved in the Sierra Leone timber, diamond, and other mining industries are not usually fair-minded."

"You're not telling me anything new, Ben. I've met with many of those who use their power to refute my efforts."

"This is a very complex situation." Ben nodded thoughtfully. "The acceptance of your association has already gone far and above what I ever envisioned. But I don't expect you to restrict people from continuing their way of life, as they have always known it will not only affect them personally, but the entire country politically, economically, and socially. We're still trying to catch up with the modern world, and I sense so much uncertainty in the government and throughout the country. That could devastate your efforts. In the meantime, we still need our farmers to grow more food, we need to tap our mineral resources, we need to develop more and better roads, and we need to build dams for a vastly improved water supply. You must be sure your solutions are workable."

*Smoke in the Kitchen*

"Thank you for your words of caution, but I know what I'm doing. I know how I'm going to handle it. Don't worry, Mr. Economic Adviser."

Ben laughed and gave Sara a quizzical look. "When you need Mr. Economic Adviser, please let him know. In the meantime, I'm heading for bed. You're welcome to come join me anytime you're ready." Halfway through the doorway, he turned. "By the way, Mr. Economic Adviser is very proud of his wife."

Sara worked for another two hours and then joined Ben, who was already fast asleep and snoring. Long after she had turned off the bedside lamp, she lay awake thinking of the reforestation project and the positive impact it would have in her generation and the ones following. The depletion had been going on for centuries. However much they planted, they would be unable to recover from the devastation caused by her grandparents and those before them.

She considered it an honor to correct some of their mistakes, however. She thought of Grandma Corinthia and all the historic information she had shared concerning their direct link with the forests of Sierra Leone. Some had been woodcutters and charcoal producers. Her own use of three fireside stones with firewood had stemmed from her roots. Her grandma could identify the best firewood with only a glance, and she had taught Sara the same skill.

Grandma Corinthia's papa had been a laundryman—a *washman,* as she had referred to him—well-known in the neighborhood. He worked with his wife, who assisted him with the ironing. In those days, he contracted with the military and government agencies to launder and iron the uniforms of government officials, including the military, the navy, and customs officials. Not many people had those privileges. As there were no running taps then, they had to do laundry by hand in huge washbasins; the work was backbreaking and hard. The navy uniforms were the most difficult to handle, but with his expertise, it had posed no problem for him. He may have used millions of charcoal pieces during the ironing process over his lifetime of service. Even with the military contracts, he couldn't afford to purchase a wood truck, but had used a wheelbarrow to cart the charcoal he needed between his buying sources and place of work.

There were no standpipes for the required water supply, so Grandma Corinthia and the children of other neighbors had had to fetch water from the stream. Fetching water was often fun, she said. She and her friends would compete to see how skillfully they could balance a bucket of water on their heads. That wasn't the fun part, though—the fun part was when the bucket of water tilted and drenched the unskilled person. In order to maintain a good balance, they would create a support, called a *kata*, made of fabric wrapped into a loop and placed on their heads. The bucket would rest on this looped fabric. When her papa was doing the laundry, Grandma Corinthia would have to make several trips to fetch water to fill the forty-four-gallon container.

After her papa finished washing the clothes, he skillfully ironed them with a charcoal iron. He had quite a few of them in different sizes, from the smallest to the largest. The charcoal pot, made of scrap metal, was about three by three feet and six inches deep.

*Smoke in the Kitchen*

A tray collected the ash as the charcoal burned. As the charcoal heated, her papa placed the irons atop the coal. If the irons became too hot for certain fabrics, he dipped them in an enamel bowl of water, reducing the temperature. The smallest charcoal iron was used to press the pleated cotton dresses for women and girls and the shirt collars of men. The largest and heaviest were used to press the military khaki uniforms.

Saturday was the busiest day, because most customers collected and dropped off items to be cleaned. The neighbors' eyes would be on their house when the military trucks stopped at the entrance to drop off and collect the uniforms. Most of the men who drove the trucks were the colonial white men from England. They would stay to laugh and chat with them. Even though they couldn't communicate very well, they seemed to understand each other. The children in the neighborhood would wave to them and call out *"whetman, whetman."* They would wave back and sometimes give them chocolates and sweets. It was fun. Sometimes the soldiers would give Grandma Corinthia's mother canned food out of their rations. The unusual foodstuffs gave interest to their usual diet of local *plassas*, rice, and *foo-foo*.

Sara turned over in bed several times as she thought about her family and their way of life. It was not any different from those of villagers to this day. Then, just as she grew weary and was about to drop off to sleep, she thought of Esther and Joseph. Too much time had elapsed since her meeting with Leona Murray. Both Ben and Othneil Baker had urged her to be patient. Investigation took time, and they didn't want to alert any of the Murrays to their activities.

Breathing a silent prayer for her wounded confidence and debilitated sense of trust, she finally accepted that if her life were to be sustained just as it was for another day, week, or month, she must continue to keep her hope alive.

## Chapter 24

The day for the formal launching of the Reforestation Association finally arrived. Sara had worked feverishly to enlist people from all walks of life as participants—from the grassroots level to top government officials. She had sent out invitations and organized a sumptuous reception down to the finest detail. She had ordered specially made placards listing the names of various people representing every governmental and nongovernmental organization, and the individual names of every market woman, woodcutter, charcoal and timber producer, laborer, farmer, teacher, student, and housewife to be prominently displayed throughout the facility.

Now, as guests enjoyed the reception and the live calypso band music, they introduced themselves and shared their enthusiasm for the association's goals. Sara had even commissioned the writing of a special calypso theme song, and it had been played at every rally for weeks. It had also been played often enough over the airwaves and via mobile trucks sent through the neighborhoods and villages that everyone at the reception could sing it. It spoke of the importance of the project and how citizens throughout the nation should participate. She had chosen this means of spreading the word about the association because of the high illiteracy rate in the country.

The children loved the calypso beat, and whenever the mobile music trucks came within earshot, they would chase them while singing and dancing to the rhythm. Adults heard it on their car radios to and from work. The lyrics embodied the theme of the association.

> If you cook with firewood . . .
> We say plant a tree.
> If you cook with charcoal . . .
> We say plant a tree.
> If you sit on wooden chairs and sleep on wooden beds . . .
> Then plant, plant, plant, plant, plant.
>
> If you build a house . . .
> We say plant a tree.
> If you work in mining . . .
> We say plant a tree.
> If you cut our timber and send it overseas . . .
> Then plant, plant, plant, plant, plant.
>
> Don't deplete our forests and don't erode our land!
> To preserve them for our children
> And preserve them for our country's pride . . .
> We say plant, plant, plant, plant, plant!
> We say plant, plant, plant, plant, plant!

Reforestation was a new word in the country's vocabulary. Even though the ideology of guests differed, all were curious to see what the launching entailed. It was great for such a diverse group to gather for the same cause, other than to celebrate holidays at public affairs. The speeches given in English were translated into the lingua franca and pleased the village headmen and elders representing their tribes.

Sara was most pleased that Ambassador Mark Harris from the United States embassy had kept his word and agreed to be the keynote speaker. Ever since his arrival in Sierra Leone, he had been considered an icon because of the encouraging role he played in any worthwhile endeavor. When invited, he would visit self-help projects in villages and advise young men to form cooperatives. When she sent him the letter requesting his presence at the launching of the Reforestation Association, he had sent a cordial acceptance. Now he approached the stage to a round of applause.

"I want to thank all of you for coming this afternoon," he said. "I especially want to commend Mrs. Sara Moses for her initiative in organizing this remarkable national project. I am looking forward to working with her and with all of you to see that the goals of the association come to pass. The association's slogan, *Replant and keep our forests green*, is most appropriate and meaningful.

"You have already learned that natural forest reproduction does not keep up with human demand. Man must do his share to help with the process. That is why you have agreed to serve on the Sierra Leone Reforestation Association, and by doing so, you will join with other countries worldwide that have already initiated reforestation practices. I am proud to say that the United States Forest Service plants approximately 1.74 billion trees every year, and this means our reforestation efforts have actually *grown* the size of our forests over the past hundred years. Although most efforts are focused on replacing trees, reforestation is not limited to only this purpose and can be expanded to include all forms of natural or transplanted plants and bushes."

Ambassador Harris paused to look over the crowd, listening with rapt attention. "You know, my friends," he said, "you will greatly benefit from your reforestation efforts. Once all those hundreds of acres of abandoned mine land have been replanted, you will once again see the return of clean water and wildlife habitats, and the elimination of rampant land erosion. The opportunity for commercial forestry will not diminish; it will endure for generations to come. Trees and forests are a vital part of your existence. You depend on your forest resources for constructing your homes, for medicine, for cooking purposes, and for a long list of other things, including recreation, hunting, and simply enjoying as part of the country's beautiful landscape.

"But, my friends, in the short time I've lived among you as a representative of my country, I have learned that Sierra Leone is only moderately forested. If the rate of forest depletion were to continue unabated, with no measures taken to restore these areas, you and your neighbors would, all too soon, be without the wood required for everyday living and would have no areas left in which to enjoy nature as it was intended.

"Now, because you heard the call of alarm from Mrs. Moses and have rallied to support her through membership in the Reforestation Association, all this will change. It is possible to change our old ways and to live each day with a conscious determination to do whatever we can to replenish and grow our natural resources. I pledge my support and the support of my country. We will work with you to ensure Sierra Leone's forests are returned to their former state, insofar as it is possible."

The applause for the ambassador was loud and prolonged. Sara quickly flicked the tears from her eyes and introduced several more speakers. One was already well-known in the community. With smiles from all those closest to him, the director of the Department of Agriculture strode to the podium in a dark green suit. Jacob Winters was one of Ben's best friends and had already assured him that the government gave 100 percent support to the association.

He began with high praise for Sara's hard work in forming the association and for gathering such strong backing from collaborative organizations. "While the government is equally enthusiastic and in accord with the association's objectives," he added, "none of you should sit back and wait on the government to do everything. As was said by many of our esteemed speakers today, it is everyone's responsibility to use their personal expertise in areas where they can contribute effectively. There are two sides to every coin." He dug one out of his pants pocket and held it up. "Let's say that the first side represents the reforestation program, which involves the members of several economic and social entities; the other side represents government participation through new laws and regulations and financial support. Both are important and necessary. One can't work without the other."

When Cano finally took his place behind the podium, Sara could see that he was nervous. He had never made a speech in public before, but he had assured her he would be able to do so. It was because of his urging that the firewood cutters were supporting the association's plans, and as their spokesman, he was determined to speak on their behalf. Though he was not dressed in a conventional suit, as were most of the other speakers, he was well-dressed in an ankle-length African embroidered caftan.

He waved to several of his friends, who were loudly cheering for him. "Aunty Sara is a star!" he shouted, and they cheered again. "My friends and colleagues, in order for this woman to get each of us involved in her program, she was willing to risk going into dangerous areas of our mountain villages in order to meet us at the forest. She had to leap over logs, watch for snakes and lizards, and on one occasion, dodge a baboon who leaped from a tree above her and landed right in front of her. She said she was only pretending to be brave, but she was willing to trek along with us to experience our lifestyle, in order to understand exactly what we go through on a daily basis. We face many dangers in our forests, and she learned firsthand about that."

Cano turned and grinned at Sara. She nodded and waved to him, remembering many of those excursions with him. The forests they worked in were inhabited not only by deer, birds, and squirrels; they contained wild cats, wild pigs, and even wild cows that often objected to the invasion of humans into their personal habitats.

"She is a brave woman," Cano repeated, "and we like her spunk." Everyone applauded, and Sara mouthed a thank you to Cano and others in the audience.

*Smoke in the Kitchen*

"All of us will need to become farmers in the future, because we have to plant a tree for each one we cut down," Cano said. "There is a saying that we never appreciate the importance of a shade tree until the tree is cut down. We don't want to say that about our forests. Madam Moses, other members of the Reforestation Association, my fellow woodcutters, and I are going to do whatever we can to make the forests expand and live again. And that's a promise you can count on."

Wild cheers and whistles from his fellow woodcutters accompanied him as he returned to his seat. Sara's smile broadened, and she poked Ben. "Wasn't he wonderful?" she asked. "I'm so proud of him."

"The speech of the moment is about to be delivered," lecturer Dan Samuel said as he introduced Sara. "She is the researcher, the founder, a true pioneer, and the bravest lady I've ever met," he said. "You have been reading about her on the editorial pages of the *Daily News* for the past few weeks. All of us who have been enlisted to work with her have admired her courage, her tireless devotion to the cause, and her undeniable love for our country and its people. *All* its people. When she says we need to work to save our forests, we believe her."

Sara walked confidently to the podium dressed in a green custom-made cotton *kabaslot,* with a tree-shaped design. It had elaborate yellow embroidery and frills on the sleeves that looked as though they were patterned from an ostrich's tail. Her head tie was elaborate, and that added flair to her outfit. Each step she took revealed her canvas shoes, *carpet sleepers,* artistically handcrafted with green and yellow wool, the same shades as in her dress. She had draped a customary black satin rectangular sash over her right shoulder. Everyone stood in her honor, and their applause was deafening. Overcome by the ovation, she finally raised her right hand to stem the clapping and noticed that Ben was the last person to finish.

"My friends," she said, speaking clearly and taking time to look as many people in the eyes as she could, "I want to begin by thanking my dear husband, Benjamin Moses. His support and advice and unending assistance have provided me the backbone for this endeavor. Without him by my side, offering encouragement and words of wisdom, I would have faltered long ago."

Again, the audience showed their appreciation with applause.

"I regard all of you in attendance for this launching as being, in every way, as courageous as I have been described by Cano. The subject of reforestation is a sensitive one. It affects the very core of our lives. The forest areas of our country are very small, considering how important they are to our socioeconomic development. We are a nation that is still developing, and the rapid depletion of our forests has already created a plethora of serious problems . . . the erosion of our land during our long rainy season, the pollution of all our water sources, which brings cholera and encourages the increased production of disease-bearing mosquitoes, which, in turn, brings malaria. Too many of our children lose their lives because we have been careless with our natural resources. No more!"

More applause and shouts of approval interrupted her speech.

She took a deep breath and glanced at her notes. "My grandparents and great-grandparents were woodcutters and charcoal producers."

Again her speech was halted as the woodcutters and charcoal producers applauded her. "Mining also has taken its toll on our forests. They must bear the responsibility to take whatever measures are necessary to eliminate erosion and pollution in the future. Reforestation is one proven method for doing this. I agree with the director of the Department of Agriculture when he said that we have to look at both sides of the coin. The work that takes place in our forests is diversified and necessary and is connected with all of us and with everything we do."

Ben's eyes lit up as she continued with her oration, and Kelitia and her siblings applauded with him. Sara couldn't stop her thoughts from roaming to Esther and Joseph. How she wished they were sitting in the audience next to their father!

"It is my intention," she said, "to provide incentives so that all of our people will enjoy planting trees on an ongoing basis. This is a national issue, not a sectional one. If anyone wants to continue to cook with firewood, our theme song reminds us . . . I will plant, plant, plant, plant, plant to make up for every cord of wood used. I will do my part and be an example to all of you. I will personally plant five trees for every tree I use in my kitchen."

Once again, she received a standing ovation as she finished and left the platform.

As the appointed chairman for the occasion, Dan Samuel of the university expressed his desire to assist Sara with educational programs for both interested workers and the general public. "The university will establish pilot programs in some of our schools," he said, "and with the permission of the Department of Education also provide seedlings for the replanting project. I'm a little embarrassed that, as an educational institution, we have done very little to save our forests. I apologize for the lapse."

He was interrupted with chuckles and giggles, which stopped when he raised his hand. "I promise to provide all the support that this program needs. Mrs. Moses has been an inspiration to me and to our entire faculty. We are in the process of expanding our curricula to include classes on environmental education and on the forest, in particular. And now, ladies and gentlemen, I am privileged to have the honor of launching the Reforestation Association of Sierra Leone."

At the end of the ceremony, Sara and the other members of the association posed for group photographs. She also requested that an additional one be taken of just her with the woodcutters and charcoal producers. Near the back of the room, guests crowded around tables where college volunteers were selling T-shirts with the logo of the association—a black silhouette of a family planting a tree.

*Smoke in the Kitchen*

Tired, but tremendously happy, Sara allowed Ben to wait on her once they returned to their home. "I am so proud, I am popping a button," he said, handing her a glass of bubbly. "You can give yourself high praise. The launching of your association was a smashing success. Not one person thought otherwise. I believe the enthusiasm is genuine and you will see mouth-dropping progress in the weeks and months to come. I can't wait!"

As Sara sipped the sparkling wine, a series of memory-evoking events passed through her mind. For most people, the accomplishment of this one monumental task would have been enough to bring untold fulfillment and personal satisfaction. But while she was undeniably pleased with the outcome of the association's formation, she couldn't dismiss the unsettled feelings that still plagued her every waking moment.

"Now," she said, "I will allow some of the others in the league to take over while I focus on bringing our children home. And, Ben, if I knew I could continue to run my family's auctioneer mart and pass it on to my children, I know I could finally be content." She placed the empty goblet on the coffee table and rose to put on some music. She needed something soothing to halt the direction of her thoughts.

"Trouble is brewing, Ben. I feel it in my bones. Something sinister is slithering through the grass and heading straight for our door."

## Chapter 25

A month after the launch, Dan Samuel arrived at Sara's office to discuss the association's progress and accomplishments. "I know several organizations have had remarkable success in organizing their planting crews and actually getting into the designated areas to plant seedlings, but I have no good idea of where we stand," she said. "There has been so much behind-the-scenes administrative work to all these reforestation activities."

Sara sighed deeply and flexed her shoulders. "I don't know about you, but some days I can't see the forest for the trees!" She laughed at her use of the cliché. "Isn't that what people say when they lose sight of the big picture?"

Dan's deep laugher followed hers. "I hear you, Sara. Trying to effectively manage all the relationships between various government entities, the private logging and mining firms, and the volunteer organizations, and then supervising the actual work operations is a full-time job for a huge team of people. If I didn't carry this notebook around with me, I'd be lost. But the good news is that we've accomplished an amazing feat in the past month."

"What's the latest figure?"

"Close to thirty thousand seeds have been germinated and should be transplanted in our designated areas!" Dan stabbed a finger on the figure in his notebook. "It's right here in black and white, and the figures agree with those provided by the company selling us the seedlings."

"We've got so many?" Sara raised both eyebrows.

"Yep! And several more planting events have been scheduled for the next two weeks."

"All that despite our being in the rainy season?"

"We always schedule more than one possible date. So far, it's worked to our advantage. I want to report, too, that several of my students have met with the woodcutters and conducted educational sessions in several villages."

Sara motioned for him to be seated. "I was invited to a meeting a couple days ago conducted by a committee of ministers of various denominational churches and the clerics of major mosques. Their members want to become activists in the reforestation movement too. They've agreed to conduct a parade through the city next week. Parishioners will carry banners encouraging citizens to join in their efforts to replant."

Dan leaned back in his chair. "That's impressive. And you will be happy to learn, Sara, that schoolchildren participated in a special planting last week. Representatives from the agricultural economics department supervised the activities. Thousands of trees in bags were transplanted into soft soil. This past Tuesday, some women planted both trees and flowering bushes in barren spots in the rural areas. Wednesday was the university's planting day. They handled planting in three locations, coordinating their efforts with students in other parts of the country."

He referred to another page in his notebook. "There was a rally on Saturday sponsored by the university and followed by a dance. We've been encouraging the students to continue with regularly planned activities. In the newsletter we send to overseas universities, we specifically mention that we would welcome forest tree and other plant seeds from anywhere. We don't want to plant the wrong trees."

Their conversation was interrupted by the phone on Sara's desk. "It's Cano," she mouthed to Dan when she picked up the phone. "He's never called me before!" She switched the receiver to her other ear. "Yes, Cano, how are you doing and what can I do for you?"

"Good morning, Aunty. I'm doing very good, thank you. The other woodcutters have asked me to request another meeting with you."

"Is something wrong, Cano?"

"Oh, no! We want to thank you for respecting us so highly. Ordinary woodcutters like us have never been asked to join such a reputable organization like this one before. We are proud."

"You *should* be proud of yourselves. You gave up your work for several days to plant trees. I am certainly proud of you. I don't think it's necessary for me to meet with you to receive your thanks, Cano. I'm the one who is grateful to you for your support."

"There are some other ideas we want to give you, Aunty."

"All right, I would be happy to meet with you then. Shall I come to the forest?"

"We want to come to the town. There are ten of us, Aunty, and we would prefer to come to your house. We can sit under the fruit trees in a shady section. We want Uncle Ben to be at the meeting, too."

"When are you thinking of coming and at what time?" Sara shrugged at Dan, who was trying to learn the purpose of the call.

"Aunty, it is left with you. You give us time. You are busy people."

"I will speak with Uncle to see when he'll be free and respond by tomorrow. Please call me either at home or in the office."

At nine Saturday morning, the woodcutters alighted from a pickup truck with Cano. Sara met them at the front door and welcomed them into the house. "Good morning, how *una* do?" she asked. She smiled and shook hands with each of them.

"Good morning, Aunty. Good morning, Uncle," they said, also shaking hands with Ben, who was standing just behind Sara.

Ben ushered them into his study, where they chatted with Ben. He had just finished putting together a secondhand computer he had purchased from one of the embassies. The men shifted from one foot to the other and fiddled with the hats they were holding in their hands. Although they were curious, they didn't want to appear too bold. They kept their eyes focused on the floor, while casting furtive glances at the furnishings in the room and at the strange piece of equipment on the desk.

Sara realized there wasn't enough space in the study.

"You have a most beautiful house, ma," Cano said.

"Yes, most beautiful, ma," Abel said, mimicking Cano's manners. "I see you have a special television with a typewriter connected to it. You can type and watch the television at the same time."

Ben smiled. "This setup is not really a television and a typewriter, although it certainly looks like it," he said. "Come closer and take a look. It's called a computer. Both Sara and I need to work at home some evenings and on weekends. This machine allows us to have a convenient office at home."

The eyes of their guests widened in astonishment. They elbowed each other and whispered their fascination with such technology.

Sara reentered the study and invited them to be seated on the back porch, where there was adequate space with chairs and a table set for the purpose. The tray she placed on the table was laden with cold bottles of Coca-Cola, Fanta, and 7UP and also a pitcher of ginger beer. "Please help yourselves," she said, letting each guest choose his preference. She poured a glass of ginger beer for herself and then seated herself on a chair facing the woodcutters.

She opened the file and removed some photocopies of the photographs she had commissioned at the launching of the Reforestation Association and passed them around. "There are enough for each of you to keep copies," she said. "You may enjoy showing them to your families and neighbors."

"Woo, look! Ay, this is good," Cano said, smiling as he showed his copies to Abel. "Aunty, we are grateful, very. You allow us to be in this important program. You show us plenty respect to our wives and children. Everywhere, people say, 'we see you in newspaper, we see you in newspaper.' We all have newspapers in house, looking at us. Like these big people say, 'I feel like a million-dollar man.'" His smile lit up his face as he patted his chest with pride.

His friends clapped in agreement and poked at him to continue talking.

"Our job is important to us . . . to our people. Now, we are no more only men who cut wood, but men who make important contributions to Sierra Leone, just like the important people in politics do. People like the Moses family. You never look down on us, Aunty. You look up to us and thank us for what we do." He glanced at his friends, who were nodding vigorously. "Two of my friends here at this meeting are new in the woodcutting business. They want to plant trees like we do." He motioned to them, and they stood up and bowed. "Jonas and Nehi," Cano said. "We are all very happy, Aunty. Thank you from our hearts." He placed both hands over his chest, and the others followed his example.

Abel cleared his throat. "Our wives are happy now, Aunty. We got to attend that rally and the dance." He moved his shoulders in rhythm to music in his head. "It costs too much money to go to clubs. This event was free for us. We danced all night long. Great."

Everyone laughed, and Sara refilled a plate of rice bread and cake and passed it around. "I am so happy you are learning how valuable you are to the country," she said. "You know, the reforestation program is rather like a three-legged stool. If even one leg is missing, it falls over. No one can use it. One leg of the program involves our government." She nodded toward Ben, who was radiating his pride in her. "They must enact laws and create organizations that will provide ongoing leadership to ensure the programs continue. They must also provide money to pay for some of the trees and labor . . . and, of course, whatever enforcement is required to ensure no one disrupts or disregards the program. The second leg of the stool represents every person, company, or organization that uses wood to produce its products. They must obey the laws for preservation and reforestation, and they must find better and less wasteful ways to conduct their businesses. The third leg represents every citizen who uses wood products. You are one of those necessary legs on the stool, and so are Ben and I."

Before their meeting was over, they had discussed how the woodcutters could form an organization that would represent its members who wanted to offer their services as tree planters on a payment basis. After the volunteer effort had dwindled, a definitive program by both the timber people and the government would be necessary, and they wanted to ensure they would receive top consideration for the hiring of their forest expertise.

The following Monday, Ben called Sara at the mart and said she should meet him at Kelitia's hotel for lunch. He had something to announce. "It's good news, Sara," he said.

Two hours later, though it seemed like an eternity, she rushed into the hotel, breathless and eager to hear the details. Kelitia met her with outstretched arms. "It's been too long since we've had a truly fun lunch together," she said, kissing her on both cheeks and hugging her tightly. "Ben hasn't come yet, but he phoned earlier and said I should get time off to have lunch with you. What is it all about? Did you get the children?"

"I don't know, Kelitia. I'm as much in the dark as you are. Ben and our lawyer have been investigating the stall in the adoption process, but I've been so distracted with launching the association these past several weeks that I haven't bugged him about it."

"Well, knowing Ben, he wouldn't ask us both to be here if it weren't for a good reason." She peered over Sara's shoulder. "Here he comes now."

Ben crossed the lobby of the hotel in long strides. When he reached them, he pressed a kiss onto Sara's forehead. "Am I lucky or what? I've got two gorgeous women to share lunch with me. Did you reserve us a good table, Kelitia?"

"The best," she said, offering her cheek for a kiss. "And you'd better not keep us waiting for dessert to tell us why we're sharing this lunch either!"

Ben took each of them by an arm and led them toward the restaurant. "A little waiting will do you both good. I think we should discuss the second term of Prime Minister Thatcher and the thrilling event of the first woman in space on the *Challenger* . . . wasn't her name Sally Ride? Looks like 1983 has been a red-banner year for others, as well as for the Moses family."

"Ben, don't you dare chatter on and on about such things!" Sara protested. "Not after teasing us over the phone with the mention of special news. Why is this a red-banner year for *you*?"

They were seated at a table dressed in starched white linen and presented with menus by their waiter. "We'll each have a glass of your best champagne," Ben said.

Kelitia looked at Sara with widened eyes. "Must be something good," she said. "This is to be a celebration."

"It is, indeed," he said. "Ladies, you are looking at the new chief economic adviser for the government of Sierra Leone."

"Oh, Ben, that's wonderful!" Sara exclaimed. "You deserve the promotion. I'm so proud of you. Tell us all about it. How will your work change?"

"Well, as head of my department, I'll be working closely with the three divisional heads of research, planning, and communication. They'll report directly to me. I'll be organizing in-service training programs to keep everyone in my department abreast of current events and how they affect our country economically. Of course, my travel schedule is unlikely to change. It may even increase. I'll still need to make frequent trips abroad to participate in conferences, seminars, and workshops, and on occasion, to be the featured speaker. I'm hoping you'll be able to come with me on some of them, Sara."

"Of course," she said, patting his hand. "Now, tell me more about how all this came about. Your staff must be pleased, dear."

The waiter had brought them each a goblet of champagne, and they had a toast. Ben opened the menu and peered over the top at them. "Let's order a fancy lunch and enjoy ourselves for the next hour or two. We deserve it."

"When do you plan to let your aunty know?" Sara asked after she had placed her order for barracuda with prawns. "She'll be very upset if you don't make it soon."

"I'll send word to her one way or the other. I won't have time to go to her potholed neck of the woods."

Kelitia wagged her fingers at him. "I've got a suggestion: send the message through the Bush Radio system!" She giggled. "That means has always been an effective way of communicating bad news. It should work just as well for good news like yours. Everyone in this country lives by their Bush Radio setup. You're an important man now. You can simply make one phone call to the radio station and ask them to make the announcement of your promotion every hour on the hour. Your Aunt Philomena will hear the message and tell all her friends and neighbors. She'll find a way to show up on your doorstep with some of her home cooking."

"Great! Just what we need," Sara said, rolling her eyes.

"Since you're paying for this, Ben, I'm going to splurge on fresh lobster," Kelitia said.

Ben didn't bat an eye. "I'll join you," he said. "Lobster sounds perfect."

For the next hour, the three of them enjoyed their meal with pleasant talk and considerable laughter. Only once did Sara allow herself to think of the disappointment she felt that the news hadn't been about bringing home her children.

\* \* \*

Weeks had passed since Sara had met with Leona Murray at the children's center. As she turned the pages of her desk calendar, it was hard to believe it was already August. Still no word came from Othneil, and she had long ago grown tired of calling him only to receive the same response. "Be patient, Sara. I'm working on it."

Wherever she went now, people recognized her. They'd seen her so many times in newspapers and on television news shows that some who had never even met her reacted as though they had known her forever. Before her marriage, she was known as the daughter of the man who owned the auctioneer mart. Then for some time after her marriage, she was known as the wife of Benjamin Moses, a senior government official. But now, she was Sara Moses, the president, founder, and pioneer of the Reforestation Association.

"Your recognition is growing as fast as the new trees in our forests, and that has been good for business," Ruth contended at the office one day.

"Sometimes it gives me a good feeling," she replied. "Whenever I appear in public, I can hear the whispers, 'she's that reforestation woman,' or 'that's her,' or 'I saw her picture in the newspapers.' Makes me feel like somebody very important! Women *should* have their own identities."

Sara insisted that Kelitia accompany her on a shopping trip one Saturday following the activities of reforestation. Sara picked up her sister at her house. Dressed in a turquoise *boubah* top with a matching cotton *lappa* that made her look younger than her age and matching turquoise and black half-slippers with two-inch heels, she nevertheless felt like Kelitia's mother. Her sister was dressed in a simple white blouse and blue skirt that looked remarkably like a schoolgirl's uniform.

"I want to stop first at the post office," Sara said. "I need to mail a few letters and send a parcel to Dan Samuel."

"Good," Kelitia said. "I need some stamps."

When they found a parking spot a short distance away and headed to their destination, they found an unusually long line of customers waiting to enter the post office. "What's happening?" Sara asked a lady who was in front of the line.

"Bus and *poda poda* strike," she said angrily. "I am told there is only one cashier."

"We can't spend the entire day here," Sara concluded despite taking her place in the long line.

Thirty minutes later, Sara and Kelitia were hustling back to their car. They went to the store, purchased a few items, and headed back home.

Just as they were about to drive past the museum, Sara applied her brakes and pulled to the side of the road. "Jeremiah! Jeremiah!" she shouted at a young man crossing the road.

He whipped around and shaded his eyes against the sun. "Is that you, Mrs. Moses?" He came running over to her. "How good it is to see you again!"

She motioned for him to climb into the backseat of the car. "Kelitia, this is Jeremiah. He used to work at the mart, until he went off to college. He's the nephew of the matron of the children's center. Jeremiah, this is Kelitia, my sister."

After shaking Kelitia's hand, Jeremiah turned his attention to Sara. "Congratulations on your great success, Mrs. Moses. Your name is everywhere on campus. In fact, several of us have asked our professor if you can be our guest speaker at a rally we're planning to kick off our own replanting program."

"I would be most pleased to do that, Jeremiah. With the support of the young people of our country, we can be assured of having our forests for decades to come." She peered at him over the front seat. "I have a question for you now. What's going on with your Aunt Madeline? Where is she?"

"She is on vacation in Liberia."

"I am so upset that the adoption of Esther and Joseph fell through. I was told your aunt traveled out of the country, Jeremiah. Do you have an address or a phone number for her?"

"She did what she had to do before she left. I feel bad for you, Mrs. Moses. Yes, you can have her number. She should be back soon. One of my cousins is getting married. I believe she'll be back as soon as that is over." Jeremiah wiped the sweat off his face. "Before she went on vacation, she was thinking of leaving her job."

"Leaving her job!" Sara was taken aback.

"That's what I wanted to tell you. She and that Mrs. Murray almost came to blows. I spoke to her before she left."

Sara twisted around in the seat so she could face Jeremiah. "They had an argument? Whatever happened?"

"When Mrs. Murray was appointed the interim chairman after Dr. Emmitt went to the hospital, she ordered that all adoption procedures were to be put on hold, especially yours. Aunt Mad told her that wasn't what the chairman wanted. They had already sent out the letter granting you approval. The children were to become yours within a couple days. No one knows what went into that woman's head, Mrs. Moses. She was adamant. She must have been embarrassed to speak to you." Jeremiah shook his head, clearly upset by the situation. "It seems Mrs. Murray hates you, Mrs. Moses—that's what my aunt said."

"Someone should have called me."

"I believe she felt embarrassed to speak to you. I apologize for not making much more effort to get on to you. I didn't know the children wouldn't have been with you after all these months—"

"It wasn't your responsibility. I don't hold it against you. We've just been at a loss as to what to do. We did learn that Mrs. Murray's husband is the attorney who is the brother of Salma White. Do you remember the ruckus she created at the office when she tried to sell all her household goods in the absence of her husband? We wouldn't allow it."

Jeremiah groaned. "That's got to be it! According to Aunt Mad, Mrs. Murray asked her for the files on pending adoptions and locked them up and held onto the keys."

"She did *that*?" Kelitia interrupted their conversation.

"It's a shame the chairman got sick. Maybe this would never have happened," Jeremiah said.

"I understand he had to have an emergency surgery and was flown overseas," Sara commented. "How . . . how can I get in touch with your aunty?"

Jeremiah looked out the open window next to him. "I shall let you have her contact number."

"But how soon do you think she might return to Freetown."

"I don't know . . . If I get any information, I promise to let you know, Mrs. Moses."

Neither Sara nor Kelitia had much to say after Jeremiah left the car. Sara turned her attention to manipulating the car through the traffic back to her sister's house. Finally, she voiced her thoughts with a calmness that surprised even her. "If we hadn't gone to the post office and done some shopping, we wouldn't have driven past the museum at the very moment Jeremiah appeared. It was God's providence at work. He has been teaching me patience these many weeks. He has been teaching me about the very serious problem concerning legal adoptions in Sierra Leone. He needs me to do something about it. And that is exactly what I intend to do."

Kelitia pinched her lips. "I don't know how you can remain so composed. I am fuming inside. I would be compelled to barge into that center like a bull and wreck everything in sight. Right now, I am seeing red. It's not fair that one or two people can work so hard to ruin the lives of people like you and Ben."

After dropping Kelitia off at her house, Sara drove home feeling more hopeful. She expected to get Mrs. Brown's contact soon. She now knew more of what had happened at the center that horrible day when the courier had come with the second letter.

Ben wasn't home when she got in. He had been there earlier and left a note to say he was with Aunty Philomena. Too tired to prepare dinner for only herself, she resorted to eating bread and butter. She wanted to put her plans in writing.

First on her list would be to pay a visit to her lawyer. It was time for action—action that produced results!

## Chapter 26

Othneil Baker's office was on the ground floor of his two-story concrete house. He was a well-established lawyer, whose clients consisted of Freetown businesses and individuals in the top 20 percent of the economic scale. He was also associated with overseas partners in at least three countries. Although Sara retained him for her business, she had wanted him to take on the investigation of the Freetown Children's Center because of his clout and business connections. He knew people who knew people who could ferret out information from uncommon sources.

But he had been working on her cousin's lawsuit against the mart for more than a year and not gotten anywhere. And now, months had passed since Ben had contacted him about the halt in their adoption process. If he couldn't give her any satisfaction today, she would embark on her own investigation. Her patience had worn thin and was festering with each passing day like a painful boil that wouldn't heal.

Sara had an eight-thirty appointment, and even though she arrived slightly late, at eight forty-five, the lawyer had just finished with another client. "Come in, come in," he said, shaking her hand and ushering her into his office. After asking his secretary to serve them coffee, he turned to her with eyes warm with admiration. "I can't begin to tell you how impressed I am with the zeal you've shown in establishing the Reforestation Association," he said. "Ben must be popping a few buttons these days. And I just heard about his promotion to chief of the Economic Adviser's Department of our government. We are lucky to have a man of his caliber in such an important position." He went on for another couple minutes extolling her ingenuity and propensity for hard work.

"Thank you, Othneil," she said, swallowing some of the hot coffee and then placing her cup and saucer firmly on the edge of his desk. "I am dedicated to the project and hope the goals we've established will become a routine part of how the timber and mining industries conduct their business in the future. No more lackadaisical practices and no more willy-nilly depletion of forest areas without a firm commitment and system for replanting. But that's not why I'm here. I want to discuss the progress you've made in solving my two personal problems. Exactly what have you learned about my cousin Thomas's progress on obtaining ownership of my business, and exactly what have you learned about what is going on in the children's center?"

Othneil smiled and leaned forward, shoving his coffee cup further away from him to keep from knocking it over. His eyes danced with amusement. "You're not going to cut me any slack this morning, are you, Sara? You're on a hunting expedition and are determined to bag your prey. I understand your frustration. I'm experiencing it myself."

"I don't want platitudes, Othneil. I am beyond being frustrated."

Sara deftly swung their casual banter to the serious discussion of matters dear to her heart. "And I want my two children home where they belong. They should not spend one more day in the center because of the vindictiveness of one woman, if that's the crux of the problem. How can someone acquire so much power to do whatever she likes?"

Othneil's smile faded. "I hear you, Sara. I am painfully aware of how frustrating working within the law can be for those who need its guidance, especially in a country that often flouts the law or tries to find ways to confuse it. Unfortunately, even seasoned lawyers find doors locked tight and mighty hard to break down." He opened the file in front of him. "Things are not going as fast as I had anticipated. I hired private investigators to locate the center's matron, Madeline Brown. We have spoken to every member of the board; these are people who volunteer their time. They were told the same thing you were told. She is on vacation. They don't seem to want to get involved. Until we can learn more about what went down between her and Mrs. Murray, a huge and important part of the puzzle is missing."

"Can't you ask some of the members to request a meeting in the absence of the chairman?

"Mrs. Murray is to convene this meeting. It appears she is acting both as chairman and matron."

Sara was silent for a moment as she thought of her conversation with Jeremiah. "I have learned the whereabouts of Mrs. Brown, Othneil. I unexpectedly ran into her nephew. She is in Liberia and may not return to her job until the chairman returns."

"That's wonderful. Not that she may not return until then, but that you learned her whereabouts. Did you learn anything else?"

Sara shared all she had learned. "Surely the organization has rules set up about how adoption transactions are conducted," she said. "I want to see a copy of their bylaws and learn what our rights are in this matter. I want a copy of it today, if possible. No more delays. I want to know why this Leona Murray made such a hasty decision and whether she had the authority to make it without the accord of the board members. I'm wondering if it was a hasty decision after all, Othneil. It seems to me that she had a plan in the works all along. It was so coincidental that the matron was proceeding on vacation the moment the chairman fell ill. I am surprised the matron didn't call me. Ben and I couldn't contact anyone upon receiving the letter rescinding the adoption. Don't you think it was a calculated move to send the letter on a Friday evening, when the center would be closed for the night and for the weekend?"

"I can't answer most of those questions, Sara, but we have learned that Mrs. Murray has not been in her office most of the time. I also learned she was working hard to place the children in another home, but I strongly suggested to certain other board members that they absent themselves from meetings, if there are any, so there would be no legal quorum."

Sara struggled to maintain her composure. The idea of Esther and Joseph being placed in someone else's home was not something she had even contemplated, and the suggestion was unexpected . . . and frightening.

Othneil's hands slid to the armrests of his chair, as though he were about to boost himself out of it, and then returned to rest on his desk. "What I also did was to talk to several of the center's donors about the situation. I must tell you, they are not happy, Sara. They have assured me they will apply pressure if I ask them to do so."

"Have you spoken with Dr. Emmitt?"

"Unfortunately, I understand he was flown out of the country for further treatment."

"I wonder whether a couple who applied for a baby at the same time we applied to adopt Esther and Joseph had their process stopped too," Sara quietly interjected. "A Mr. and Mrs. Fisher."

"The Fishers received their baby . . . . I saw all of them in church."

Unable to control her exasperation, Sara rose and paced the room. "The inspection has been on my mind recently," she said. "Have you thought of establishing whether or not there was a link between one or all three of the inspectors and Leona Murray? The man—Albert North—was quite hostile and had nothing encouraging or nice to say on that day."

Othneil reached for a pad and jotted down his name. "I'll look into his background and associations and try to get a copy of his report."

"According to Jeremiah, Mrs. Murray locked up all the documents in the file cabinet."

Sara paused and stared blankly out the window of Othneil's office. A steady stream of traffic was going by, and for a moment, she was lost in thought. Finally, she turned to face her lawyer, who was stroking his whiskered chin. "Do we even know if the children are still in the center?"

He hung his head and played with the pen on his desk. "Again, Sara, I can't answer your question. I feel ashamed to admit I never thought of asking. As you know, legal adoptions of children are rare in Sierra Leone. Usually, families just accept one or more into their homes informally."

"I know. That's how Kelitia became my sister."

Othneil rose and came to her side. "I have, however, made some progress on the lawsuit. I've been communicating with James Murray, in an effort to get him to reveal more about his investigation. In my last communication, I quite firmly stated I have gone through the documents in the registrar's office myself and found no evidence to support anything illegal in the inheritance transactions concerning your father's acquiring the rights to the mart or yours from him. I also insisted that we receive the address of your cousin forthwith, as we wish to communicate in person."

"And have you had a response?"

"He insisted all communication with your cousin should be done through him."

"I am going to do a little investigating of my own, Othneil. I intend to put out the word to my uncle and have him spread the word to old neighborhood friends of my cousin. It may be that one of them has kept track of Thomas better than I have."

Sara left his office at eleven and went directly to her office. Ben found her there at five, still working on a list of potential contacts. Her anger at her cousin had dissipated into resolve. She looked up at him with flashing eyes. "I have decided to apply for a place on the Freetown Children's Center Board of Directors."

Shocked at the announcement, Ben sank onto the sofa at the far end of her office. "Are you serious?"

"Yes, I want to know what's happening in there, and this may be the only way I can learn what we need to know. Besides, I'm unhappy with the way in which things are being run. If other potential parents are going through what we're being made to endure, the system needs changing."

"You can't do this on your own . . ." Ben said, assuming Sara wouldn't change her mind.

"There is always a beginning." Her eyes veered away from his.

"Well, if that's what you want, I have no doubt you'll find a way to do it. If you need letters of recommendation, I don't think you'll have any trouble gaining a position. You're known and respected throughout the entire country now. Mrs. Murray won't know what's hit her once she is inundated with personal requests."

"I saw Othneil today and—"

"What did he say?"

"I was stunned to learn that Murray had made preliminary arrangements for our children to go to other parents. Othneil spoke with certain board members and got them to agree to stop attending board meetings so no legal transactions could take place because of the lack of a quorum."

"What about the mart . . . anything new there?"

"Not really. James Murray is still mum on providing the information we need; he wants all communication with Thomas to go through him. Othneil has been hesitant to issue court orders or to be too firm with him, because we need to tread lightly until we know his connection to our adoption process, if any. It's hard to believe he isn't at least advising his wife about how far she can go to stall proceedings."

Ben rose and crossed the room in long strides. "You've had a rough day, Mrs. Moses. Let's go home."

Sara's eyes glittered with purpose. "I won't be mollified by you or Othneil, Ben, but don't let me become bitter if none of this turns out the way I want. Maybe I'm not supposed to become a mother. Maybe I'm supposed to focus my entire energy on the Reforestation Association. Goodness knows it's a full-time responsibility, and I'd be doing something worthwhile with my time and education."

Ben looked deeply into her eyes. "You will have children, my dear. Maybe we won't have our Esther and Joseph, but we *will* have children. All we want. All we can reasonably take care of, considering our busy lives. Believe that." He steered her toward the door of her office.

With her head held high, Sara willed herself to remain strong. She would not allow herself the luxury of any more tears. Why life had to have so many twists and turns, so much pain, so many trials was beyond her comprehension. It hurt to know there were those who despised her and were so eager to ruin what little happiness she had found. Her faith would have to sustain her, as it had so many times in the past—her faith and Ben's love. She understood now that real love was an emotion that couldn't be turned on and off like a stopcock. It was part of the very fiber of your being. She and Ben loved each other, and whatever experiences they shared would enrich their lives. Still . . . there were the *if onlys*.

On her way home, with her husband's car behind hers, she pushed away the hurt she was feeling despite her outward bravado. Her pain was real, the wound deep . . . too deep to properly analyze. Maybe tomorrow would bring some good news. There was always tomorrow.

## Chapter 27

After deliberating all night long, Sara decided her first task would be to invite Uncle Jabez to her home for dinner. She would question him about Thomas, without going too far into the details about why she needed to find him. First, though, she would call Kelitia and invite her too. Kelitia could distract him when too many questions forced her into a corner.

With trembling hands, she dialed Kelitia and related the events of the preceding day. "I'm at my wit's end. It's taking too long for Othneil to learn anything substantial. I have to take matters into my own hands. We women have our own ways. So, I need you to assist with Uncle Jabez. Will you come?"

"Of course! I've always enjoyed chatting with Uncle anyway. Count me in."

About to send her driver to take a letter to Uncle Jabez, Sara was disrupted when her office door opened. "Mrs. Moses," Ruth said, "Stephen Paul, the editor of the *Daily News,* is here to see you. Remember? He called yesterday. He wants to do an article about the Friday rally for the paper."

Great! That was all she needed. Another interruption. Sara forced a smile and waved for Ruth to usher him in. Rising from her desk, she extended her hand. "Good morning, Stephen. You're right on time. Won't you be seated?" She gestured toward the chair fronting her desk. "Ruth, would you bring in coffee for us?" While flexing her shoulders to relieve the tired aching in them, she returned to her desk chair. "It's good to see you again, Stephen. Thank you for giving us such extensive coverage in the paper these past several weeks," she said. "It was a tremendous help in getting our citizens motivated."

Stephen Paul accepted the cup of coffee from Ruth and watched without speaking as Sara received hers and then dismissed her secretary. "It was news, and we're in the business of giving our readers objective accounts of whatever is going on of interest," he said. He crossed one leg over the other and sipped at his coffee, eyeing her with a frank stare. "You've had remarkable success with your newest venture. Tell me about the rally."

"Friday's rally will be the last for a while. The association is well enough organized now to go on without my continual hands-on attention. We've established contacts in all district and provincial headquarters and set up a governing council to discuss issues and make decisions. Each district has representatives, and they will work with members from the government and the timber and other industries. Professor Dan Samuel is our chief coordinator. Now, I guess you have a few questions for me." She reached for her cup and stirred the dark brew with a spoon.

"Who are the featured speakers at this rally?"

"Actually, other than myself, we decided it would be more effective to have shorter speeches from various representatives. Enthusiasm comes when the locals hear from those in their various areas. So, we'll have students, market women, village heads, woodcutters . . . people like that. Last time, I heard from an amazing number that they don't like to hear what they call 'white men bosses from companies or offices tell them what they ought to do and why.' They prefer hearing from *their own,* their neighbors."

Paul jotted several notes on his pad. "What's your message going to be this time? More of the same?"

*Watch out*, she warned herself. Editors could be nosy, and they had their own ways of digging up information to put a twist on things, even ones as friendly toward her as Stephen Paul. Laughing softly, she said, "It does seem like we're all repeating ourselves, doesn't it? This time, I'll offer a very short report on our progress. Our target is one hundred thousand trees and bushes. That's quite a remarkable feat, considering we recently launched this association. We hope the government will adopt all of our suggested resolutions. We are doing this without putting the jobs of our citizens at risk. Educating everyone to the reasons why reforestation is necessary has worked. We're having fun, and most importantly, the barren areas of our forests will soon be growing again."

Paul nodded and scratched more notes onto his pad. "Anything else?"

"Well, yes," she said. "The association is going to advocate, both nationally and internationally, that financial incentives be given to everyone who plants a tree. Hopefully, this will encourage more of our less financially secure brothers and sisters to participate. We can't keep them from using wood as fuel and cooking, but we *can* inspire them to use it more judiciously if we offer to pay for the work they do in replanting the trees they use up."

"So you're not going to push the disuse of wood for such purposes."

"Of course not. It would be foolhardy to even think of such a thing. Until our entire country has been modernized, that isn't even feasible. If all of us stop using firewood today, it will have a profoundly negative effect on the incomes of our woodcutters and their families and subsequently our country's economy. If we strike against the use of timber for any purpose, it will affect the economic viability of the country, as well as the incomes of the timber producers. What we want to encourage right now is the simple fact that we must replant what we cut down, or eventually we'll have no forests and our land will erode into mud piles during our rainy seasons."

Once again, she paused to stir the coffee she hadn't drunk. She eyed the editor as he wrote his notes and wondered what he was thinking. She had subscribed to the newspaper for several years. Her advertisements for auction sales were regularly posted in it. They had known each other for a long time.

Paul stuffed the pad into his suit-jacket pocket and the pen into his shirt pocket. He was quiet for a long enough time for Sara to grow uncomfortable.

"I sense a hesitancy, Stephen. Is something wrong? Have you heard something about the association or the rally I should know about?"

He coughed into his hand. "No, it isn't that, Sara." He peered over his shoulder as though to see if anyone else were in the room and then lowered his voice. "I received a rather disturbing letter about you . . . one that was intended for publication. It would constitute important news, and I can't, in all good conscience, ignore it. I . . . I thought it would be important for me to get your side of the story first."

Feeling his intense scrutiny, Sara struggled to maintain her composure. *Another letter.* With her heart throbbing, she smiled. "My goodness, Stephen, what is this all about? You look positively in agony. Surely it can't be as bad as you're letting on."

He pulled a document from his briefcase and handed it to her. "I wrote back to request more evidence, but I am still awaiting the information."

Sara felt heaviness in her face, and embarrassment shrouded her entire being as she read the letter. No wonder the editor of the only widely distributed newspaper in Freetown was so upset. The letter stated that Sara's paternal grandpa had gifted the property to Sara's papa. Upon her papa's death, the property should have gone to a male grandchild, but Sara, a female grandchild, had converted and registered property as the *bona fide* owner. She gave it back to him. "My cousin Thomas initiated a lawsuit against me at least a year ago, Stephen. He has hired James Murray to represent him, and Murray has spent time and money at the registrar's office trying to dig up any sort of evidence that could prove that I wrongly inherited this property from my father upon his death. Thomas wants the mart. I don't know why. I haven't seen my cousin in years. My lawyer, Othneil Baker, has been working diligently to find Thomas. We can't find him. It doesn't make sense that he hasn't shown up here to confront me in person."

Again, Stephen Paul coughed into his hand, more uncomfortably this time. "It was my impression that this was a family matter, but because it involves such an important and well-known business in our community, I should consider the merits of the story."

"You don't need to apologize, Stephen. I quite understand your dilemma. I ask that you wait on the story, however, as we are learning more things and need to put them all together. I will tell you what we know if you promise to keep it confidential until the matters come to a close. Then you'll have your headline story."

For the next several minutes, Sara recounted what she knew about James and Leona Murray. "I can't help wondering if my cousin is somehow involved in this too, Stephen. That's why we need to find him, and that's why we're trying to make contact with the matron."

"I have no trouble holding the story, Sara. Thank you for trusting me with your side. If I can learn anything from my angle, I'll be sure to let you know. Our newspaper has a good reputation, and I wouldn't want to publish a libelous article that would create problems for us."

"When did Thomas send this letter to you, by the way?"

"Three weeks ago."

"Is there a return address?"

"It came to my office through James Murray."

For the next hour, Sara sat at her desk, too numb to act on anything. The newspaper was the last place she would have expected Thomas to go. Surely if he were keeping abreast of the news in Freetown, he would have seen the articles about the Reforestation Association and her close ties to it. He must know she was well-liked and respected in the community. Obviously, he felt the positive publicity would injure his claims. He would have to malign her reputation so that everyone would doubt her integrity. Her husband was now the chief economic adviser, and any suggestion of impropriety would be embarrassing to them both.

What would all those she had worked with think . . . the woodcutters and their friends? What about the Reforestation Association's personnel? And more importantly, what would the members of the children's center board think after reading such drivel and not knowing if it were true? She couldn't swallow the hurt that had balled up in her throat. Thomas was not only going to destroy her image in the public's eye, but also her life as she knew it. Never mind if he lost the case and she retained the mart—would anyone ever believe her again once her reputation had been sullied? People would always wonder. Was her father a crook to claim property that wasn't his? Was she? Were they a moneygrubbing family?

Picking up the empty coffee cup on her desk and draining it into her mouth, she swallowed air. She felt mentally drained. She would send the note to Uncle Jabez and get him to her house by Friday evening. By hook or by crook, she'd find her cousin and have it out with him. Hopefully Stephen Paul would keep his word and not publish one word about their conversation until she gave him the go-ahead.

No news was good news when it concerned the potential destruction of the Reforestation Association and its elaborate maze of supporting organizations and citizens. As important as the mart was to her, she couldn't—wouldn't—risk its failure because of a family feud.

## Chapter 28

It rained all that afternoon, as Sara made her way home and into the evening. At the sink, she methodically rearranged the plants that decorated the windowsill while staring out the window at the scene, imagining each flash of lightning was stabbing her in the heart. She hadn't mentioned her meeting with Stephen Paul to Ben. She had chattered about inane business and then turned the rest of their dialogue to his new job.

Ben said from behind her, "Are you going to tell me what's on your mind? Do you honestly think I didn't know you were holding something back during our meal? It was delicious, by the way."

"Your suspicious mind is on the loose again," she said, flashing the semblance of a smile.

"I prefer to call it my caring mind, especially when it comes to you. Let's have it. What's bothering you? Something happen today at work?"

She fixed her sober eyes on his face. "You know me too well. Yes, something happened today." By the time she had watered the last plant, which was the hanging golden pothos, she had finished telling him about the editor's startling revelation. "I don't know whether or not Stephen will honor his word, Ben. He may feel the accusations in the letter are too hot to sit on. After all, his paper is in business to make a profit. Can you imagine the vast number of newspapers he'd sell? Can you see the headlines? Why did my father pass the mart onto me? He should have willed it to Thomas. Men have always been company owners. What chance would I have?"

"Sara, listen to me." Ben held her arms. "Thomas is your cousin, not your brother. Your father inherited the property, and he had every right to will ownership to you, his only heir."

"Thanks for your comforting words, Ben." Her voice was calm, despite the avalanche of emotions that racked her insides. "But I have this gnawing fear that any day now, the front page of our newspaper will shout that I am a fraud."

Ben was silent for so long, she pulled away to peer up at him. "What are you thinking?"

"I'm thinking that we must focus all our efforts on finding Thomas. I was also thinking about what other means we have, other than Othneil's investigation."

"His strategy is to remain on speaking terms with Murray, because of his likely involvement in the children's center issue."

"You're probably right. We don't want to foul that up. Maybe we could trick Murray and his wife and get them into the same room together and then lock the door until they come up with the answers we need."

Sara couldn't help herself. She had to laugh. "I think you'd better let me handle this, Ben."

The next morning, Sara took her time dressing and ate a leisurely breakfast, forcing herself to have two cups of coffee. Ben had left early and wasn't home to disrupt her thoughts.

She had worked hard all her life. First, she had put every ounce of effort into obtaining her college degree. She hadn't been distracted with dating. When Willy came along, he had swept her off her feet; she hadn't been prepared to deal with the emotions that love instigated. After that, she had made a long series of mistakes, and then, grieving over the loss of both Willy and her baby, she had turned her thoughts and emotions inward. During that same time, she also had to cope with the deaths of her grandmother and both parents. Actually, she hadn't managed that well either. She had, instead, used every waking hour of her energy to see that her business flourished and grew. Yes, she had continued her usual routine, teaching Sunday school and entertaining on occasion, but her heart hadn't been in it. Not really. It was like she was dead inside.

Then she'd received word that her cousin was about to turn her world upside down yet again. Her emotions had taken another tumble, and it seemed like she should prepare for a life of regular disappointments. No amount of sermons from Kelitia could convince her that life was worth living. "*Sara John*," she'd said sternly, "*God has never promised us a life without problems. Everyone has them in abundance. When something is worthwhile, it's worth taking a risk. You need to get yourself out there and throw yourself into every situation that can use your skills and intelligence. Don't hide in your house and become a hermit."*

Then she met Ben.

Once again, she saw the sun and all that life could be. Her childhood dreams returned. She envisioned the laughter and joy that would come with filling the house with children. For a brief moment, she had even set aside thoughts of Thomas and losing the mart.

By the time Sara reached her office, it was approaching eleven o'clock, and she was greeted with mountains of folders and notes from Ruth, including at least a dozen phone messages. Ruth followed her into the office.

"Mrs. Moses, a man called the office an hour ago. He wouldn't leave me his name or his telephone number, but he sounded very eager to meet with you."

"Never mind, Ruth. If it's important enough, he'll call back."

"I think you can expect that call. He said he was your cousin."

"My cousin! My *cousin*?" Sara gasped.

"He sounded like someone from overseas."

"I . . . I only have *one* cousin, Ruth, who lived overseas, and I've been trying to reach him for over a year!"

"I'm so sorry, Mrs. Moses. I didn't know. I-I would have tried harder to get more information from him."

"It's not your fault, Ruth. If he calls again, though, get me on the line immediately, and if I'm not here for some reason, get his phone number and address and find out if I can meet him somewhere. It is critically important."

The second the door closed behind Ruth, Sara reached for the phone and dialed Ben. "I must speak with him immediately," she said. "I'll stay on the line until you find him." It took his secretary a full three minutes to track him down.

"Sara? What's the matter? Are you all right?" Ben's voice registered his anxiety.

"I'm fine, Ben. I had to let you know . . . Thomas called my office this morning!"

"He phoned you? Where is he? What did he say?"

"I wasn't in the office. I arrived late this morning. Ruth took the message. Thomas wouldn't leave his name or number. He just said he was my cousin."

"You're sure it was Thomas? Not a hoax?"

Sara caught her breath and sank onto her desk chair, swiveling so that she could see out the window. It was still raining. The gray sky cast a gloom on both her office and her mood. "I-I didn't even think of that, Ben. Of course, it's a hoax. The same people who are playing with our emotions over the adoption are—"

"Don't even go there, Sara. I'm sorry I mentioned it. I'm going to do some investigating over the next hour. If Thomas is in Sierra Leone, we should be able to find him. He'll be in Freetown, not some other town or village. Let's not worry until we have something to worry about."

Ruth entered her office with a folder of faxed messages. "These are all labeled urgent, Mrs. Moses." She handed Sara the file.

"Thank you. I'll get to them in a minute or two." Ruth had her hand on the doorknob when Sara called her back. "Ruth . . . can you remember exactly what time my cousin called?"

"I have the details in my notebook. I'll get it." The phone was ringing, and she dashed out of the office without closing the door. "Hello. Family Auctioneer Mart. May I help you? Hold on, and I'll connect you. *Oh, no! Mrs. Moses!* It was your cousin again, but we were disconnected when the power went out!"

Sara threw her hands in the air. Both her desk lamp and the overhead light had flicked off at the same time a bolt of lightning, followed by a crack of thunder, made her jump from her chair. "Is someone turning the generator on?" she shouted. She had installed a small generator to run the fax machine, telephone, electric typewriter, and the computer, which no one in the office really knew how to use. Once the generator was running, at least the lights would come back on. The telephone was another issue.

Depending on whether there were a malfunction, it could take a few minutes, a couple hours, or days or even months to rectify. Nothing was repaired in an efficient manner in the country. Waiting was part of living.

For the next several minutes, she paced the floor. Events were not proceeding as she had predicted only moments ago. Wringing her hands, she worked herself into a frenzy. Myriad thoughts raced through her mind. Had Thomas found his proof? Was he about to present her with an ultimatum: give me that business or I'll destroy your reputation? Choose one or the other: the children or the business?

Even after the generator had provided the power necessary to turn on the office lights, she found it too challenging to produce satisfactory work. The fax folder remained closed. She stared at the telephone, willing it would come back on, but it was a futile effort. She would receive no more calls from Thomas or whoever was pretending to be him. She would not be able to reach Ben either. She had known this day was coming, but had chosen to remain hopeful.

Finally, Sara gave up her determination to be productive. By the time the rain had stopped and the sun peeked out on occasion from behind still-saturated clouds, she had made a decision. Maybe she couldn't make future plans for the mart today, but she would not turn her back on hope. Sara's driver dropped her off in time to prepare dinner for Uncle Jabez and Kelitia; he then headed to Uncle Jabez's house. Sara would still use him to track down Thomas. The calls were simply practical jokes. She would march steadily toward her goal.

Kelitia arrived shortly before five o'clock with Uncle Jabez in tow. Beaming at Sara, he shuffled across the threshold of her home. "When I hear and read 'bout you, I feel proud as a peacock, Sara. And your Mr. Ben, too. Good man, that one. Look at this palace he *give* you." He peered at her through his wire-rimmed glasses. "You look sickly. You okay?"

"I'm fine, Uncle. It's the rain and the work. Kelitia, take Uncle into the living room. I have to get something from the kitchen."

He had barely seated himself on a chair when she returned with the tray. "I have brought your favorite, Uncle. Star beer." She spoke brightly, winking at Kelitia.

"You know I don't drink it cold," he groused.

"It's room temperature. Right from the carton, not the refrigerator."

"Thank you, my dear."

He sipped his beer slowly and then set the bottle firmly on the table next to him, making sure it was placed on the coaster. Then he carefully removed a clay pipe from his shirt pocket and a pouch containing crushed tobacco from his jacket pocket. After he had filled the pipe bowl with tobacco, he searched his many pockets and finally found his matches. Puffing several times, he was finally able to light the tobacco. A curl of smoke wrapped around him.

"How is that husband of yours doing?" he asked, taking another gulp from the bottle. "I understand he got himself a promotion. He's a big shot now. A big-shot government man. You 'bout to have those children you always talking about?"

Sara glanced at Kelitia, who lifted her shoulders in a shrug. "We're all very proud of Ben, Uncle. He's worked hard for that promotion. He's the chief economic adviser now, and that makes him busier than ever. In fact, he travels quite a bit. Fortunately, he'll be able to join us for dinner." Sara looked at the clock on the mantle. "Speaking of dinner, I'd better finish cooking. Just relax and enjoy yourself, Uncle. It you want to roam about the rooms or come to the kitchen, you're welcome to do that."

Just as she reached for the pot holders to remove a saucepan from the cooker, the phone rang. Startled, she almost dropped the pan. Placing it firmly on the range top, she dashed to remove the receiver from the hook on the wall. "Hello."

"Hello, dear, Ben here. You'll never guess who I have with me."

"Don't play games, Ben. I'm finishing dinner, and Kelitia and Uncle Jabez are already here." Her eyes were on the clock.

Just then, Kelitia entered the room and mouthed, "Who is it?"

"Ben," Sara said, placing her hand over the mouthpiece.

"Sara, listen to me. I have Thomas here in the office with me. I'm bringing him home for dinner."

Sara dropped the receiver and had to fumble for it. Finally, with shaking fingers, she brought it to her ear again. "I-I don't think I heard you correctly, Ben."

"Yes, you did. Stay calm. We'll be there in forty-five minutes. Set another place at the table."

Clutching her throat, Sara turned to face her sister. No words came from her open mouth. If it were possible for a black woman to suddenly become white, she knew her face would be as pale as the moon.

"What is it, Sara? You're scaring me." Kelitia rushed to her side.

"It-it's *Thomas*. He finally showed up. Ben is bringing him home. He'll be here in, uh . . . forty-five minutes. What will I do? I-I can't face him when Uncle is here. I-I just can't, Kelitia. Thomas is set to ruin my life, and Uncle will come up with all sorts of inappropriate comments. I-I don't know what I'll do . . . what I'll say."

Kelitia gathered her into a tight hug. "I know what to do. I'll pack up a dinner for Uncle and take him home. We don't need to be here for such a traumatic moment for you. He'll understand. I'll fill him in on only a bit of what has been happening. Now, find me a container or two. I see you've made your famous jollof rice. He'll enjoy that."

Within five minutes, the food had been packed into containers. Kelitia hustled the old man from the house amid lots of chatter and the pretense that Ben had called and asked Sara to meet him urgently.

Within fifteen minutes, Sara heard Ben's car stop in the driveway. She had swiftly removed the additional settings from the table and had rushed to the mirror in the downstairs bathroom to check out her appearance and to splash cold water on her face. Frightened eyes stared back at her, and she saw that she was visibly nervous. Breathing a quick prayer for serenity, patience, and understanding, she walked toward the entrance as Ben opened the door, followed by a man only a couple inches shorter and just as broad-chested.

"Sara, my dear, dear cousin," Thomas said, the smile on his round face spreading from ear to ear and infusing his slightly bulging eyes with a sparkle. He strode toward her and kissed both cheeks, before gathering her into a surprising hug. "What a great pleasure to see you again after such a long, long time." He hugged her again. "Why have you been hiding from me?"

Sara couldn't believe her ears. Surely he was jesting. What sort of game was he playing? Well, she could play games too. "You're right, Thomas. It has, indeed, been a long time since we've seen each other. It has been such a long time, I'm not sure I would recognize you if we passed you on the street." She peered at Ben over Thomas's shoulder and gave him a quizzical look. He merely shrugged.

"Becca sends her love. She told me that if I failed to get in touch with you this time when I'm here in Freetown, I'd be in big trouble when I get home. I have phoned you a few times, but you and your husband are so busy, I've never connected. Office people always said Ben was out of the country, and your phone was either not going through or when I eventually got through, you were in some village or at some gathering giving a speech on reforestation. Unfortunately, I am always on the road too."

Was Thomas putting on an act? Or was he merely trying to soften her up before telling her the bad news?

"How is Becca?" she asked, working hard to retain her sense of social graces.

"Pretty well. She has two young boys and a pretty little girl. They are growing like weeds these days and keeping her busier than she'd like to be some days."

"How many children do you have now?"

"Three sons and a preteen daughter. When school is on holiday next time, I must bring them here to meet you. They talk about their aunty all the time. I have regaled them with stories."

Was she having a nightmare? The conversation seemed so surreal.

"What about you, Sara? Any children? I know you've just been married a year, but we're not getting any younger."

"No children yet." Sara glanced at Ben, who was standing by with his hands in the pockets of his pants watching them. "I'm eager to hear how you found Ben. Why don't you go wash up? Dinner is ready. Ben, will you show Thomas where the washroom is? Then take him directly to the dining room."

Back in the kitchen, she hung over the sink and tried to quell her gagging. The nausea roiling around in her abdomen had weakened not only her body, but her resolve. How could she continue with this charade? How could she play hostess to a relative who had threatened her for more than a year and caused so much emotional stress? How could she look him in the face and not throw daggers? How could she serve him her best jollof rice and pretend he was a welcome guest at her table?

Reaching for a face towel, she wiped the perspiration from her face and then washed her hands. She could do it, because she wouldn't stoop to his level. He didn't seem like the sort of person who would take her business from her. Maybe there was a reasonable explanation for everything. She would give him the benefit of the doubt.

As they were seated at the table, she pointed out the dishes she had prepared—krio salad, jollof rice, and stew.

"Mmm, mmm. This is a feast, Sara." Thomas helped himself to a generous helping of each.

"Feel free to eat as much as you like." She fussed over her napkin and took only a small portion of a couple items, hoping Ben wouldn't notice. She had lost her appetite.

"You've taken over where your Gramma Corinthia left off, Sara. I remember when we were young; she used to cook such tasty food for all of us. I do believe your jollof rice is better, though. The best I've ever had."

All during the meal, Thomas heaped praise on her. "I've been reading about you in the papers. What a remarkable thing you're doing for our people and our country. I'm not at all surprised, though. You have been a hardworking person as long as I've known you, and generous to a fault . . . always giving of your talents and your time. To tell you the truth, Sara, I was always a little jealous of you. Even my crotchety old man would brag on you." He took a sip of the wine from his goblet. "You asked earlier how I was able to finally find Ben. It wasn't difficult, actually. Everyone in town knows him. I asked the taxi driver, and he took me directly to his office. I gave up calling."

Ben laughed like they were long-lost friends.

Sara stared at Thomas with her fork poised halfway to her mouth. Had her husband jilted her for a man with a glib mouth and courtly manners?

"What's it like to be married to such a famous woman, Ben? She's such a popular figure these days—is she ever home to make you jollof rice like this? Or is her famous cooking talent reserved for a company-only affair?"

Ben chuckled again. "I didn't tell him any of that stuff," he said to Sara. "Your cousin knew all about your Reforestation Association and how you've become as renowned as a movie star."

Thomas raised his wineglass and offered a toast. "Here's to our health and longevity and to our renewed relationship."

Sara clinked his glass, but couldn't drink a drop of the wine. She'd likely choke on it.

"How's the Family Auctioneer Mart doing?" Thomas asked.

Ben seemed as startled as she was by the question. With her heart throbbing in her throat, she was about to say he ought to know! Instead, she swallowed and said, "It's doing well, actually. It's hard work, but I have a good team working for me." She excused herself to carry dirty dishes to the kitchen and prepare dessert before another mart question was posed. While in the kitchen, she could hear Thomas and Ben chatting about business, the economy, and the two countries. It seemed as if they had known each other for a long time. She wondered if it were his sister who had asked him to initiate contact with her or whether Thomas had wanted to do so himself. And why was he pretending to not know anything about the mart?

Irritated by the farce, she tightened her lips and decided to bring up the subject herself.

"This is a beautiful house," Thomas was saying as she reentered the dining room carrying a cake.

"Thank you." She placed the cake on the table and returned to the kitchen for the tray that held dessert plates and the coffee service.

As soon as they had finished dinner, amid more stilted conversation, Ben rose and announced that he would get the wedding album. With a sense of panic, Sara was about to protest, but knew she had to finally take the bull by the horns and talk about what had been on her mind for months. A sudden chill passed through her when she thought of the letter Stephen Paul had shown her. She cast a quick glance at her cousin before focusing once again on her coffee cup. Why couldn't she just come out and ask him? Ben had done his part by bringing Thomas to her; she had to do her part.

"Why don't we go into the living room, Thomas," she said, pushing her chair back. "You can refill your cup and take it with you. Or would you prefer more wine?" She reached for the half-filled bottle on the table, the second one they'd drunk during the meal.

"I believe I'll have a little more wine," he said, taking the bottle from her. "How about you?" He held it over her glass.

"No, no. I've had enough." She turned and headed toward the living room, wishing she could guzzle down the entire bottle and find some of the nerve she knew she usually had in such situations.

Once they were seated, she smiled stiffly, and her eyelids fluttered. "I-I think we have a few important things to discuss, Thomas. I can't pretend any longer that I'm happy to see you."

He looked at her with puzzled eyes. "I don't think I understand, Sara."

"Yes, you do. You know exactly what I mean, Thomas! Don't pretend otherwise. Our relationship has been broken for a long time. We haven't spoken to each other for years, and yet you've been working behind my back to ruin my life. We inherited a broken relationship from our fathers, and now you're determined to carry it into perpetuity, all because of your father's animosity toward my father! You've hurt me in a way I'm not sure I'll ever be able to get over. Your actions these past several months have devastated me, and—"

"Wait! I don't know what you're talking about, Sara," Thomas protested, pushing his empty wineglass onto the table next to him. He shook his head in bewilderment. "*What* actions? What have I done to upset you so much?" His nostrils flared, but his voice remained calm.

"I don't know how you can sit there and . . . and deny knowing what I'm talking about, Thomas. You want to deprive me of my inheritance . . . the property willed to me by Papa! You want to take the auctioneer mart away from me!"

He grabbed her hand and placed it over his chest, holding it there while he stared deeply into her eyes. "As God is my witness,

I don't know what you're talking about, Sara. I have no intention of doing that. It has never crossed my mind to do that. Wherever did you get that idea? Becca wasn't happy that whenever I travel to Sierra Leone, I never stop by to see you. I don't want to do that again. I want us to be cousins again. I don't understand what you are trying to say."

Sara yanked her hand free and jerked to a standing position. "Why are you trying to sweet-talk me into believing you're innocent, Thomas? I received the papers. Your signature is on them. You've already instigated a lawsuit against me. For months now, I've had to wonder when the shoe would drop and we'd end up in court. I've tried for months to get hold of you. Your lawyer wouldn't give me your address or your phone number. We've tried and tried. And now, you've sent a letter to the *Daily News* editor saying despicable things about me. Things that will ruin my reputation. You've declared me a liar and a fraud. You've said I forged documents to obtain ownership of the mart and—"

Thomas leaped to his feet and grabbed hold of her shoulders. His face was dark with anger. She was perplexed to see no remorse in him. "Look at me!" he demanded. "I don't know where all this is coming from, but I am categorically denying everything you've just hurled at me! I am *not* suing you. I don't need your business. I have *not* sent a letter to the editor of any newspaper."

Sara twisted free and temporarily lost her voice. What was he saying? How could it be? She'd seen the papers herself. Othneil had spoken with his lawyer many times. She'd read the letter. Yet here he was, standing in her living room, lying to her about it. *Denying everything.*

Her lips curled under, and she spat out her disgust. "You don't have an ounce of integrity, Thomas. I'm not blind. I'm not stupid. I read the letter. I saw your signature. Are you having remorse at this late date? Have you changed your mind? Are you here to . . . to *apologize*?"

Thomas turned away and paced the room in long, agitated strides. He threw his hands in the air. "What can I say to convince you? Show me these documents! Who is this lawyer you say is working for me?"

"James Murray! That's who you've hired to work for you. And his sister is the acting chairman/matron of the Freetown Children's Center. The night before Ben and I were to . . . to receive the two children we've adopted, she . . . she rescinded the contract. Tore it up, Thomas! R-refuses to let us adopt, and . . . and I can't have any ch-children of my own." She crumbled back into her chair and covered her face with her hands. Loud sobs escaped from deep within her. She couldn't hold them back any longer.

At that very moment, Ben reentered the room. "What's going on here? Why all the shouting?" He rushed to Sara's side. "Can you explain this, Thomas? Why have you been shouting to the extent that Sara is crying?" His lips narrowed into a thin line and his eyes into slits.

*Smoke in the Kitchen*

Thomas sighed and again threw his hands into the air. "It appears that someone has been perpetrating a heinous crime against my cousin, Ben. This person is using my name to go after Sara and her business and is using fraudulent tactics to achieve this purpose. I promise on all that is holy that I have not done any of the things she has just accused me of doing." He sank onto the sofa and leaned forward with his elbows on his knees. "I am so sorry. So very, very sorry."

Sara raised a hand to touch his shoulder. "I-I believe you, Thomas. God help me, but I believe you." She lifted her tearstained face to Ben's. "What do we do now?"

## Chapter 29

Throughout the long weekend, Thomas worked feverishly with Ben and Sara to develop a plan. Thomas called his wife to say he would be delayed due to unexpected business and he would tell her all about it when he got home. Since no one in the city had expected him, he could keep his presence in town a secret until he had made a surprise visit to James Murray in his office. In the meantime, he placed calls to three of Murray's office employees who knew him personally and would likely know what their boss was up to. "Office gossip is always available for a price," he said. "I intend to offer enough to encourage loose mouths and then tight lips."

"Put on your boxing gloves, Sara," Ben said. "This may not be easy, but we're finally head-to-head in the match we've been angling for these past several weeks."

"Murray won't know what hit him," Sara said fervently. "I intend to be the immovable force that puts him away where he belongs. It angers me no end that someone would put his own agenda before the happiness of innocent, hurting children, Ben."

Thomas had agreed to spend the weekend in the guest room that Sara had already decorated as Joseph's bedroom. "When we finally bring Joseph home, it will be my great pleasure to tell him his Uncle Thomas slept in his bedroom," she said, giving him a warm hug.

## Smoke in the Kitchen

On Saturday morning, while Thomas was out meeting his contacts individually at different places in town, Ben worked the phone. He called a government official in Liberia and asked him to use all means possible to find a Madeline Brown who arrived from Sierra Leone on vacation. Within four hours, he had a return phone call from him with the information they needed. "I'm disappointed that Jeremiah didn't come to your office with her phone number, but then I remembered what it is like to be a new college student. Can't fault him for forgetting."

Pushing her troubled thoughts aside, Sara glanced at the clock. "I'll call Mrs. Brown. She knows and likes me." Thirty minutes later, she had explained to the speechless woman what was about to happen. "We need you here in Freetown," she said. "If you're agreeable to returning by Monday morning, I bet there are flights coming in then. I'll arrange for a return airline ticket and have a driver meet you at the airport. Monday? That would be wonderful, if it isn't an imposition. And one more thing . . . I would prefer that you not speak to anyone about this. We mustn't tip off anyone who may go to the Murrays."

By Saturday evening, Thomas greeted them with a broad smile, although he looked decidedly tired. Dark circles were more pronounced under his eyes. He accepted a cold Star beer and stretched his long legs in front of him after finding a position on the sofa. He had only begun to relate the astonishing plot behind all the subversive dealings that had turned their world upside down when Sara stopped him. "I'm going to call Othneil Baker right now and invite him to the house on Monday morning for breakfast. I think we need to let him hear all this and then discuss the legalities of any strategy we intend to use to put an end to Murray's machinations, Thomas."

It was very late before the three of them finally said good night to each other. They had agreed that Sunday would be a quiet day.

Sleep was the furthest thing from Sara's mind on Sunday night. She had gone to bed, but after tossing and turning and suffering from a prickle of uneasiness, she had finally risen to dress and get to her kitchen. Nothing calmed her down like cooking. If she had her druthers, she'd be in her outdoor kitchen, but her modern one would have to do. While she prepared coffee, she cracked eggs and beat them up in a mixing bowl to cook omelets for breakfast. Her thoughts centered on what was to transpire in the next few days if everything went as planned. Already she was beholden to her cousin Thomas. How could she have thought the worst of him without any proof of his intentions? Now, she had nothing but admiration for the way in which he had taken on the challenge of getting to the bottom of their longtime nightmare.

The wind was howling with renewed energy outside the window, and it pelted the rain against the house. Rainy season in Sierra Leone was always depressing, to say the least. Now it only added to the tormenting thoughts that bombarded her concerning all the things that could go wrong. She poured the ingredients into the oil already heated in the frying pan and then moved to the refrigerator and selected some oranges to make fresh juice. For Sara, multitasking in the kitchen was innate.

## Smoke in the Kitchen

An hour later, she heard footsteps coming down the stairs and soon Ben poked his head into the kitchen. "Nice smell . . . . I woke up and found you missing in our bed," he said. "How long have you been down here? Have you gotten any sleep at all?"

"Only a couple hours, and no, I couldn't sleep. Too much on my mind. I'm excited and scared to death at the same time." She reached into the cupboard for four cups and saucers and then four plates. "I am a muddle of emotions, Ben. What if Thomas is wrong and things don't go as expected? What then? Will we have any other recourse? Murray is well-known in Freetown. He has a lot of powerful friends. And Thomas said—"

"Sara . . . again I have to say, let's wait until we have something to worry about. Let's just stay centered on what we've decided to do. Othneil will give us his professional opinions, and we can go forward from there."

"I agree with your husband, Sara. You'd better listen to him." Thomas entered while working on the knot of his red tie. "When did you say your lawyer will be here?"

Sara glanced at the clock over the sink. "In about an hour. I've already got the coffee on. Want some?"

"Sounds great. Although I'm already more than a little psyched. I haven't been this excited about anything for years. Nothing like a good fight to energize you, especially when it means a low-life impostor is exposed for his underhanded schemes."

Ben patted his shoulder. "Do you know how glad Sara and I are to have you here, Thomas? We'd still be waiting for Othneil's people to uncover the plot that you've exposed in one day's work. It pays to have even a casual relationship with those in a position to know something." He pulled out a chair from the table and motioned for Thomas to take it. Then he pulled one out for himself.

Sara placed the omelet on the dining table. "We won't start until Othneil arrives; I'll toast the bread then," she said. She poured coffee for all of them. "No reason we can't begin on the coffee. Enjoy, gentlemen."

When the doorbell rang, Ben leaped to his feet. "I'll get it. Stay where you are. We can all sit around the table. No sense in being formal." He returned shortly with the lawyer dressed in his Sunday best. Ben had already received his umbrella and placed it in the stand by the entrance.

"So this is the long-lost cousin," he said, extending his hand to Thomas. "You've led my clerks searching everywhere for you. I'm certainly glad to see you. Sara tells me you were as much in the dark as we've been over certain events this past year."

Thomas grasped his hand in both of his and shook it warmly. "That's what I hear, Mr. Baker. Sorry about that. We men aren't very good about writing letters, and I'm no exception. It's a poor excuse for not keeping in touch with a relative, but my busy job and family activities take up all of my time. I just happened to be in Freetown on an unexpected business trip."

"Take a seat, Othneil. I'll get your coffee," Sara said, still busy at the kitchen counter. She placed a cup of steaming brew in front of him and pushed the milk mug and sugar bowl across the table. She poured the freshly squeezed oranges into four glasses and placed them on the table. "Now, we can enjoy this while Thomas fills you in on what he's learned in just one day."

The lawyer pushed his briefcase behind his chair and then quickly downed half the juice before Sara served everyone omelet. He helped himself to two slices of toast. "Mmm, delicious, Sara. You should open a restaurant one of these days. I'd be first in line every morning if you'd do breakfast." He glanced up at Thomas. "How'd you find Ben? Sara said you showed up in his office Friday."

Thomas grinned. "It didn't take much sleuthing, actually. I merely told the cab driver I was looking to find the economic adviser of the Sierra Leone government and his name was Benjamin Moses. I asked if he could get me to his office. He drove directly there. Said Mr. and Mrs. Moses were well-known in town. Everyone knew where they lived and worked."

Othneil nodded. "That's true. They are two of the finest people in our community."

Sara rattled the spoon in her cup. "I'm sorry, that's all the small talk I can endure. Let's talk about why we're seated at this table together. I learned Friday that my cousin knew absolutely nothing about the lawsuit or the letter to the editor, Othneil. He did not hire James Murray and had no knowledge of what the man has put me through this past year. The documents are forgeries."

"That's so?" Othneil peered closely at Thomas over the rims of his glasses.

"That's a fact, sir. When Sara threw all the accusations at me, no one could have been more surprised than I was. After learning more details and seeing copies of the documents, I came to believe that Murray was after the mart for himself and we'd best find out why. When she told me of the added misery perpetrated by his wife at the children's center, I sensed collusion. I decided to conduct a little information gathering of my own. Fortunately, I know three people who work in Murray's office. One is a junior lawyer, one is a longtime paralegal, and the third is a secretarial assistant."

"He met with them on Saturday morning, Othneil. Just wait until you hear what he learned," Sara interrupted.

Thomas rose from his chair. "Wait a minute while I get my briefcase." He returned and pushed a document across the table toward the lawyer. "Those are the names of the three I interviewed."

Othneil quickly scanned it. "How do you know what they told you is the truth?"

"First, I have no reason to doubt that any of these three acquaintances would lie to me. Then, I met with each of them alone on the pretense of simply having a casual get-together to reminisce over old times. None knew I was meeting with the other two. I had asked each not to spread the word I was in town, because I didn't have time to see everyone and didn't want to upset anyone. They had no time to formulate a story. Also, I would have recognized a similarity in the way in which they answered my questions."

"Good. Good." Othneil nodded and then pushed his plate far enough forward on the table to make room for his elbows. "Now," he said, "let's hear what you learned from these people."

Thomas motioned for Sara to refill his coffee cup. He leaned forward, his brow furrowed and his dark eyes glistening. "I pretended I was in financial constraints and hoped to find a lucrative solution to my problems soon. I asked how things were going at Murray's firm, if they were happy there, and if they thought James might be able to use me. Imagine my surprise when all three mentioned there was something going on there that would soon put them all on easy street. They thought I was already in on it, since it involved the acquisition of the auctioneer mart property! A few more questions, and I learned Murray was after personal ownership of the mart for a bombshell reason—he needed the facility and location to move the transport of gold to foreign markets."

"Gold!" Othneil sat back in his chair and folded his arms over his chest. "That's a little far-fetched, don't you think, Thomas? This country has considerable gold, but it's not being mined to any great degree. It's a small industry compared to diamonds."

"I agree with you, but Murray's sources have evidently convinced him that gold is the next big export from our country. India consumes a great deal of it, and the American currency is based on the gold standard. Rumors are that some big importers of diamonds are planning to cut their losses and suspend any mining dealings here. World attention has focused on the extent of child labor in the mines, and the issue is receiving too much negative press."

"Hmm," Othneil muttered. "So Murray decided to get in on the gold business from the get-go, and the most valuable property for his venture just happens to be Sara's auctioneer mart."

Ben was up pacing the kitchen. "That man has the nerve of a hungry snake!"

Thomas nodded. "I agree with you. He needed a property that was close to the water for easy access to shipping. Murray intends to smuggle gold to other neighboring countries. Decades ago properties near the sea were used as a conduit for smuggling hard liquor by carting it into fishing boats from Freetown to countries along the Atlantic. The auctioneer mart would still be run as it is but be used as a cover for the illegal transport of gold."

"I don't understand why he pretended you were after the mart. Why didn't he just go to Sara and make an offer? Why all the subterfuge?"

"Because everyone in town knows she'd never sell. It's a longtime family business. She has increased its business substantially, and she does a great service to those in need of both furnishings and money. She's fair-minded and doesn't overcharge for her services."

## Smoke in the Kitchen

"So, Murray has spent untold hours over the past several months poring over every document on file in the registry office, hoping to come up with something smelly to convince Sara she'd lose the mart anyway if she didn't turn over ownership to you."

"Can you believe it, Othneil?" Sara curled her fingers around the handle of her cup and schooled her emotions. "I never suspected a thing. I believed Thomas was behind the lawsuit. Murray had probably already had his own people search for Thomas and they came up with nothing, just as yours did. He thought he'd be in the clear."

Thomas laughed. "And here I am, all hale and hearty!" He turned serious again. "My three contacts told me all about the scam regarding the mart. The thought of having enough income to improve the lives of their family members was too powerful for them to have sleepless nights. So . . . I played their game. I asked what they had been promised in the way of cold hard cash and then offered to double it if they'd remain quiet until I confronted Murray to get my take out of the scheme. After all, the man was pretending to be me! I handed them enough money to ensure their silence until we have our chance to deal with Murray. We'll figure out how to reward them properly after all this is over."

"We've got to act on this immediately," Ben said, turning to Othneil. "We can't dawdle,. Time changes things for everyone. We've learned that firsthand."

Othneil scratched his ear and turned his gaze to the ceiling to think. "Where is all this gold supposed to be mined, by the way?

I'm not doubting your word, Thomas; I'm just trying to get the full picture."

"I understand somewhere in the Northern Province."

"Makes sense. I'm not totally deaf to the buzz of gold in the north."

Ben agreed. "The government has talked about it more often in recent months but has been reluctant to push involvement in any other minerals. Diamonds have been the 'gold' of choice for such a long time now." He dropped onto his chair again. "I'm sure part of their reluctance has to do with our still unstable currency. Although gold would most likely stabilize it and allow more of our companies to do legitimate business with neighboring and other countries, the expressed concern is that increased trading usually results in illegal trading. Murray knows that, but with all his connections, he's probably not worried. He knows it takes time and effort to set up a system of issuing licenses and authorizing a legal buy and sell system based upon the proper valuing of the gold. Knowing what I know of him now, I wouldn't put it past him to have a few choice government officials in on the scheme."

"You're right, Ben," Thomas nodded.

Othneil listened without comment. Finally he nodded. "I believe you're on the right track, Thomas. Murray wants the mart himself. He's pretending to be you. But exactly how does he intend to get Sara on board?"

"It's as plain as the nose on your face, Othneil!" Sara said, her passionate voice filled with the anguish she felt. "He got his wife, Leona, to overturn our adoption of Esther and Joseph! She knew how much Ben and I want those children. James Murray decided to use that ploy to his advantage. The unexpected illness and emergency surgery of Dr. Emmitt worked right into their plans. Leona Murray moved in and took over. They knew their plan wouldn't work unless they got Mrs. Brown out. Coincidentally she had been scheduled to proceed on vacation, but Leona Murray pushed her out before she knew it."

Othneil rubbed his face with his hands and readjusted his glasses. "Despicable the way greed entices people to turn on their neighbors and friends. We've long heard that money is the root of all evil. That's true worldwide, not only in Sierra Leone." He turned to Thomas again. "What do you intend to do about the information you've gathered? Sue Murray over illegal use of your name?"

"Eventually I may need to do that, but my concern is how to ensure Sara and Ben can welcome the children they already love into this lovely home." Thomas rolled up the sleeves of his shirt. "I've got a plan. I've already told Ben and Sara about it, and they feel it may work. We need your legal advice and cooperation to pull it off."

"I'm all ears." Othneil removed his suit jacket and draped it over the back of his chair. He reached into his own briefcase and pulled out a legal pad and pen.

Thomas cleared his throat and drank the already cooled coffee in his cup. "This is what I plan to do. I'm going to show up at Murray's office tomorrow. He'll be quite shocked to see me. I'm going to tell him I know all about his scheme to get the mart by pretending to be me, and I want to be in on the action or I'll expose him to the public and take him to court for fraud. I'll feed into his belief that the family feud still exists . . . that not only was my father upset over not inheriting the mart, but I am equally irate that the business wasn't passed down to me, as the only male grandchild. Nothing would make me happier than to see that Sara loses her business. I'll tell him I will continue with his plan and seek ownership for a cut of his gold profits. When I see that he intends to fulfill his part of the bargain, I'll sell the mart to him before I leave the country."

Sara looked from one man to the other to see how the plan was being received.

"And just how can you convince him that Sara will sign over ownership to you without going to court?"

"I'll tell him that I know Sara; she wouldn't want a long drawn-out court case. He was right about thinking she wants those children more than anything else in the world. I'll tell him to call Sara and Ben into his office and confront them with an ultimatum. Either they sign the papers giving me ownership of the mart, or they will never be able to adopt Esther and Joseph. For that matter, no children from the center, because that fake letter will be published in the newspapers and their reputations will be ruined. Sign the deed, and they can take the children home that very day."

Sara listened to the men plot the details of their own trickery and felt the full force of her frayed nerves. Was her long ordeal finally going to come to an end? Would she be able to move forward without dragging the heavy load of anguish behind her every step of the way?

Ben glanced at her and then at Othneil. "First thing—" The phone ring interrupted Ben. "Excuse me." He picked up the phone and stepped into the parlor.

After speaking for about ten minutes, he returned, smiling. "That was Dr. Emmitt."

"Is he back?" Sara sounded upbeat.

"He has requested an appointment to see us not at the center but at his house at 10:00 a.m. tomorrow. He arrived last night. My bet is that he knows nothing about Leona Murray's deceitfulness."

Thomas rose and pushed his chair under the table. "And I will arrive in Murray's office at the same time tomorrow. Catch him unaware. I'll be my wily best and show him I can be as devious as he is!"

Long after Othneil had left, Sara listened to the two men talk. Finally unable to stay around any longer, she returned to her kitchen to prepare dinner.

## Chapter 30

With no particular fanfare, Sara and Ben were ushered into James Murray's office by his assistant on Wednesday morning. They were accompanied by Othneil Baker, who greeted Murray with professional civility, shaking hands in a gentlemanly manner.

Sara took in the sumptuousness of the furnishings and knew the lawyer charged big fees and had established a lavish lifestyle. The walls were paneled in solid mahogany to blend in with the inbuilt bookcases holding law journals and objects of art. His desk, library table, and other furniture pieces in the room were also in mahogany—most likely imported from overseas. It was far and beyond anything Othneil had in his modest home office. With shaking knees, Sara walked across the expansive room, hanging on to Ben's arm, hoping she could remain in full command of her emotions.

"Ah, Mr. and Mrs. Moses, it's good of you to come this morning. It should take no time at all to complete our transactions. I have the documents ready for your signatures." Murray extended his hand to them.

Ben grasped and shook it in a perfunctory manner, too well-mannered to ignore the gesture. Sara took one of the three chairs strategically placed in front of his desk and ignored extending the same courtesy. She was quivering with emotional upheaval, hardly able to breathe normally, and knew that if she didn't sit

## Smoke in the Kitchen

immediately, she might crumble to the floor in a dead faint. A long list of what-ifs paraded through her mind. What if Murray knew Thomas had been lying? What if he ordered his henchmen to follow him after the meeting and learned Thomas was in contact with Ben and Sara, too? What if the documents had been doctored and they wouldn't achieve their goals? Then what?

Once Murray had seated himself, he opened a folder on his desk and riffled through several papers. Then, clearing his throat, he looked up with a tight smile. "As you know, I have been in contact with your cousin, Thomas John, in recent days, Mrs. Moses. As I indicated to you through your own lawyer"—he nodded at Othneil, who nodded back—"Mr. John is eager to resolve this matter in a most judicious way. A long, drawn-out court procedure would not benefit anyone in the long run. He is well aware that you have invested considerable time and effort into maintaining the auctioneer mart business passed on to you after the death of your father, but documents have surfaced showing his original inheritance of the mart and the deed of gift to Sara was illegal."

Another flash of another tight smile appeared and disappeared so quickly on his face, Sara could hardly identify it as one. She lowered her eyes to focus on her securely folded hands, which lay in her lap. She had been warned not to comment on anything without Othneil's approval. Who was this man to talk about laws when he had built his entire so-called case on a plethora of lies? Pinching her lips together, she concentrated on what he was saying.

Just then, the office door opened and Leona Murray entered. She crossed the floor with confidence, as though she were accustomed to conducting business in her husband's office. She carried a folder with her and handed it to him without speaking. She cast only a cursory glance at Sara and Ben before seating herself on a sofa to the right of the desk, crossing one leg over the other and swinging one beautifully clad foot as though the proceedings were an everyday occurrence of no serious consequence.

"One question, sir," Ben said, after looking directly at Leona, "if Sara's cousin has proof that the mart belongs to him and you helped him find that proof, why is it that we are having to make such a momentous decision today? Why is Sara being essentially forced to sign over the deed to her cousin if we are to be allowed to adopt the two children we already believe to be ours? Why was the adoption procedure halted by your wife? I think we are owed an explanation. What does one have to do with the other?"

Sara's eyes moved from Murray's face to that of his wife. Had she seen a look pass between the spouses? The woman fidgeted with the lapel of her custom-made suit but kept her head propped at a slight angle while wearing a closed-lips smile. She didn't blink but stared directly at her husband, waiting for him to make the explanation.

Again, Murray cleared his throat. His eyes flicked over at Othneil for only a brief second and then lowered to the folder on his desk. "I will confess, Mr. Moses, that Mr. John suggested we use the children as a bargaining chip. He is eager to obtain ownership of the mart to get on with his life. It is his rightful inheritance."

Sara glanced sideways at Ben. His eyes were as cold as ice, and he wore an indefinable expression on his face. How could Murray sit there and purposely create one lie after the other about Thomas? She bit her tongue, but it didn't do any good. "I am absolutely appalled that you would stoop to such—!"

Othneil coughed into his hand. Sara threw him a glance from the sides of her eyes and saw him almost imperceptibly shake his head.

"Thomas was right," she said in a softer voice. "Nothing would make me happier than to become the mother I have always wanted to be." She felt her eyes become misty and blinked several times. She pulled a clean hanky and dabbed at her eyes, hoping her act was having the right effect.

Murray seemed to be taken in by her show of emotion. He nodded. "It is with that understanding that I have gone to great lengths to have the legal adoption papers here this morning, Mrs. Moses." Murray opened the folder brought to him by his wife. "They are here and ready to be signed." He pushed them toward her.

Sara reached for the papers and glanced through them quickly. Then she handed them to Othneil. "Will you look these over to ensure they are in proper order, Mr. Baker? We have been told that once we sign them and I sign over the mart to Thomas, we will be able to pick up the children from the center today." She turned and looked directly at Leona. "Is that right, Mrs. Murray? You have the children ready for us? There will be no more delays of any kind?"

The woman finally blinked. "None whatsoever. I have asked the staff to have the children ready for you."

Othneil handed the papers to Ben. "They look in order, Sara. You and Ben may sign them. They have already been signed by the members of the Freetown Children's Center Board and Mrs. Murray, as the interim matron. Once your signatures are on the papers, the children are legally yours and no one can take them from you."

Ben had already removed a pen from his inside suit jacket pocket. He quickly scrawled his name on the documents and handed the pen to Sara, who was about to add her name below his.

Murray seemed to panic. "Wait a minute!" he said. "Not yet. Mrs. Moses should sign the deed documents first." He rose and pushed the other folder toward her, thumping his finger on a particular line at the bottom of the sheet. "Sign right here."

But Sara had already signed the adoption papers. "There," she said. "We are now the proud and legal parents of two beautiful children." She swept up the papers and handed them to Othneil, who took them from her with a broad smile.

"Now," he said, rising from his chair, "I believe we are through here."

Sputtering in anger, Murray pounded his fist on his desk. "Oh, no, you aren't. Do you think you put one over on me? A deal is a deal! Sign the deed papers immediately, Mrs. Moses, or—"

"Or what?" she asked, barely keeping her voice civil.

"You agreed to the procedure that you'd get the children if—"

"If we signed illegal documents to turn over the mart to you to use as a depot for the equally illegal transport of gold from Freetown to foreign buyers?"

Murray seemed taken aback. His jaw dropped open until he could find his voice. "I-I don't know what you're talking about! The mart belongs to your cousin, Thomas John. I'm his attorney. You can't just walk out of here and—"

"They know everything, James. You're not my lawyer, and I have no intention of stealing the mart from Sara."

Murray's eyes flew to the face of Thomas as he pushed open the office door and strode into the room with Stephan Paul, the *Daily News* reporter. Right behind them, a photographer was snapping pictures, the flashbulbs on his camera illuminating the office with flickers not unlike lightning in a moonless night sky.

Murray held up a bent arm to shield his face. "What are you talking about, Thomas? You said—"

"How does it feel to be dealt with in the same manner as you deal with others? Did you honestly think you could get away with this?" Thomas draped his arm around Sara's shoulders. "I love my cousin. I have never harbored ill will against her. The disagreement between our fathers and our grandfather took place a long time ago. Our grandfather had every right to pass on the auctioneer mart to the son who was the most likely to take care of it. That person was not my father. Fraud and deception may have been his game, but not mine. I'll have no part in it."

Leona Murray had already risen from the sofa and moved closer to her husband. Her eyes were wide and frightened. Clearly, her tough demeanor was only a pretense used when she had an agenda forced on her by her domineering husband.

"Have you signed the adoption papers?" Thomas asked, looking down at Sara.

Sara nodded. "The-the children are ours, Thomas." Her eyes clouded over as she held up the papers and she offered him a tremulous smile.

"Good. Then I think we're through here. Do you have any questions, Mr. Paul, or do you have all the details necessary to write your article?" He peered over his shoulder at the editor. "Your readers will enjoy learning about the counterfeit letter written by Mr. Murray intended to ruin the reputations of two innocent people."

Stephen Paul grinned. "If Mr. and Mrs. Moses wouldn't mind, we'd like to accompany them to the children's center to snap the first family photograph."

Othneil faced James Murray, who had sunk onto his office chair, cowed and intimidated by the swift turnabout. "I believe our business here is finished, my friend. My office will get in touch with yours first thing tomorrow morning. Of course you know I have no recourse but to turn in a detailed report of your unprofessional conduct to the authorities. What they decide to do about the charges of forgery and fraud is up to them."

"What . . . what do you intend to say in your article?" Murray asked Paul, his voice almost a whisper.

"The truth, Mr. Murray," Paul said. "Just the truth." He motioned to his photographer to take one more picture of Murray, his face drawn and his mouth downturned.

His wife cowered in the corner of the office behind him. "Wh-what about me?" she asked. "What's going to happen to me? I-I didn't want to impede the adoption of those children. I-I was told to—"

"Quiet, Leona!" her husband barked.

Suddenly another man appeared at the door of the office. "Good, I'm glad you're here, Leona. Your services will no longer be necessary at the center. As of this moment, you are forbidden to set foot on the property."

Everyone turned to identify the man's voice. Dr. Emmitt stood there with Madeline Brown's arm firmly hooked through his as though to help him to stand erect. "The board has decided unanimously to terminate your duties as the interim matron," he said. "We hope to reassure the public that no shenanigans will ever again be allowed to interfere with the way in which we conduct our legal adoptions. The children should not be made to suffer because of the greed of any citizens who place their own agenda before the children's welfare."

Squaring her shoulders and holding her head high, Madeline Brown bravely met the hostile gaze of the woman who had replaced her. "I've learned something valuable from Mrs. Moses in the past several hours," she said, her voice firm and clear. "If people of honor allow those bent on destroying their jobs and good names through intimidation and fear-mongering to succeed, they will only be contributing to the continuance of crime and corruption in our country. That's why I have decided to continue working to uphold the good name of the Freetown Children's Center. My aim is to rename it after the woman who gave tirelessly to our abandoned and orphaned children. It is because of people like Grandma Abigail that these children will grow up to become contributing citizens."

She glared at the silent woman. "And, Mrs. Murray, you should be ashamed of yourself for agreeing to such an underhanded scheme as the one perpetrated by your husband. You have a voice. Use it! You have a heart. Only the worst kind of woman could look into the faces of the children at the center and deny them the right to loving parents and the safety and comfort of a real home. Don't deny yourself the feeling that comes from doing what's right. No amount of money is worth exchanging your soul for it."

Two hours later, Sara walked to the entrance of her home holding tightly to the hands of Esther and Joseph. "This is your home, my darling children," she said. "It will always be yours and no one can take you away from it. It is my prayer that you will be happy here and come to love your father and me as your new parents." Her voice was choked with the emotion that had been building steadily over the months, but especially after she had firmly written her name on the adoption papers. Finally . . . *finally*, she was the mother she'd always imagined in her dreams since she was a girl the age of Esther. She peeked over her shoulder at Ben, her heart in her eyes for him to see.

At that very moment, the front door to their home opened and Kelitia stepped out. "Welcome home!" she cried, holding out her arms to the children. "I am your Aunty Kelitia, and someday I have a very special story to tell you about your mother." She ushered them into the parlor, which she had decorated with balloons and a banner that said WELCOME HOME, ESTHER AND JOSEPH MOSES!

For the next several minutes, there were lots of hugs amid laughter and lots of chatter. Throughout the day family members and friends visited and made themselves known to the new members of their family. There was plenty of food, drinks, and reminiscences.

As she looked upon her extended family and especially on the two children who wore never-ending smiles of happiness, Sara's eyes misted with tears as she wrapped her arm around the waist of her husband. "Isn't this a wonderful day, Ben?"

"I just spoke with my other son's mother," he said, nodding. "She has said they will not be moving to France after all, and she has promised that he can visit us very soon to meet his new brother and sister."

"Oh, Ben," Sara cried, "that's wonderful!" She rose up on her tiptoes and laid her cheek against his. "That news is the high point of this remarkable day. No one could be happier than I am. Thank you for supporting me during this difficult period. We have the children I've wanted for so long, and no man could be a finer father for them. They will grow to love you as much as I do."

A smile tugged at his lips. "It pleases me you no longer have to worry about losing your family's auctioneer mart, darling. It will be there for our children to inherit."

The laughter that bubbled from Sara's throat drew everyone's attention, and both Esther and Joseph ran to throw their arms around her. Lifting her face to the heavens, she mouthed a thank you to the God who had given her the strength and fortitude to pursue her dreams and keep hope alive.

# Epilogue

**Sierra Leone, 1996**

The graduation ceremony took place on a typical Sierra Leonean day that was bathed in spirit-drenching heat and humidity. Most attendees looked as though they had just stepped out of a hot shower, but their attitudes remained upbeat as they cooled themselves with a variety of handheld fans and the graduation booklets. Sara Moses wasn't at all concerned with the sweltering temperatures. She walked proudly to the microphone to deliver the commencement address to the newest graduating class of her alma mater, knowing she looked elegant in her royal blue cotton gown with its intricate gold embroidery. She had had it made specially for the occasion. Only the best would do, and that meant it had been custom-made by one of the area's finest tailors.

Sara was eager to share some of her life with the young people seated in the front rows. She had overcome a long series of life-changing events, the kind that too often crippled those who allowed such adversities to steal their aspirations and render them hopeless. She wanted to instill in them a passion for life and a determination to prevail, no matter how difficult the odds.

As she adjusted the microphone, she caught a glimpse of her daughter beaming at her from the second row of graduates. For a moment, Sara's eyes misted, and she blinked rapidly several times to banish any possibility of spilling tears. This wasn't the time for them. Speaking loudly and clearly, she spoke to Esther and her classmates, relating several personal and professional stories about the necessity for following their dreams and what was required of them to see their realization. She spoke of the necessity and impact of persistence, unwavering faith, a deep commitment, and individual discipline. She spoke of the importance of being a giver as well as a taker and of how community involvement through voluntary activities would enrich their lives. She spoke of self-respect and the development of competence, integrity, courage, and generosity.

"As young adults in Sierra Leone, you are not unlike the trees of our forests—sturdy, strong, and beautiful," she said. "You are already well-grounded in our culture and have become resilient to many negative influences that could have deterred your intention to reach this milestone. It is your time to take on life's challenges and make a name for yourself—a name that will bring honor not only to you, but also to your family and to your community and country. Never lose your thirst for knowledge. Never give up striving to reach your next goal. Become a hero in the eyes of the next generation—a hero known for solving problems and accepting responsibilities and giving generously and selflessly to those without your talents and education. I congratulate all of you on earning your college degree. Use it wisely and well. May God bless you."

As she watched the promising young adults accept their certificates, Sara smiled broadly. This is a day for the victory column, she thought. But even as she rejoiced over what the occasion represented, she couldn't help but pray that her daughter's future would be less turbulent than her own past.

Her eyes searched for and found her husband as he sat proudly next to their two sons, Ben Jr. and Joseph. Ben Jr and Joseph had expressed their firm intention to work toward the democratization of a better Sierra Leone.

Hope, Sara thought. What could she have accomplished without keeping her hope alive? Now she must encourage her children never to abandon their hopes. Sadly, that meant they would need to risk pain and failure. There was no other choice for those who cared about the downtrodden in Sierra Leone. The greatest hazard to a quality life was to risk nothing. Hope wasn't at all like smoke in the kitchen. It didn't rise to meet the clouds and then dissipate in the air. Hope endured as long as there was the smallest ember of it burning in their hearts. She would teach them that when the world says, "Give up," hope will always whisper, "Try one more time."

The End

# About the Book

*Smoke in the Kitchen* is about second chances. This book, set in Freetown, Sierra Leone, tells the story about forty-three-year-old Sara Moses, who happens to find life's purpose where she least expects. The challenging situation she faces is not uncommon to Sara. Following the untimely death of her fiancé and her unborn daughter, her life becomes empty and meaningless. With much persuasion from her sister, she picks herself up, dusts herself off, and begins a new life. She falls in love and marries Benjamin Moses, a government official. Still plagued by her challenging circumstances, including her desire to have children, she starts the process of adopting two children. This doesn't go well due to retaliation from an unknown source. Feeling devastated, Sara channels her energy by forming a reforestation society and encourages an entire nation to replant the forest. At the end, Sara provides a second chance to nature as well as to two innocent children.

Made in the USA
Lexington, KY
24 July 2014